THE SEASON OF LOVE

After dinner Daniel invited Freddie to follow him into the drawing room, where he wished to have a few words with her. He smiled as charmingly as he could but was disappointed to see that it didn't completely wipe away the wary look in her eyes.

"Miss Hendry," he said, as soon as he had settled her on the rose-colored settee, "I wish first to apologize for any discomfort I may have caused you yesterday."

She sat with her hands folded in her lap, looking at him as if she expected him to fly up into the rafters at any minute. He could tell that his speech and manner had not produced the proper mood he had hoped for, even though he was trying his very best not to be so stiff and proper. "It was my misconception of circumstances, not yours, which caused the problems. I'm sorry." He took a deep breath and sat down beside her. "I should have known that you could not have been a selfish person."

Freddie's eyes were now alight, and Daniel wanted to keep them that way. She turned those chocolate eyes on his face, and he watched, mesmerized, as her gaze traveled from the top of his head, down one cheek, across his chin, up the other cheek, and down his nose until it settled on his lips. Daniel moved closer to Freddie and wrapped her in his arms. "Will you forgive me for accusing you of being mean-spirited?"

Freddie started to speak, but the minute he held her, Daniel's emotions began rolling downhill so fast they could not be stopped. "If you do find it in your head to forgive me, will you marry me and be my countess?" He placed a finger on her lips, which again prevented her from speaking. "Don't try to say anything right now, because I'm going to kiss you."

And he did.

Books by Paula Tanner Girard

LORD WAKEFORD'S GOLD WATCH

CHARADE OF HEARTS

A FATHER FOR CHRISTMAS

A HUSBAND FOR CHRISTMAS

THE SISTER SEASON

Published by Zebra Books

The Sister Season

Paula Tanner Girard

Zebra Books
Kensington Publishing Corp.
http://www.zebrabooks.com

ZEBRA BOOKS are published by

Kensington Publishing Corp.
850 Third Avenue
New York, NY 10022

Copyright © 1998 by Paula Tanner Girard

All rights reserved. No part of this book may be reproduced in any form or by any means without the prior written consent of the Publisher, excepting brief quotes used in reviews.

If you purchased this book without a cover you should be aware that this book is stolen property. It was reported as "unsold and destroyed" to the Publisher and neither the Author nor the Publisher has received any payment for this "stripped book."

Zebra and the Z logo Reg. U.S. Pat. & TM Off.

First Printing: October, 1998
10 9 8 7 6 5 4 3 2 1

Printed in the United States of America

One

"You know why I am here!" Daniel's words sounded appallingly like gunshots, echoing round the cavernous room. "I have come to decide your future." Having said that, he asked himself what the devil he was going to do with them.

Daniel Douglas Durham, the seventh Earl of Chantry, was a strong young man of military bearing, with hair the flaxen yellow of his Saxon ancestors, eyes black and sharp as a raven's. Dressed from head to foot in somber mourning apparel, he paced back and forth in the vast hall of a rambling manor called Knocktigh nestled deep in the Cheviot Hills, appraising the eight young ladies seated in a row of high-backed chairs in front of him, their heads bowed in obeisance, hands clasped demurely in their laps.

They were now his charges, his responsibility, his sisters and half sisters, most of whom he had never seen before in his twenty-six years. Nor they him.

If it had not been for the totally unexpected request made by his dying father, the man he admired more than any other, Daniel vowed that he certainly would not have traveled so deep into this remote area west of the small border town of Cornhill-on-Tweed three hundred miles north of London. Definitely not! Especially in this raw miserable month of March.

A few feet away the Honorable Mr. James Pettigrew, a thin angular scarecrow of a man who had been the late earl's faithful secretary for over eighteen years, anxiously watched his young

master's face for any giveaway to his thoughts. He had handed
Lord Chantry a list of his sisters' names and the year of births
for each, which he'd obtained from Mrs. Ash the elderly housekeeper soon after their arrival, but his lordship seemed too en-
grossed to peruse it.

Daniel was indeed so preoccupied with his own dark musings
that he gave the sheet no more than a penny's worth of attention.
"What have I done, Mr. Pettigrew, for the Fates to have played
such a quixotic trick on me? The days of romantical knights in
shining armor are long past."

The last six years of his life Daniel had spent on the Continent,
fighting for his country, for his king, and just trying to stay alive.
No sooner had they whipped Old Boney at Waterloo than he had
received word to return to London. Not to celebrate with his
fellow officers as he should have done, but to mourn the death
of his father, Lord Chantry, the sixth earl; one of the wealthiest
men in England, diplomat extraordinaire, close friend and trusted
advisor for many years to King George the Third.

Daniel stopped his pacing. The girls appeared to be all hair
because that was all he could see of their bowed heads. He
would have worried that they had no noses or chins if he had
not observed differently when he had first met them upon his
arrival little more than an hour ago. Their drab frocks bespoke
that they were still in mourning. He likewise had forsaken his
bright scarlet regimentals for more somber black, and even
though nine months had passed since that sad day, no small
armband would suffice for what he owed his father. From what
he'd glimpsed of his sisters' faces they were not unattractive,
but what bewildered him was their timidity, their inability to
look him squarely in the eye. Did they think him some sort of
beast who had come to devour them?

As the silence grew more profound, Daniel cleared his throat
in an authoritative way since he was accustomed to addressing
soldiers not sensitive young ladies, and studied each one indi-
vidually. To his annoyance this only made the girls clasp their
hands tighter and continue to stare down at them.

A frown creased Daniel's forehead. He had not managed to extract more than a dozen words from them since his arrival, and he couldn't understand why. He had tried to be all that was polite, and if he did not find it easy to smile, he'd at least tried his best to be pleasant. They had known he was coming for he'd posted a letter several weeks ago informing them of his schedule. In fact, he had even arrived a day earlier than expected. Punctuality was an attribute which Daniel prized highly on his list of essentials.

"On his death bed, my father—"

Mr. Pettigrew coughed discreetly.

Only the most discerning eye would have detected the tightening of Daniel's jaw as he corrected himself. "On his death bed *our* father expressed his deep regret in a letter to me that he had not fulfilled a pledge he had made years ago that when each of my sisters—" Daniel was interrupted by yet another fit of coughing. He waited for it to stop then proceeded. "Each of my *sisters*—when she reached the appropriate age—was to have a Season in London."

A variety of snorts and wheezes which grew steadily more consumptive forced Daniel to turn about. "Mr. Pettigrew, is something the matter?"

"Beg pardon, my lord, but I believe your father said, *my daughters*."

Daniel had found over the last few months that Mr. Pettigrew was not only a loyal servant, but also a stickler for exactness. This was another quality which the young earl respected, and he therefore made allowances for the man's forwardness. However, logic had been one of Daniel's favorite pursuits at Oxford, and he never could resist a challenge to put forth his own reasoning, especially when he felt he had the right of it. "It is one and the same, is it not? My father's daughters are my sisters," he said, cocking a brow.

Mr. Pettigrew, in his own somewhat obsequious way, was just as persistent. "Yes, my lord, but you were stating that your father said *sisters*, and I do remember him saying *daughters*."

"Thank you Mr. Pettigrew. I concede. You were the one who was there, of course."

Daniel swung round in time to catch the girls exchanging surreptitious looks with one another. His eyes narrowed. They would soon learn that very little escaped his scrutiny. When he'd mentioned their father's promise to give them a Season in London, their skeptical expressions hadn't gone unnoticed. Unfortunately, as soon as they observed his penetrating gaze, they returned to their docile state.

His purpose had not been to frighten them, but it was hard to forgo being Major Durham, aide-de-camp to the Duke of Wellington, and step into the more genteel role of the Earl of Chantry in so short a time. However, he felt his sisters had to know that there were compelling reasons why their father had not been able to carry out his promises.

"The earl was extremely busy," Daniel said in defense of this man whom he'd tried to emulate all his life. "Duty was always uppermost in his thoughts." He could hear his father so clearly the old earl might have been standing right there in the room, and Daniel attempted to repeat the words in the same roaring spirit to his sisters, so that they would be inspired as he had been. " 'Duty, my boy! Duty to king and country! Duty is the highest calling to test a man's valor!' " he said, shaking his fist at them the way the late Lord Chantry had done.

Unfortunately Daniel's performance did not seem to impress his sisters. He saw a little booted foot slowly move from under the faded bombazine skirt in the fourth chair to nudge one beneath the fifth chair's faded wool. Perhaps if he toned down his voice they wouldn't be so skittish, he thought, but active service in His Majesty's army did not breed soft-spoken officers.

Then the shoulders beneath the brown tresses began to tremble, and two enormous velvety-brown eyes, shiny from unshed tears, opened up to his, but closed again so quickly that Daniel wondered if he'd imagined it. Was it ungentlemanly of him to continue his effort to persuade them? The rough lessons he'd learned in the all-male institutions he'd attended had not prepared him for dealing with sensitive young ladies. What was he to do? The lower the timbre of his voice the more he seemed to terrorize them. Yet, for some reason, he felt it more imperative than ever that he redeem his father's stature in the sight of his daughters. He tried again. "The government entrusted our father with many responsibilities during the terrible fighting: there were the peace talks in Vienna . . . Amiens . . . and so forth . . ."

But, alas, when Daniel saw a hand shoot out from a black bombazine sleeve to squeeze the fingers of the little brown mouse whose tiny figure was now shaking all over, he let his voice trail off. He would confuse his sisters no longer with matters of state nor frighten them with tales of war. His role was to assure them.

"As your brother and now head of the family, my duty, of course, is to fulfill his lordship's promises. It was his wish—no, I take it as a command—that I am to see each and every one of his daughters . . . you . . . my sisters . . . shall have her Season."

Mr. Pettigrew enthusiastically nodded his approval.

Daniel had no sooner congratulated himself that at least one person in the room appreciated his efforts to be honorable, when the reality of the situation struck. His eyes glazed over, and for a moment he looked as if he'd turned to stone. Egad! Eight sisters!

Mr. Pettigrew put the tips of his fingers to his lips, pushing the corners of them upward.

What was there to smile about? Od'sbodkins! The man was relentless in his pursuit to make a picnic out of this fiasco. Daniel had thought when the war was over he could return to England, sell out his commission, and sample a bit of the delights of London. Perhaps even look into the marriage mart himself, for it was about time he began to think of producing the next heir to the Durham dynasty. He would be a relic by the time he finished getting all of his sisters situated, though, for that was part of his father's provision. Not only was he to see that they were presented at court, but that they were married as well.

The sudden realization of possible complications, unforeseen until now, forced Daniel to study the girls even more closely. He had to admit that he'd expected to see a wider range of years among his sisters, not eight fully grown females. But when a young woman reached a certain maturity, how was a man to tell? All were well formed—very well formed indeed, Daniel was shocked to acknowledge.

The oldest would be his own full sisters, Ruth and Rebecca. The only ones whom Daniel remembered. His mind calculated quickly. He had been six years old when they were born, which would make them twenty and far past the time when they should have debuted. He located two young ladies with the same shade of yellow hair as his own, but they were not seated together. In fact at opposite ends.

Frowning, he consulted the list in his hand. Mr. Pettigrew had indeed proved his competency in collecting and listing his data. By comparing the years of birth, Daniel made an interesting discovery. It seemed that his father had sired four sets of twins in as many years. The thought of being able to present them two at a time overshadowed the mathematical probabilities of this happening and sent an unexpected sense of euphoria through Daniel. It took a great deal of control to keep himself from shouting, *Hallelujah!*

Four sets of twins, four come-outs, four years to complete the task of finding husbands for his sisters—not eight years.

With some measure of relief, Daniel checked the next two on the list: Georgette and Winifred, nineteen. Then Antoinette and Babette, eighteen. The last two were Margaret and Mary, seventeen years old.

With this new fascinating prospect of cutting the campaign in half, he looked up and tried to sort out the pairs by hair color, but they were in a complete hodgepodge; black, carrot, yellow, and that single brown-haired girl who went into a twitter every time he spoke. Where did she fit in? Daniel's jaw tightened.

"You are not in order," he barked. "How am I to be expected to identify you if you don't conform to Mr. Pettigrew's list?"

The seventh Lord Chantry—Daniel had been trained to fill

this role of privilege from the day he was born—was finding that habits created over a lifetime do not change as easily as one wishes. First as a student in strict boarding schools, then university, and finally as a member of the military, he had lived by order and discipline. It was his decided opinion that both were essential to good health and well-being.

Disregarding Mr. Pettigrew's wildly dancing eyebrows, Daniel stood at attention, clicked his heels, and said, "You will arrange yourselves according to your birth year. Immediately!"

The girls rose as one body and, with neither a glance to the right or to the left, switched seats with the precision of a well-trained troop of soldiers. Daniel watched with surprise and no little admiration.

When all were in their proper places, seated, hands in laps, heads bowed as before, Daniel was more inclined to look upon his sisters with benevolence. If they were a bit dull, they were at least obedient and biddable. A generous smile lit up his face, making it quite handsome to anyone who happened to glance his way.

"Ah, that is more the thing," he said, marching up the line and calling muster. Ruth and Rebecca, their pale golden hair identifying them, were now at the head of the line where they should have been in the first place.

"Lady Georgette?" he asked the dark-haired beauty in the third chair.

She nodded, looking up through long sweeping black lashes.

"And Lady Winifred," he said, directing his words to the brown locks. Both nineteen, he noted from Mr. Pettigrew's list, not taking time to give her more than a glance. Obviously they were not identical twins, but that would simplify his telling them apart.

However, another problem arose at the next two chairs. Eighteen-year-old Babette and Antoinette resembled Georgette so uncannily that they could have been taken for triplets. Daniel recalled the day when his father had turned up unexpectedly at Harrow, only three months after his own mother had died, to introduce the elegant, dark-haired French noblewoman he had taken for his second wife.

Daniel passed these dark-haired lovelies and finally came to the freckled-faced, seventeen-year-old redheads, Margaret and Mary, who were of a certainty the daughters of the last countess and third wife, the Scottish widow whom Mr. Pettigrew said had raised all eight girls as if they were her own for fourteen years, until her death four years ago.

Mary and Margaret may have been the youngest according to the list, but their robustness, which manifested itself in some extremely visible ways, made them appear older than his tall and slender full sisters. Daniel did not dwell on the trouble these assets could lead to in the future, because he was feeling too pleased with himself at having established some degree of order.

"Now," he said, in a friendlier tone, "Since Lady Ruth and Lady Rebecca are the eldest, I shall take them to London first for this year's Season."

Puzzled when he saw no appreciable change in the girls' demeanor, no anticipated blush, no fluttering of maidenly lashes, Daniel eyed them narrowly. He had been led to believe that it was every young maiden's dream to be introduced to *Le Beau Monde.* An uneasy feeling in the pit of his stomach told him he would be wise if he took time to regroup his defenses.

Daniel allowed himself a minute to let his gaze sweep the large hall of the old mansion. His attention was captured for a moment by the far distant view of the River Tweed out the tall north window. Reflecting the shimmering grayness of the March sky, it lay like a smooth silver knife cutting this part of England and Scotland in half.

The room was decidedly plain. It had no display of weaponry or of the trappings of war which decorated so many old manor houses, and it smelled more of beeswax and the penetrating aroma of burning furze as the bundled sticks crackled in the large stone fireplace. There were no portraits of ancestors or trophies of the manly sport of hunting. Not what he would have expected of one of his father's houses. In fact, it was noticeably bereft of furniture except for several wooden chairs and a settle near the fireplace. Not even a vase of flowers to brighten the room. But then frost was still on the ground this far north, while around London the fields would hopefully soon be turning yellow with daffodils.

A wooden frame with an unfinished tapestry tacked to it stood in front of the large hearth where a black and white cat sat licking its paw. It was definitely a house inhabited by women. Aye, there was a peaceful air about it, but no matter how much he tried, Daniel still could not picture his father spending much time here.

As the enormity of his situation began to ride roughshod over his thoughts, Daniel clasped his hands behind his back and, fixing his gaze on one head after the other, marched down the line of chairs, stopped, made a sound in his throat which might have been said to resemble a growl more than a grumble, then marched back again to where he'd begun.

The merest idea of having to find husbands for eight sisters would seem a formidable task for an ordinary man. Daniel Douglas Durham, however, did not consider himself ordinary in any sense of the word. Was he going to permit himself to be overwhelmed by this responsibility?

Hardly.

Yet there was that niggling statistic that set his mind to calculating the facts again. If he brought out Ruth and Rebecca first, the next set of sisters the following year, and so forth, it would still take a devil of a long time to get them all spoken for and married.

Then another obstacle presented itself. If he accompanied Ruth and Rebecca to London he would have to leave the other six practically unchaperoned three hundred miles to the north in a house that was cold as Siberia and staffed only by a few elderly retainers, not the multitude of servants he had been led to believe by Mr. Pettigrew.

That would never do. Never do indeed. His predicament was doubly complicated because he'd been away from home so long he knew of no older female relatives or close friends of the family upon whom he could call to take in the other girls.

Daniel saw Mr. Pettigrew's brows begin to signal him to get on with it. The man had no patience. No patience at all. Didn't he know that it took time to analyze the situation? First, spread the map on the table; pinpoint the objective; take count of man-power and weaponry; then assess the opposition's number and weapons; pick the best strategy to meet the objectives; and, fi-nally, advance on the enemy. Of course, surprise was always the best policy, as was power in numbers. He certainly had the num-bers. Now all he needed was to find the most expedient policy.

Daniel pounded his fist into the palm of his hand and smiled broadly for the second time that afternoon. Terrace Palace off the Strand, which his father had purchased for his second wife, was large enough to accommodate an army. Why hadn't he thought of it sooner? "All or nothing, Mr. Pettigrew," Daniel whispered hoarsely.

The secretary nodded hopefully as the earl passed by. His lord-ship had smiled—for a second time—in less than an hour. 'Twas an occasion so remarkable that even Mr. Pettigrew took note of it and decided he would have to relate the incident to Tilbury, his master's valet, later to see what he could make of it.

Daniel stopped pacing in front of the girls. "I have decided to carry you back to London with me and present *all* of you at this year's Season."

It took a moment before he realized that his pronouncement still brought no exclamations of girlish delight. Although he did think for a moment that he heard a giggle, but he soon decided that he was mistaken. Daniel had anticipated a little more en-thusiasm over his plan. However, since his sisters seemed not to object, logically it meant they agreed.

Outside the light was already beginning to fade. The day would soon be over and Daniel wanted to conclude the interview. "I shall speak more on it this evening at supper. I will want to leave for London as soon as possible."

Not a finger, not one little booted foot, not one hair upon a head wiggled.

"We will dine at eight o'clock," he said.

Only the crackling of the dwindling bundle of sticks in the fireplace answered him.

Daniel wondered what he was doing wrong. No matter how he tried to spark their interest, his sisters showed no enthusiasm. If he were expected to say something more, he wasn't quite sure of what that should be. He'd not had younger sisters to contend with before, and he wondered if they were waiting for him to excuse them as young men were used to having done by their superiors: be it headmaster, professor, or commander.

"Company dismissed," he said crisply.

Mr. Pettigrew raised his eyes to the ceiling and mouthed a silent prayer.

The eight girls stood as if by some secret signal, then filed quietly to the end of the hall and toward the wide staircase. Doubts about the wisdom of his plan threatened to intrude on Daniel's thoughts. For all their wealth and beauty were his sisters too dull and countrified to attract worthy suitors? He refused to be discouraged. "I have led a battalion of over eight hundred men into battle, Mr. Pettigrew. How difficult can it be to introduce eight sweet, biddable young ladies such as my sisters to the London society?"

"I do believe you will find there is a difference, my lord."

"Balderdash!" Daniel exclaimed, slapping his arms to get some warmth into them. "For any siege to be successful, a competent commander only needs a workable plan and well-armed troops."

The secretary looked skeptical. "I cannot readily say, my lord. I have never known of anybody trying to marry off so many young females at one time."

Anticipation of the challenge ahead raised Daniel's spirits immeasurably. "Never fear, Mr. Pettigrew, we shall discuss our campaign during the journey back to London."

"Did you say, *we* my lord?"

"Why yes, Mr. Pettigrew. I shall be in need of an aide for this maneuver. Don't you want to have a hand in helping the young ladies find suitable husbands?"

As his eyes grew rounder, Mr. Pettigrew's eyebrows nearly disappeared into his scanty hairline. "Are you really asking me to assist you, my lord? Do you think I can possibly be of help?"

"I am, and I am sure that you will be," Daniel said confidently. "After all, Mr. Pettigrew, I have been away from England for a very long time. I know how to design a battle plan, but I will need someone who knows the field. I shall depend upon you to let me know how the *haut ton* goes on about things here at home. My sisters must be presented in the most seemly manner and with the proper decorum."

Choosing to dismiss Mr. Pettigrew's sudden inclination to dance a jig as just one more of the man's many peculiarities which he'd come to accept, Daniel continued to watch the girls glide prettily hand in hand across the room, like a string of fragile paper dolls cut from one sheet. Simpleminded or not, they looked so vulnerable that he pledged to double his efforts to have his sisters all settled safely in their own households as soon as possible.

When the last one disappeared onto the landing above, Daniel said with assurance, "I daresay, Mr. Pettigrew, we shall have them all married within the year. You wait and see."

The Honorable Mr. Pettigrew, born the thirteenth child and twelfth son of an impoverished baron, had been introduced early to the reality that he would have to earn his own living—or go hungry. He had accepted his fate with the same equanimity he accepted most all that life had dealt him. He was a dedicated man who had worked hard to please the sixth Earl of Chantry, thankful that he had found employment. He had always been there to run errands, take notes, write letters, pay bills, and meet with his master's man of business so that the earl could enjoy his clubs. Mr. Pettigrew also suffered the brunt of tempers gone amuck and pieced together the mistakes of others. To his disappointment, no one seemed to think these things important enough for any particular notice.

This unintrusive man even sharpened quills until their tips could pierce an eggshell without breaking it. That feat alone brought him some sense of pride, but it was not the end of his talents. He then would blow out the egg, paint the shell with.a tiny sable-hair brush, and place it on a little wooden pedestal, which he had lovingly and meticulously carved from scraps of wood gathered at the cabinetmakers. Mr. Pettigrew had created quite a few of these delicate pieces over the years, but no one had ever praised him for it or asked to see his collection. It was as if he were no more than a stick of furniture—invisible—until they wished to use him.

Because of this proclivity to fade into the background, there had been many times during his service to Daniel's father in which Mr. Pettigrew quite by accident had been made privy to top government secrets. Although he thought he'd proved his trustworthiness by his silence, he'd never been consulted about anything of great importance. Until this moment. Mr. Pettigrew's eyes misted. Now, for the first time in his life, he was being asked to take part in a real mission.

"Indeed, I shall try my best, my lord," Mr. Pettigrew answered with a click of his heels and a meaningful flick of his brows.

Ruth and Rebecca, Georgette and Winifred, Antoinette and Babette, and, finally, Margaret and Mary slipped quietly up the stairs, down the long hall, and through the arched portals of a large bedchamber.

No sooner had the last one crossed the threshold and slammed shut the heavy oaken door than all eight girls squealed with delight and doubled over with laughter. Ruth and Rebecca hugged each other, Babette and Antoinette joined hands and swung around in circles, and Margaret pulled Mary's hair.

"We did it! We did it! We did it!"

"We fooled him, Freddie," Georgette shouted, throwing out

her arms and twirling around the room. "Your plan worked! Lord Chantry is quite persuaded that you are his sister. Did you hear? He said he is carrying all *eight* of us to Londontown! What would we have done if we had to leave you behind?"

Freddie crossed her arms and pursed her lips. " 'Tis plain as a pike's staff. You would not have had any fun at all."

Two

"Shame on you, Freddie," Babette scolded. "You would have let the cat out of the bag right in front of Lord Chantry and spoiled everything if Georgette hadn't squeezed your hand."

"You were giggling, too, and you promised you would not," Antoinette added with a shake of her finger.

"I'm sorry," Winifred said, wiping the tears from her eyes. "It was just that . . ." She started to laugh again. "Lord Chantry looked so purposeful when he spoke of his *duty*. Especially when he called us *boys*. 'Duty, my boy! Duty is the highest calling to test a man's valor!' I was almost tempted to stick out my foot and trip him."

This sent the girls into another fit of the whoops.

"No matter what any of you say, I think our brother is quite handsome," said a dreamy-eyed Mary, hugging herself.

"For once I agree with you," Margaret said. "A most splendid specimen, indeed."

Her twin gave her a scolding look. "Maggie! You make him sound like one of those bugs you are always collecting."

"They are insects, not bugs, Miss Prissy," Margaret said, sticking out her tongue in a most unladylike way. "In fact, Dr. MacDougal said that the one I caught for him the last time he came collecting was a bush cricket. He said it was very rare this far north."

"They are creepy, crawly bugs," Mary insisted.

"Girls! Watch what you say and how you deport yourselves

or you will have us in the stew before the day is out," Freddie scolded.

"Well, for my part, I find Lord Chantry divinely formed," Mary said. "You think so too, don't you, Freddie? I saw the way you looked at him when he was gazing out the window."

"We were all *looking* at him, silly," Georgette chided. "We have not seen so handsome a man as our brother in a long time."

Freddie was not quite sure what her real feelings were. She only knew that something about the earl unsettled her, but she would not tell the other girls that. Instead she blurted out, "I do think that he will make a splendid dupe to play tricks on."

"Do not be deceived into thinking that because he is a well-looking man he is a fool, dear," Rebecca said.

Yes, Freddie thought. That is what Granny Eizel had told her. His lordship would definitely bear watching. She would just have to be more subtle when plotting their adventures when they arrived in the city.

"But your plan worked," Georgette said with admiration. "That's what is important."

Babette and Antoinette nodded their agreement.

Ruth and Rebecca hugged Freddie. "She speaks the truth, dear," Ruth said, as her twin added, "His lordship has accepted you as his sister."

"Oh, I hope so. Mama always said that she wanted all of us to go to Londontown when we grew up. She talked about the time she spent there with so much enthusiasm. Now she will get her wish." So saying, Freddie broke free of her sisters, and giving Georgette a swat upon the backside, dashed across the room and leaped onto the high postered bed.

Georgette chased after her and, grabbing a pillow, whopped Freddie heartily over the head, popping the stitches open. Feathers exploded every which way. With shouts of glee, the other girls followed. As they clambered up the stepstool and piled on top of each other, a cloud of down snowed all over the eight of them, setting off more swatting and giggling.

Freddie wriggled out from under the mountain of bodies and

rolled off the bed. "Come girls," she said, swiping a feather off her nose. "We don't have a minute to lose. We must collect our belongings and be ready to go as soon as possible."

"We don't have much to pack," Ruth said, looking down at her serviceable woolen frock.

"That just makes it easier, doesn't it? The sooner we are ready, the quicker we will be on our way; and Lord Chantry will not have the chance to think twice about his promise to bring us out all at one time."

Mary's blue eyes grew enormous. "He would not do that, would he, Freddie? How am I to find my heart's delight if I do not go to Londontown?"

"Well, if the coal dust has killed all the insects, I don't care if I go or not," said Margaret.

Mary squealed. "She's been nutty in the head ever since that bug person from the institute in Edinburgh came here. She'll spoil everything."

"Freddie, make her quit. Dr. MacDougal is a highly regarded entomologist—not a bug person," Margaret cried.

"Girls! Girls! I am sure there are enough gallant men and insects to go around for both of you in Londontown," Freddie said, trying to hide her amusement. "If he catches you acting like silly peahens, your brother may bow out altogether."

"Oh, he wouldn't. Would he?" Georgette asked.

"I feel that Lord Chantry is a man who always keeps his word," Rebecca said, linking her arm with her twin. "If he says he is taking us to Londontown, he will do it."

Ruth nodded.

Freddie narrowed her eyes. "But we cannot count on that until it happens, can we? Granny Eizel says, ' 'Tis best beware than be sorry.' "

"Are you going to tell Granny Eizel that we are leaving, Freddie?"

"Yes, I will tell her. Now do as I say, and Lord Chantry need be none the wiser."

"Yes, Freddie," the girls said in unison.

"Georgette, you move the fastest. Run belowstairs and find Dinn-Dinn. Tell him we will be needing the trunks from the attic. He is too old to lift them by himself, so fetch Gilby from the garden to help him.

"Mary, you have the most innocent of countenances. Go tell Agnes that the ticking on another pillow has popped open again and to bring the broom. And while you are there tell Flora to fetch some rags. We will need them to dust out the trunks. Now off with you. Your brother wants us to be ready to leave as soon as possible."

The girls nodded in compliance.

"The last one packed is a goose," she said, shooing the girls out the door.

As soon as the door closed behind them, the sisters gathered in the corridor.

Hands on hips, Margaret spoke first. "I don't see why Mama Gilliane did not persuade our father to adopt Freddie. If she had, Freddie would be Lord Chantry's sister legally. He would have been bound by his pledge of honor to bring her out, and it would have saved us all this hugger-muggery."

"You never listen," Mary scolded. "Mama explained that it was because Freddie is the only offspring that her daddy, Frederick Hendry, had, and she hoped that someday his father would forgive him for running off with her and accept Freddie."

Margaret tossed her head. "Well, if Lord Bellingham hasn't acknowledged her as his granddaughter by now, 'tis not likely that he ever will."

"Mama was a romantic," Mary said with a sigh. "She always believed in happy endings."

"Well, you can see what her woolgathering has brought us, Miss Prissy."

"Now girls," Ruth placated, "Mama Gilliane has been in her grave for over four years and we cannot undo what has already been done."

"Perhaps that is so—but Freddie is just like her," Georgette said. "She does anything that flits into her head. That is why she is so much fun."

"That is also why we must be careful that Lord Chantry does not find out," Rebecca answered.

"We could tell him the truth," Ruth suggested. "Our brother seems an honorable man. Surely he would not leave Freddie, even if she is not his sister."

"Oh, please, don't tell him!" Georgette cried. "You read his letter. He wrote explicitly that he was coming to fetch his sisters, and Mr. Pettigrew said that our father definitely said *daughters*. Neither mentioned anything about Freddie."

"Well, she is *our* sister," Margaret said, taking Mary's hand in a show of unusual camaraderie. "At least, half sister and that counts for something."

"We have the same mama, even if our papas were different," Mary explained to the others as if they didn't already know.

"Remember, Freddie warned us that we cannot be sure of what he would do," Georgette said. "What fun would I have without Freddie? She is my bosom bow."

The two other dark-haired beauties, Babette and Antoinette, nodded in agreement with their older sister.

"That is why Freddie said we would have to contrive so that she can come with us," Margaret added. "Besides, she is the one who copied all of Mama Gilliane's maps. We could not find our way around Londontown without her."

"Then we must all pledge right here and now to keep her secret," Ruth said.

All the girls bobbed their heads up and down vigorously.

Rebecca held out her hands for them to form a ring, the way Mama Gilliane had taught them when they were wee bairns. "Are we all in this race together?" she asked.

"Aye!" they all shouted.

"Then answer after me," she said.

"Are ye saddled?"

"Aye."

"Are ye bridled?"

"Aye."

"Are ye ready for the calf?"

"Aye!! Aye!! Aye!!!"

"Aff then an' awa'!"

Georgette giggled. "I wonder what exciting games Freddie has up her sleeve for us to play in Londontown?"

"Well, dear, we had best get packed or we shall never know," Ruth said, smiling.

Babette's and Antoinette's adorable little lips turned upward too.

"I must write a letter to Dr. MacDougal to tell him about my wonderful opportunity to collect some London insects for him," Margaret said eagerly.

Mary squealed. "If you take that box of bugs with you, I'm going to tell Freddie."

With that, the door opened and Freddie stuck her head out. "What is all the squabbling about? I can hear the ruckus all the way through this door. Now, get to your chores."

"Yes, Freddie," they all chimed, scattering like dandelion seeds in the wind.

Trying not to laugh out loud, Freddie watched the girls fondly, then closed the door and leaned against it. God Bless them! They were all her sisters whether Lord Chantry would agree with her on that point or not. She had to admit that he looked like no other male she had ever seen, but she was afraid from what she had observed already of his lordship that he was a pattern-saint who ran on rules and regulations, not on his heart. Just like his father.

Freddie gave a little whoop. What a ninny she had been to fear that she could not match wits with Lord Chantry! She remembered the mixture of curiosity and apprehension which had run through her that morning several weeks ago when Flora Doone, the cook's daughter, came scrambling up the hill where they were hunting rabbits. " 'Tis a letter come in the post, m'lady," she'd called, waving the packet like a banner high above her head—just before she'd tripped and sprawled headlong upon the ground. Poor Flora. Mrs. Doone had said that her daughter's feet were more suited to having oars attached to them than shoes.

The letter, which the overzealous scullery maid carried had announced the death of the sixth Earl of Chantry. It surprised them all for it was several months after the event, so it seemed. All the girls were saddened of course, for they had kind hearts, but it was for a personage whom they had little known or had any word from for four years.

The missive was signed by a man saying that he was their brother: Daniel Douglas Durham, seventh Earl of Chantry. It seemed his lordship was coming to Cornhill-on-Tweed to confirm that their father's dying wish had been for each of his daughters—when they came of age—to have a Season in London.

The minute Freddie had finished the letter, the other seven girls shouted and hugged each other—until Ruth saw the stricken expression on Freddie's face. "Girls, girls!" she said, holding up her hands. "Lord Chantry said nothing about Freddie. Let us go over his letter again."

Solemnly they all seated themselves on the side of the hill and begged Freddie to tell them what it all meant.

"I do not know," she said, reading through the letter again. "I shall have to ask Granny Eizel what we should do."

They knew they had a brother. Mama Gilliane had told them about him from the time they were small. But the young viscount was in school too far away to visit them, she had said, so they gave him little thought except when the late Earl of Chantry stopped by now and then on his way to Edinburgh.

On those occasions Freddie could not count the number of times they heard the name Daniel, roll off the old earl's lips, and Freddie wondered if his lordship spoke of his daughters as often when he was in his son's presence. Obviously not, from the bewildered look upon the new Lord Chantry's face when he first laid sight on them this afternoon two months after his letter had come. Neither did he seem to have any knowledge of how many sisters he had, which is what Freddie had counted on, because Granny Eizel had told her that to assure her chances of going to London she must trick the earl into believing she was one of his sisters.

Freddie had been on the upper landing when she'd heard the pounding on the front door earlier that afternoon. It took three more assaults—each louder and more persistent than the last— before their elderly butler, Dinn-Dinn, allowed that something was happening at that end of the house and shuffled forward to open it. No one came to the front door anymore, for the carriage path had long ago been lost to the weeds and rabbits.

Dear befuddled Dinn-Dinn—his memory being as it was up in the attic these past few years, and so hard of hearing that they had to call his name twice to have him attend them—had mistaken the newcomer for the old earl and ushered him in, chattering like a magpie as though the late Lord Chantry had only been there the week before.

The instant Freddie saw the girls' brother, even before he'd uncovered his head, she had known who he was. A black cape hid much of the upper half of the long black surtout. The heels of his black riding boots clicked on the gray slate at the entry, and he marched into Knocktigh as though he had been the lord of the manor forever.

He gave his riding crop to one of the two gentlemen accompanying him, removed his tall beaver to reveal a crown of blond hair much like the color of Ruth's and Rebecca's, while at the same time his dark eyes took in all that he could see in Great Hall. He handed the hat to Dinn-Dinn, then methodically pulled off his leather riding gloves one finger at a time and gave these two items to Dinn-Dinn also, who dropped the hat to take the gloves and then dropped the gloves and kicked the hat in an attempt to retrieve it, sending it rolling across the floor to where it finally came to rest under a three-legged table propped against the wall.

Freddie clamped her hand tightly over her mouth to keep from bursting into a fit of laughter which would have revealed that she was eavesdropping. Had his lordship known that Dinn-Dinn could not concentrate on more than one task at a time, he surely would not have handed him the gloves in the first place.

While the thin gentleman, whom Freddie now knew to be Mr. Pettigrew, rescued the hat from further destruction, the second attendant, who looked suspiciously like a gnome, stood on tiptoe to assist his lordship in removing his coat.

Taking back his riding crop, the earl slapped it against the palm of his hand in slow easy strokes as if nothing had gone amiss at all. The whole procedure had been executed with a certain control and elegance of style that started a tingling in her fingers which ran up her arms, wrapped round and round her chest, and finally settled in the vicinity of her heart. At the same time, as far as she could see, not one expression passed over the earl's face to indicate that anything had gone awry. He was a sly boots all right. Cool as a Highland spring.

Now that she had heard what his lordship's plans were, Freddie knew it was more imperative than ever that she accompany the girls to Londontown. Without her, they would surely make a complete mishmash of the whole thing.

Comely young men were a scarcity hereabouts, and Freddie was afraid that her trusting sisters would be so dazzled by the sight of all those dashing youths in the city they'd succumb to the first sweet words spoken.

Worse yet, what if his lordship insisted on marrying off his sisters to pattern-saints like himself, or, heaven forbid, to *doitits,* who were muddleheaded, weak-willed, clodpolls. Freddie was determined not to let that happen, for either would make terribly boring husbands. Her sisters deserved better than that.

In another part of the house Daniel entered his bedchamber whistling. Candles were burning in sconces on the walls, and a small blaze warmed the area near the hearth on which a large, half-filled wooden tub sat. Towels hung on a rack, his shaving kit lay on a nearby table, and his dinner clothes were already picked out.

Tilbury, the earl's valet, neither blinking nor showing any other signs of curiosity over his young master's surprising change of temper from that which he'd exhibited much of the last five days, stood at the ready to do the earl's bidding. Yes, something to the young lord's liking had happened below in the Great Hall to cause him to be so joyful; a part of his meeting with his siblings, no doubt, which Tilbury regretted that he must have missed when he had to go outside to scrounge for sticks to fuel his lordship's fireplace.

Mr. Pettigrew and Tilbury had conferred about their master's foul mood when they had traveled in relative comfort to the Scottish border inside the enclosed Durham family coach. They had ruled out that his ill humor on the journey was caused by his lordship's insistence that he ride, despite rain and sleet, the entire trip on that great smoky horse he'd brought back from the war. Mr. Pettigrew told Tilbury that his lordship had suffered far worse during his six years of fighting Boney. Neither was it dyspepsia, because they both agreed that nothing seemed to interfere with the young nobleman's healthy appetite. But for all his curiosity, Tilbury was not about to ask his lordship as to the source of his good humor now for fear of breaking the spell. Because he and Mr. Pettigrew had just about had enough of his nibs glums on their journey to Knocktigh, he did not want to say something that would set him back.

On the other hand, Tilbury knew that the earl would be waiting for him to make some remark—for he always did so—and if he did not, his lordship would suspect his valet had been up to something.

"All went as you expected, my lord?"

Daniel's brow rose almost imperceptibly. "I saw you in and about, Tilbury, tending to my needs, I am sure. How much did you hear?"

"All that was possible from above."

"Then it is not necessary for me to go into detail, is it?"

"Not if you do not wish to, my lord," the valet answered stiffly. Tilbury was no worm. What good was a gentleman's gentleman if he did not stick his nose into everything that concerned his master? He only wished he'd managed it better and not had to miss such a great deal of the goings-on. Now he was going to have to employ his usual devious methods to find out what had happened in the room below.

Three

Daniel was not quite certain if he had hired the valet or the other way round, but suffice it to say that they'd acquired each other to their mutual satisfaction soon after he'd arrived back in England. Edgar Buttons, Daniel's batman for four years on the Continent, had chosen to stay with his company when Daniel returned to London. His and Buttons's relationship had survived through several battles, situations in which one or both were near death and were patching up one another's wounds. He sorely was at a loss without him, until Tilbury appeared on the scene.

The roly-poly man, who resembled a barrel, had a pinched mouth, two blackberries for eyes, and plump red apples where his cheeks should have been, and when he smiled, growled, scolded, or just screwed up his face to concentrate on the task at hand, his eyes disappeared altogether.

He had been in the employ of a retired army colonel until that worthy stuck his spoon in the wall, so he was quite familiar with a military officer's penchant for persnicketiness. A gentleman's gentleman of impeccable taste—at least where it suited his master—he thought nothing of ordering the earl back like a recalcitrant schoolboy to be done over if one strand of hair dared pop out of place, while hisself sported a nest of steel gray fuzz which frizzled out from his head as though it were permanently attached to an electrical machine. Either it could not be tamed or Tilbury never bothered to try. Daniel suspected the latter was nearer the truth.

Under his care, Daniel was dressed to the nines. In addition to his military uniforms—for Daniel had not yet sold out his commission—Tilbury saw that his lordship acquired a fashionable town and country wardrobe appropriate to his new station. As long as he kept his master looking up to the ears in the latest style, the valet didn't seem to mind in the least that hisself looked like a casualty blown in from the battlefield. His suits showed no particular style or date. Most had been castoffs from his former employer—a much taller man—and although the garments buttoned around him well enough, the length left several inches of cloth nesting round his ankles. And his neckcloth, secured round his throat in a sorry knot, with one end forever loose, looked like a gray squirrel perched upon his shoulder with its tail flapping behind.

Daniel walked to the hearth and held out his hands to warm them. As he eyed the tub a deep growl of pleasure escaped him. When he had arrived at Knocktigh earlier that afternoon, he'd taken only a moment to be directed to his room to freshen up. He had not wanted to delay getting on with the purpose of his visit. There had only been time for Tilbury to brush off some of the dust of the road from his breeches and give his boots a quick rub before going down to meet his sisters.

Now the round little man helped the earl out of his coat and waited for him to hand over his cravat and shirt. "Do you wish to take a lie-down, first, my lord?"

"No, no, Tilbury. The tub will do," Daniel said, then laughed. "You can pry me out of it in an hour. That should give me time to dress for supper."

Six wooden buckets of water sat in a row on the hearth while a large copper kettle, steam rising from its spout, hung on a hook over the flames.

Ordinarily four buckets of water would have been sufficient, but since they all leaked in various amounts, tiny rivulets ran off the hearth and into and out of the cracks of the planked floor, and from there, raced toward the door.

Daniel looked down at his feet. "There is a puddle forming around my boots, Tilbury."

"If his lordship would just step a few inches to one side he would not be in the path of the stream."

"I suppose you are right, but why did you get leaky buckets in the first place?"

"That was all I could find, my lord." Tilbury was not about to tell his lordship the scant supplies he'd found belowstairs.

"Well, never mind—we shall be out of here as soon as possible," Daniel said, shedding his small clothes. He stepped into the tub and eased himself down into the warm water. With knees drawn up, he lay his head back upon the folded towel which had been placed under his neck, closed his eyes, and waited to be shaved.

"How long do you think it will take my sisters to be ready, Tilbury? A week? Two weeks?"

"I have no idea, my lord. I would think it would take at least the latter to gather all the fribbles and geegaws that a woman accumulates."

"Well, I hope no longer than that. It took us only two days to be on the road for here."

Tilbury reckoned it would be of no use pointing out that at his lordship's Albany set of rooms, he'd had a houseman and a cleaning woman who came in during the day, not counting Mr. Pettigrew and hisself to do all the packing and running about for him.

"But the young ladies will be coming to London for the whole Season, my lord," Tilbury said, as he handed the earl a steaming-hot face linen and began to put away the shaving materials.

"That is true. I will allow them two weeks, no more than that. It will give me time to inspect Knocktigh's assets with Mr. Pettigrew and speak to the steward. I did not even know this estate existed until Mr. Pettigrew informed me that my sisters lived here."

Several minutes later, Daniel, his eyes covered with the cloth, had begun to drift off when a knock sounded on the door. "Whoever it is, Tilbury, send them away."

After a brief discussion in the corridor, the valet came back.

"It is Mr. Pettigrew, my lord. He insists it is most important that he speak to you."

Daniel mumbled from under the cloth. "Tell him I'm sure it can wait."

The valet made another trip to the door and another back to the hearth. "Mr. Pettigrew says it is a matter of which he thinks you need to be informed."

"Oh, hell's bells!" Daniel said. "Tell him to come in, Tilbury. I refuse to move."

The valet had had enough of this hither and yon. He was not after all an errand boy. "Come in, Mr. Pettigrew," he shouted across the room. "His lordship will see you."

Daniel removed the cloth from over one eye. "What the devil is this emergency that is so great that you should disturb me in my bath, Mr. Pettigrew?"

The secretary's brows twitched simultaneously, one up, one down. Daniel wondered how he did it. "There is a matter that has arisen . . . that is . . . something that I do not know how to handle."

"Od'sbodkins, Mr. Pettigrew. I have never known anything which you cannot take care of."

Mr. Pettigrew wrung his hands. "It is about the young ladies, my lord."

Daniel groaned. "Have my sisters finally found their tongues? If it has taken them this long, I am sure whatever it is they have to say can wait until dinner time."

"I don't believe so, my lord. They may not be here that long. They are down in the Great Hall with their trunks, and I overheard Lady Winifred instructing the servants to start carrying them out to the carriage house. I thought you should know."

"What?" Daniel shouted, rearing up so quickly that water cascaded over the rim of the tub, once more flooding the wood planking. "They've run off?"

His eyes growing wider by the minute, Mr. Pettigrew jumped nimbly to one side as the earl scrambled over the rim of the tub and began pulling on his boots. Tilbury scurried to hand his lordship a towel with one hand, his small clothes with the other, but the earl was already buttoning up his shirt, wrong.

"I shall catch those ungrateful runagates and bring them back," Daniel said, making a grab for his dinner jacket.

"On the contrary, my lord. They are still here."

Daniel stopped midway to the door and whirled around. "What do you mean they are still here?" He pushed away Tilbury's arm as the valet tried to hand his master his pantaloons. "I thought you said they had left."

Mr. Pettigrew blanched. He'd never seen Lord Chantry in such a state of dishabille; one side of his shirt longer than the other, sloshing boots, and no trousers. After he'd caused his master such distress, Lord Chantry would never want him to be his aide. "I meant, they were still in the Hall a few minutes ago."

"Then I shall stop them before they escape."

"My lord," Tilbury said, sternly. "I will not permit you to go out of the room without your breeches."

Daniel glanced down at the bare knees showing beneath his shirt and pulled himself up straight. "Of course not, Tilbury. I had no such intention. Quickly, Mr. Pettigrew, waylay my sisters for as long as it takes for me to dress. We shall get to the bottom of this treachery once and for all. I will not accept such insubordination. Even from my sisters."

The secretary was not even out the door before Tilbury waddled into action.

"Must you be so slow, Tilbury?" Daniel complained as the valet tugged off his boots so that he could redress him properly from inside out. The earl rejected the small clothes, rebuttoned his shirt himself, accepted the trousers, and refused the evening pumps, pulling his riding boots back on, while grumbling about the probability that he would be on horseback before the hour was passed. He would have skipped the waistcoat also if Tilbury hadn't insisted that he put it on. Finally, the bedeviled servant commenced to try, with little success, to create a decent waterfall in his lordship's neckcloth.

"Confound it, Tilbury! It will not matter what I look like if

Mr. Pettigrew has been unable to stop my sisters and I must chase after them over hill and dale in the dead of night."

Tilbury had never seen his young master in such a lather. Wisely, he said nothing while twisting his lordship's neckcloth so tightly that the earl had to stop his squirming or face the possibility of being strangled.

Daniel knew the signs, and as soon as he saw the valet's eyes disappear into the folds of his cheeks, he surrendered. "I do not understand it, Tilbury," he said in a much more mollified tone. "I have ridden in the foulest of weather for five days to attend them; I have had my hat crushed; and, I swear, they have not had the courtesy to speak more than a dozen words to me since I arrived. I have offered to take them away from this dismal place; I have had my bath interrupted; and now, I find they are trying to run away from me. Are all females so ungrateful a lot or is it only sisters?"

"I could not say, my lord. I never had a sister to compare— and would your lordship please stand still so I can tie your cravat. I will not permit you out of this room looking anything less than a gentleman."

Finally, after Daniel had fussed and fumed and mussed up his hair for the third time while shrugging into his dinner jacket, Tilbury was quite happy to be rid of him. Even so, he could not but feel a sense of pride as he watched the young man leave the room. His lordship, of course, even looked up to the mark with a layer of dust on him. But, the way he was turned out now, the young ladies could not help but be impressed.

Daniel, his mouth set in a stubborn line, strode with long, determined steps down the corridor. When he had arrived this afternoon, he'd anticipated a far different welcome from his sisters than what he was receiving. If not expressing girlish joy in finding they had a protector, at least they could show some enthusiasm for their chance to go to London. Of all the reactions he had rehearsed in his mind, desertion was the one he would have thought least possible—and the one he would not accept. By the time Daniel arrived at the top of the stairwell overlooking the Great Hall below, he

was in a temper to ring a peal over his sisters' heads and therefore not at all prepared for what he saw below.

All eight girls, their hands folded in front of them, stood
beside four tattered and worn trunks, looking up at him, smiling;
Mr. Pettigrew was with them, smiling; Dinn-Dinn stood stiffly
nearby in a frizzled grayed wig long past its prime, a full-skirted
faded black coat, and, beneath his breeches, wrinkled white silk
stockings that clung precariously to spindly legs. There were
silver buckles on his black shoes and a white linen cloth was
draped over his arm, and he was smiling. A thickset, broad-
shouldered man servant in rather reprehensible faded green livery, whom Daniel took to be a footman, was positioned behind
the butler, beaming pleasantly upon one and all as though nothing was amiss. Daniel had the uncomfortable feeling that there
were other retainers peering out from darkened doorways. Probably all of them were smiling too. It was a conspiracy of monu-
mental proportions, but he would not be taken in by their efforts
to whitewash the girls' mutiny.

"Lord Chantry," Mr. Pettigrew said, stepping forward in an
obsequious attempt to smooth the waters, "I humbly beg your
pardon for my previous misrepresentation of the facts."

"I think the facts speak for themselves, Mr. Pettigrew," Daniel
said, gesturing with a sweep of his arm toward the trunks. "What
are those, pray tell?" he asked, feeling oddly that he looked the
clown for asking. "Do you now contend that they were not running away?"

Everyone's gaze followed to where the earl pointed at the
baggage, except Lady Winifred. Now that she stood in a row
with her sisters, Daniel realized for the first time how tiny in
stature she was. The little brown mouse with the chocolate eyes,
who had been so frightened of him only an hour before, now
boldly kept her gaze riveted upon his face. She even had the
audacity to smile as if the whole affair was a joke.

"But we only did as you told us and packed as quickly as
possible," Freddie said, trying her best to look contrite and humble. She feared she did not succeed and bowed her head so Lord

Chantry could not see the laughter in her eyes. *Did he really think they were running away?* "We were going to have the luggage carried to the coach before dinner so that we would be ready to leave for Londontown in the morning."

"Whatever you had taken out will have to be brought back in. We are not leaving tomorrow," Daniel said. He was about to tell her that he had heard better Banbury tales, when he was stopped by Mr. Pettigrew, who began to choke out several nonsensical words which the earl took to be affirmations of his sisters' good intentions. Then, from the manner in which the others all nodded, he was almost flummoxed into thinking them innocent as angels.

It was then that Daniel saw behind the crowd a long trestle table covered with white linen, sitting in front of the great stone hearth. A silver candelabrum placed in the center illuminated the ten place settings, four on either side and one at each end. The fire had been rekindled and burned brightly with a welcoming warmth which even he could appreciate as the heat rose up to meet him.

They were not running away after all. There was a moment of complete silence as the earl stood motionless at the top of the landing. Then as though he had just newly come upon the scene, he descended the steps calmly and bowed to the ladies. Whereupon, Ruth and Rebecca hurried forward and after curtsying prettily, each took one of his arms and, before he knew it, he found himself being ushered to the head of the table.

When Freddie first saw Lord Chantry upon the stairs, her mouth dropped open. She could do naught but stare. What a splendid picture his lordship made standing above them dressed all in black, a halo of golden hair encircling his face, a fierce slant to his brows, his dark eyes snapping. She once more felt the tiny fingers playing up and down her spine, and wondered what it meant. She had hurried the girls to be packed and ready to go in the morning. Not that there had been much to put in the trunks. They had exhausted their supply of fabrics months ago and had even cut up most of the draperies to make frocks for the winter.

At first, Freddie could not imagine what the earl had to be angry about, until she realized that he really thought they were running away. The corners of her mouth threatened to curl upward and she had to squeeze her lips together to keep from giggling. His lordship had actually become unraveled. If he could be thrown into the dithers so easily, what fun they were going to have with him in Londontown, she thought wickedly. But she could hear Granny Eizel in her head, telling her to behave, so Freddie kept her own counsel and signaled Ruth and Rebecca to approach the earl as planned.

They were quite tall for girls, but now as he walked between them, Freddie realized that Lord Chantry was not of as great a height as she had first thought. He was, however, so divinely built that his wide shoulders made the two slender girls look dainty beside him.

As the rest of the party followed, Freddie placed a finger on her cheek and contemplated the scene for a minute. Then, taking her place at the foot of the table, she thought of the few encounters with the male sex she and her sisters had experienced during the last four years. With Dinn-Dinn looking like a reed ready to break, and Gilby resembling the mastiff owned by Dr. Shivers in the village, and Loof, their old stableman, more a picture of an overgrown, silver-bearded elf, the menfolk of Knocktigh had not prepared them for the contrast of a man like the earl. If the gentlemen of Londontown were half as comely as their brother, she feared she might have difficulty keeping her girls in check.

Dinner proceeded quite smoothly—actually better than expected—but if Daniel thought that he had broken the spell and loosened his sisters' tongues, he was soon disillusioned. The Honorable Mr. Pettigrew, being the son of a baron, joined them, but once seated among eight young ladies that timid soul did not prove to be a fountain of eloquence either. However, it was an enjoyable meal deliciously prepared, though there seemed to be an overabundance of dishes featuring rabbit and chicken, potatoes, and apples. And although the beverages were more cider than wine, this did not take away from the uniqueness of the occasion. The several removes were served by the butler, the footman, and a plump, rosy-cheeked maid. Perhaps they were not as efficient as many of the Quality would insist they should be, but Daniel had to admit that they worked with a great deal more enthusiasm.

And if his sisters did not prove to be as loquacious as he'd hoped, it did give Daniel an opportunity to study them more closely. When they had been lined up in the Great Hall he'd taken note that his full sisters were the tallest, Margaret and Mary were of medium height. The dark-haired girls were only a tad shorter. But the smallest of all was the little mouse . . . and yet, surprisingly, she had been the first to have the courage to speak up to him.

Daniel had fond memories of his own mother and vaguely remembered the dark-haired French noblewoman, but he'd never met the Scottish widow whom his father had married in Edinburgh. Upon seeing the carrottops of his youngest half sisters, he reckoned that the third Countess of Chantry had been redheaded as well. It was the plain brown of Georgette's twin's tresses which puzzled him, and he wondered if his father's hair had been brown at one time. For as long as he could remember, the late earl's hair had been a misty gray-and-white, similar to that of Daniel's horse.

He also wondered why it was Lady Winifred who positioned herself opposite him at the other end of the table. He deduced that it had to be because his full sisters Ruth and Rebecca wished to be seated on either side of him at the head of the table. And since it was Lady Winifred who was situated nearest the servants' entrance, it was only logical that they should ask her for direction. He was pleased with this show of courtesy on their part. Although they refrained from speaking to him directly, he did see the shy glances Ruth and Rebecca cast his way.

Daniel was contemplating how he should respond when it occurred to him that some of his sisters might still harbor ill will toward him for accusing them of running away. Perhaps, an apology, and an assurance that he was not such a black-heart as they had thought, would smooth the waters and loosen their tongues. "I am sorry that we had a misunderstanding," he began. "If it appeared that I would be so cruel as to snatch you away before you could say your goodbyes to your friends and neighbors who will miss you . . . I did not mean to do so. You do not need to feel hurried, for it will take a few days more for me to see the bailiff and assess my property."

Daniel had not even finished the sentence when one of his dark-haired sisters choked and began to cough quite uncontrollably. Was it Babette or Antoinette? Or Georgette? Devil take it! Would he ever get them straight in his head? No, it had to be Georgette because she was sitting next to Winifred who was at the foot of the table where rightfully Ruth and Rebecca should be. He looked in that direction and saw that he was right, for the dark-haired one was wriggling in her chair at the other end of the table. Winifred had her hands clasped over her mouth, and from the way her eyes bulged he feared she may be about to have a fit herself.

Then either Babette or Antoinette was coughing, again, and while Ruth or Rebecca patted her on the back, one of the redheads—was it Mary or Margaret?—knocked her fork off the table onto the floor, then bumped heads with her twin when they both dove to retrieve it. The maid, rushing to pick up the fallen cutlery, and the eager young footman in green, who was hurrying in the contrary direction with a beaker of cider, collided with a great crash and clatter. Giggles and more coughing ensued, and a number of people whom Daniel had not seen before appeared wielding brooms and mops, and bearing clean cutlery. They swept through, and in a matter of minutes disappeared to whence they had come, leaving everything neat and tidy.

Suddenly silence once more descended upon the Great Hall. The girls sat demurely in their chairs, eyes shielded under long lashes, and began once more to eat as though nothing unusual had occurred. Daniel, himself was not sure of what had happened, but he *was* certain that they had probably forgotten what he'd been talking about. He knew he had.

Clearing his throat, he began anew. "I shall be making an inspection of the premises tomorrow with Mr. Pettigrew to take inventory of the manor, outbuildings, livestock, and so forth. I am especially interested in the stables. Arrangements will have to be made, of course, for the care of the horses when I carry you all to London."

The girls' heads popped up and turned in his direction. Daniel held up his hands. "These are my responsibilities now. You need never concern yourselves over such matters again."

Although his sisters seemed to place all of their attention on the meal, he caught them watching him with sidelong glances now and then, frequent smiles lighting up their faces. For the first time that evening, Daniel was once again inclined to look upon his sisters with benevolence, deciding that what had occurred had been a rare happenstance and that their manners were all they should be. In spite of their drab ensembles—which *did* bother him—Daniel was pleased to say that each of his sisters in her own way was more becoming than he had at first thought. Even the smallest, the one with the chocolate eyes, stood out because she was different. It pleased him to think that his mission to get them all to the altar didn't seem an impossible goal after all.

But on the downside, his attempts to draw them into sensible conversation still seemed to be failing. Mr. Pettigrew, who turned red every time one of the young ladies looked his way, was proving to be no help whatsoever. So Daniel found he was left to his own resources to figure out what one did say to sisters.

There was always the social art of flirting. The earl had never considered himself successful at it, but then one did not flirt with one's sisters anyway. Gentlemen flirted with ladies who were not kin; students flirted with barmaids; soldiers flirted with farmer's daughters and camp followers.

Daniel had attended gatherings of the Fashionable Set in Brussels before Boney escaped from Elba, and although he'd now been back in England for nearly nine months, he still had not made it a habit to frequent many balls or soirees where it required him to hold lengthy exchanges with the opposite sex.

Teasing was what one did to sisters, but Daniel wasn't very good at that either. He remembered visiting a chum from school, Spooney Packard, who had invited him to spend the holidays with his family in Hampshire. Spooney had two sisters and he'd teased them unmercifully, until they'd cried sometimes. Daniel had decided he would never tease anybody if it made them cry. He did not think it a very pleasant thing to do, and he could not understand why Spooney seemed to derive so much pleasure from it. Not that Daniel cared that much for Spooney, but it was better than spending the holidays alone at Durham Hall in Oxfordshire under the scrutiny of sixty-four servants. His father had written from London that the countess was not feeling quite the thing and that as soon as she was better he promised to fetch Daniel to London for a visit. Which never came to be.

Now the earl took a long look at his sisters. Perhaps it was better that they did not talk. Without silly female chatter, he could eat in peace. He began to relax, and to his considerable relief they finished their meal with a certain aura of contentment all round.

Four

After Daniel had dismissed his sisters, the old butler brought the two men some port, a bit of which he spilled after the cork was drawn. It painted a scarlet path across the white cloth before reaching the crystal glasses.

Daniel wondered if spirits were in short supply here at Knocktigh. "You may leave the wine, Dinn-Dinn," Daniel said, reaching for the bottle as it tipped dangerously. He had hoped to rescue his clothing from a similar fate as that of the table linen, but just as Daniel thought he had his fingers firmly on the bottle, the old man jerked up, ripping it away from him.

"Wot say?" Dinn-Dinn shouted, leaning forward.

Daniel managed to grab the bottle, held firm, and spoke a little louder. "I was pleased with the service this evening, sir. You may retire."

The wrinkled hand withdrew its shaky hold on the container to cup an ear in the earl's direction. *"Wot?"*

"I said, you did fine, Dinn-Dinn! You may retire now!"

A toothless grin spread quickly across the craggy face until it reached both ears, and the servant bowed himself from the gentlemen's presence.

Daniel collapsed back into his chair, wiped his forehead with one hand, and lifted his glass to his lips with the other. He would have relished a good cigar right then, but he'd left the box up in his bedchamber and wasn't sure he could trust the old man to make it safely up and back again. He couldn't ask Mr. Pettigrew to run the errand either—after all the man was his guest for the evening—so Daniel decided to leave well enough alone and poured himself another drink. Tilting back his head, he let the soothing gobbet of liquid run down his throat until the last drop was gone.

Mr. Pettigrew watched intently. Never before in all his years of service had he been asked to sit down to dinner with his employer, let alone been privileged to share an after-dinner drink. Afraid that he might do the thing improperly, he mimicked—to the best of his ability—every movement the earl made.

Daniel sucked in a deep breath. Shaking his head as though to clear it, he raised his empty glass and stared intensely through the tiny faceted windows of crystal at the miniature flames, dancing. After a moment of reflection, he filled their glasses again. "I do believe I have tasted every flavor of wine that Portugal had to offer, but I have never savored the likes of this port, Mr. Pettigrew. Put it on your list to have me shown the wine cellar while I am here. I must find out what this is."

"Yes, my lord," the secretary said with a crooked grin, while the earl poured them another drink. A little twinge of excitement ran through Mr. Pettigrew as he watched. Then, upending his tumbler, he swallowed the whole in one gulp.

Daniel blinked several times to enable him to see Mr. Pettigrew more clearly. He did not know the man's history except that he recognized genteel poverty when he saw it. What had been the circumstances which had forced this humble man to seek employment he did not know, but he judged the secretary to be not more than ten years older than himself. Much the age as his batman had been. He had become used to having Buttons to talk to of an evening.

Mr. Pettigrew seemed an agreeable sort—easy to talk to, Daniel reflected. "I had no idea until you told me that my father owned such a sizable piece of property this far north. The stories you told me led me to believe that the estate was far more up to the mark than what I am seeing." Daniel reached for the wine bottle and refilled their glasses.

"I do not understand it, my lord," Mr. Pettigrew said apologetically. "When I accompanied your father on his visits to Knocktigh I recalled the manor house as being well maintained and full of fine old period furnishings. There was an abundance of servants, and guests occupied every bedroom. The countess did love to entertain, and I remember she kept the stables filled with the finest breed of hunters for their pleasure."

"By George, Mr. Pettigrew, you have indeed whetted my appetite to see what treasures of fine horseflesh I have acquired!" Daniel said with gusto, raising his glass to the surprised secretary before draining it once more.

"Today has been taken up with becoming acquainted with my sisters. Tomorrow we shall check the stables first thing. And I will want to see what equipage is available to us in the carriage house. We will need more conveyances, other than my traveling coach, to transport my sisters and their maids. I shall also need to find out who was appointed trustee of Knocktigh. If my father did not have it entailed I may want to sell it, or at least take some of the cattle to another one of my estates farther south."

Mr. Pettigrew finished his drink, stifled a yawn, and raised his eyebrows as high as he could in an attempt to keep his eyes open. He was not in the habit of imbibing so much fruit of the vine. "It *hash* been a long and eventful day, my lord."

Contrariwise, Daniel, at that moment, was of a mind that he could beat the daylights out of Gentleman Jackson had he been around to challenge him. He'd have to ask Dinn-Dinn what vintage of wine had been served them, but since Mr. Pettigrew, with his head nodding and his eyes slipping closed, was the only male around, the earl, having some pity in his soul, said, "I fear that if you do not take to your bed soon, you will not be able to pry your eyes open before noon. What say you that we make it a night?"

Mr. Pettigrew set his glass down carefully on the white linen, and holding the table edge for support, rose. "Ashhh you say, m' lord," he said, weaving his way over as quickly as he could to hold the earl's chair.

A few minutes later, Daniel made his way to his room with a feeling that all was going well, very well indeed.

Tilbury was not only waiting up for Lord Chantry, but appeared not the least sleepy, as he often was in London when his lordship had spent an evening at one of his clubs. In fact, from the florid tint of his cheeks, and the slightly breathless tone of his voice as he greeted Daniel and helped him out of his coat, one would have thought the man had been running a race.

Daniel turned around, tugging at the knot on his neckcloth. "I was surprised to see that a couple of my sisters wore the same frocks they had had on this afternoon, Tilbury. They had changed them with a lace collar or a knitted shawl, but I could tell."

"Perhaps it is because they had packed all their clothes thinking you wanted to leave tomorrow, my lord," the servant said.

Daniel was so busy trying to think of what he could have said which made his sisters believe he'd meant to leave tomorrow that he failed to wonder how his valet could have known what had transpired on the floor below earlier that evening. "I cannot imagine how they had come to that conclusion. I thought you told me it would take a lady as much as two weeks to be ready. But, aside from that, I have been in London long enough now to know that my sisters' dresses are sadly out of style. Of course, I am aware that they will need a few new frocks for parties and balls. I don't suppose they have been to many parties or assemblies, living out here in the hills as they do and the countess dead these past four years."

"London is full of shops, my lord . . . and dressmakers. I am sure the young ladies can find all that they desire for the Season there."

"But I have no idea what is appropriate for a young lady to wear. You know all about fashion, Tilbury. After all, that is your livelihood, is it not? I'm sure you can advise them quite adequately."

The valet's mouth dropped open, and his eyes suddenly appeared twice their usual size.

Daniel looked at him quizzically.

"But, my lord, I have you to think of."

"Never you mind, Tilbury. My wardrobe is quite complete. It shall not be a long assignment, for remember, I am skilled at executing the most intricate maneuvers. Already plans for my campaign are taking form in my brain. I shall have them all married within a year. You wait and see."

"That is what you told Mr. Pettigrew, my lord."

"Ah, yes . . . You are undoubtedly about to tell me that you also accidently overheard our conversation when you were tending to my needs."

"Just so, my lord."

"And Mr. Pettigrew said what?"

"That he believed you will find there is a difference in the habits of soldiers and those of young ladies."

"And with whom do you agree, Tilbury?"

"I tend to favor Mr. Pettigrew's opinion, my lord."

"Tell me, Tilbury, what do you think of my sisters?"

"It is not for me to comment on your kin, my lord."

"No, but I know that you have a keen eye for the ladies and are dying to tell me. You will anyway, if I know you, so you might as well spill it."

"They are very comely, my lord," Tillbury said primly.

"Then I see no reason why you and Mr. Pettigrew do not think it is possible to have them all married off by the Season's end."

"But—"

"But what? You cannot disagree that I shall be able to find men willing to wed them."

"You should have no trouble finding them admirers, my lord . . . but what about the young ladies accepting them?"

Daniel looked at the servant as if he'd just announced that he didn't believe in king and country. "What has that to do with anything? They have nothing to say to the matter. I am their guardian. I shall pick their mates."

"It is not the same as leading an army, my lord."

Daniel raised an eyebrow. "If I remember correctly, Mr. Pettigrew said that also."

"Then that gentleman and I are in agreement. Young ladies are a different breed from men altogether."

"Ho! I think you are wrong there, Tilbury. There are leaders, and there are followers. The only difference is that it is the nature of the female to be a follower. That leaves the men to lead."

"As you say, my lord."

"I am right, Tilbury. Therefore, I shall look the field over and pick the men I think most suitable for each of my sisters. Then I shall introduce them. That should take care of the matter."

Tilbury's eyes disappeared into his cheeks. "Oh, I am certain that it will, my lord," he said, handing the earl his nightshirt.

Pulling the garment over his head, Daniel hid a crooked grin. He wasn't about to tell his servant that he had another enticement in the back of his mind. He'd decided to offer a twenty-thousand-pound dowry with each girl. He could well afford it, and such a substantial amount should turn the trick to have all eight of his sisters off his hands before the year was out.

"Wake me early tomorrow morning, Tilbury. I am anxious to see what surprises await me in the Knocktigh stables."

Georgette finally fell asleep, but Freddie lay awake letting her imagination conjure up all sorts of delightful pictures. She should have been just as exhausted as her sister, for they had whispered absurdities and laughed and tried to list all the things they wanted to do in Londontown for an hour after they had crawled into bed. But the giggles which kept bubbling up in Freddie's throat kept her awake, and she had to pull a pillow over her face to keep them from disturbing her partner.

"If you wish hard enough," Mama had said, "anything is possible. You wait and see." But Mama had gone to heaven and left them to wish and wait without her. They had not expected that. After Mama left they lived as well as they could, but Freddie was never quite persuaded that her mother had really gone away. If she covered her ears with her hands she could hear Mama's laughter; if she squeezed her eyes shut she could see Mama on the chestnut mare, her orange-red hair flowing out like wings as she flew over the Cheviots. She had died as she would have liked—out on her hills, riding in the moonlight one summer night. The horse had come back the next morning without her. They found Mama lying on the ground with her head cradled in her arms as if she were sleeping.

While the countess was alive Knocktigh seemed to be over-flowing with people. Only when Lord Chantry came on his way to Edinburgh did she send all of her guests away. Freddie re-membered the gifts he'd brought Gilliane; jewelry, bolts of beautiful fabrics, and the one which lit up her mama's eyes the most: a spirited chestnut mare with flaxen mane and tail, which he had brought back for her from the Austrian Tyrol after one of his conferences. She was a sturdy, surefooted little animal, bred for the mountains

When the earl came to visit, the girls would hide upon the landing and watch through the banisters along the walk above the Great Hall. They would shush each other and try not to snicker so they could hear what was being said below. She was about twelve years old when they heard Lord Chantry tell Mama that Daniel had become a soldier. Freddie could not interpret from the earl's tone of voice whether he was angry or proud. Perhaps it was both.

Lord Chantry seldom came after that, but Freddie liked to imagine what the viscount looked like dressed as an officer. He would be unexceptionably handsome, of course, and he would commit himself to doing brave and noble deeds. She would picture him with blond hair one day, then give him brown like her own the next. At times he had red hair the shade of Mama's horse or it was black like coal—even silver sometimes when she made note of his father's hair.

When Mama was still with them she sometimes took them shop-ping in Cornhill-on-Tweed or on over the bridge to Coldstream in

Scotland, where the king's soldiers passed by sometimes riding fine horses. Their scarlet or blue coats sported decorations of gilt brass buttons and twisted gold cords and broad bands of lace. There were gray breeches and blue, and the kilts of the Highlanders. Rounded hats of black fur and tricorns and tall plumed bonnets vied for their attention. In her mind's eye Freddie had dressed Daniel accordingly, in one uniform after another.

Although she had found that the new Lord Chantry was not as tall as she had expected she was not disappointed, for he was ever so much better-looking than she could have ever imagined. His eyes were intelligent and she was sure they missed nothing. His mouth was firm and strong. Ruth and Rebecca thought it showed honor and purpose. That might be true, but Freddie didn't think he used it to laugh very much.

Several months after Mama died, the earl arrived and placed a wreath of evergreens upon her grave. They had buried her on the side of the hill beside Freddie's daddy The Honorable Frederick Hendry.

The mare would not be caught, so they let her stay in the hills. The girls glimpsed her now and then when they rode their donkeys.

They never saw Lord Chantry—nor heard from him again. Freddie had thought they'd slipped his mind altogether until the letter from the new Lord Chantry came four years later, telling the girls that their father had died. To Freddie it became self-evident that women were only as important as the men they married. Therefore, it was imperative that her sisters find good matches.

Knocktigh perched like a deserted eagle's aerie far and away from all but a few other hilltop habitations. Only those hearty souls who had serious business or were more curious than most attempted the winding, stony road to the manor. Dr. MacDougal from Edinburgh still came into the Cheviots during the summers to study insects, and Margaret continued to follow him about. Otherwise, time stopped. Mama's friends did not come anymore, and the girls did not know how to send word to their father. Most of the servants sought positions where they would be paid. Only those who were too old or who had nowhere else to go stayed on.

Mama had told them it wasn't until she'd married the sixth Earl of Chantry and had lived in Londontown for a whole year that she found out most young ladies desirous of entering Society were given what was called a debut. Mama didn't have to have a come-out to be an Incomparable because as the countess of Chantry she was invited to all sorts of parties and balls and musicales, the theater and gardens. She even met the queen at St. James's Palace and was asked to a reception at Carlton House, given by the Prince of Wales. She kept all her girls enthralled with her tales of how grand it all was, and she said that if she had her rathers when they grew up they would all travel to Londontown.

Mama had laughed when they'd wanted to go right away. "You must be patient. Learn to wait," she'd said. So they waited. And while they waited, they contrived to make do with what they had and only sold what was necessary to get by. Mama also had said, "Never stop wishing." So every night they chanted, "Twinkle, twinkle, little star." Then they made their desires known whether they could see any stars or not.

When the years passed and no one had come to carry them to Londontown, Freddie insisted that they must keep playing the learning games which Mama had taught them so that they would be well educated when they made their come-outs. They had *The Book* to go by. They made up new dances to add to the ones Mama had already shown them. They read aloud to each other so that they would not be considered dullards when asked to recite a poem or two.

They caught the donkeys that ran wild in the Cheviots so they would not forget how to ride, because Mama had told them that fine ladies and gentlemen rode their horses in the parks of Londontown. And they only raided their neighbors' storage houses every once in a while, when it was necessary to replenish their larder. Now, after four years, their wishes were going to come true.

Freddie finally fell asleep, hoping that Lord Chantry didn't take too long to make his inspection of the outbuildings because she wanted them to be on their way to Londontown before he had time to change his mind.

The following morning Daniel was already up, and had just finished shaving himself when Tilbury came to wake him.

"My lord, you should not have done it," the servant said, his lips quivering with disapproval. The black leather riding boots which he carried, and which he'd cleaned the night before, were allowed to drop with a deliberate *thunk* upon the hard-planked floor.

Daniel continued to remove a spot of lather from his left ear. "I am fully capable of dressing myself, Tilbury."

The valet was already beside his master, handing him a clean towel as he ripped the wet one from his master's hand. "You are the earl now, not a soldier at the battlefront, and well you should remember it. Everybody has set responsibilities, my lord. Dressing you is mine."

Daniel didn't know why he should feel guilty, but he did. As he wiped his face with the fresh linen, he watched the pudgy valet scurry across the room, baggy pants swishing from side to side like a sack of potatoes in motion. Hustling back and forth, Tilbury first went to the chest of drawers where he pulled out a black shirt and neckcloth, and after he'd handed Daniel those, it was back to the clothespress for trousers and waistcoat.

When Tilbury returned from picking up the boots he had so unceremoniously dropped by the door, he found Lord Chantry had already pulled on his black Hessians with the lovely bell-like silver and gold tassels Tilbury had personally chosen to dangle down from the little peak at the front, assuring his young master that their brilliance did not break his lordship's resolve to remain in mourning, only added to his exalted consequence.

"I believe your more serviceable riding boots will do quite

well, my lord," Tilbury said, glancing anxiously at the footgear already on his lordship.

Daniel rose from his chair. "I beg to differ," he said, trying to see his reflection in the smoky cheval mirror without much success. "Image is most important when a new master is meeting his retainers for the first time. I am going no farther than the stables and outbuildings, and since the ground has not yet thawed, I don't have to contend with mud. Neither do I plan to ride today, though I might be tempted if the Knocktigh cattle are anything nigh as splendid as Mr. Pettigrew said." Daniel held up a hand to stop his valet from speaking. "No, Tilbury, I know I am right. I was made sadly aware last night that tasteful dress has been badly neglected here at the manor. My father would never have permitted any daughter of his to appear in such humdrum attire—especially at dinner. I am afraid their mother was negligent in her instruction."

"I understand that the countess has been dead these four years past, my lord."

"That is of no account when it comes to neglecting the proprieties. If the rules had been well enforced, her daughters would never break them. Letting down on standards only sets a bad example for the staff. From what I have observed so far, I am afraid I shall have to undo the damage. First, I must set the highest example. Must I not, Tilbury?"

"Aye, my lord, but I still believe your tasseled Hessians are not the thing." Tilbury stuck his nose in the air. He was miffed. If Lord Chantry did not care to listen, then he just wouldn't tell his nibs that he'd already made a quick study of the field when he was out and around gathering sticks the night before.

Daniel didn't notice. "No, indeed, Tilbury. I am only going to inspect the stables and carriage house. I shall wear the Hessians. A good image must be maintained. Perhaps I should have worn my regimentals. Since they do command a certain amount of respect. But I have sworn that I would wear full mourning attire until the entire year is up."

"And your sisters, my lord. Will they be expected to wear dark clothing in London, as well?"

Daniel frowned. "I had not thought of that." There were more problems popping up every minute with this coming-out business.

Freddie shaded her eyes with her hand and peered up at the upper story dormer, waiting for the signal. The air had warmed considerably during the night, and there had been a smattering of rain. But now the skies were surprisingly clear of clouds in the east, and the sun's rays were painting the tops of the lower hills with a pale yellow.

Then it came. A flicker of two candles held up to the glass windowpane. All was clear. The night before Ruth and Rebecca had agreed to play lookout from an upstairs window. One candle was the signal to tell them that someone could still see them. Two candles meant all was clear.

"Hurry, girls," Freddie urged in a husky whisper, "or it will be too late for us to hide ourselves in the barn before they come out."

It didn't take long before Margaret and Georgette disappeared round the sprawling stone structure. Antoinette and Babette were already halfway across the rear courtyard.

Mary was the only one who hesitated to venture out onto the cobbles. "It looks muddy," she complained, "and I have holes in my shoes."

"Mistress Mary, quite contrary," sang Freddie, giving her younger sister an extra tug out the kitchen door.

"But you heard our brother say at supper that he was going to inspect the stables," Mary said, gingerly sticking out the toe of her leather half boots to test the ground.

"If we hurry we can be out of sight by the time he reaches the barn."

"But his groom and coachman may still be in their rooms over the carriage house."

"If you had not been lingering in the doorway like a silly-nilly, you would have seen that Ruth and Rebecca held up two candles. Now I am going whether you want to or not, goose, for I will not miss the party," Freddie said. With a laugh she dashed pell-mell down the herb garden path, and lifting her skirts to jump over a fallen post, crossed what had once been a holding pen attached to the large stone building. As she expected, she heard Mary's squeal behind her.

"I was not lingering. Don't leave me, Freddie! I'm coming."

Five

The earl allowed his valet to make a final inspection. "That is enough, Tilbury, I am starving. You must be too. As soon as I leave take yourself belowstairs and see to your meal."

"If you say so, my lord. Thank you," Tilbury said, screwing up his face until it resembled a prune.

"I do say." Daniel stepped through the portal info the corridor. "And it is no use, Tilbury, your theatrics will not work on me this morning. I will not change my footwear."

Tilbury let out a loud sigh, shook his head, and tried to catch a last glimpse of the shining Hessians with their silver and gold tassels swinging so prettily from side to side.

Mr. Pettigrew was at that very moment hurrying down the corridor from his own room, the brown leather portfolio, which held his writing materials, tucked under one arm.

They met at the landing. "Good morning, Mr. Pettigrew," Daniel said with a vigor and a certain lilt to his voice which the secretary was relieved to hear, and which confirmed the secretary's opinion that his master's good spirits from the night before were still with him.

"And to you, my lord," he replied. Mr. Pettigrew, too, seemed ready to take on the world, for he had a spring in his step and took a little hop-skip just before he started down the stairs. He loved to dance. In all the years he'd worked for the late earl, he'd never been invited to attend the balls at Terrace Palace, but he had enjoyed watching from some vantage point during the parties, and he would practice the intricate steps later in his room.

"If I read the signs right we are to have a more pleasant day than we have had all the past week," Daniel said.

"I dare say you are right, my lord. The window in my room faces the east, and I do believe I saw a decided tinge of gold upon the horizon. That is . . . gold with a tiny bit of cadmium yellow mixed in." Mr. Pettigrew was very particular about getting his hues right.

Daniel, however, was taking in the rich smells floating up from the floor below. A distinct aroma of mint hung in the air along with another pleasant odor which seemed deliciously similar to that of the hot porridge he used to love as a child— with nuts and raisins, which he'd chosen to pretend were little boats floating in rivers of honey and melted butter.

They had now reached the bottom of the stairway. The trestle table with a fresh white cloth spread over it still remained in front of the huge fireplace. There were no telltale signs from the disaster with the wine the night before, but from the scattering of crumbs and a damp ring on the tablecloth he would have said that someone else had already been down to break their fast. There was no sideboard with their victuals upon it, neither did he see a single servant. Yet, the pleasing aromas grew stronger.

Just as they approached, Mrs. Doone herself came hurrying in with a basket of fresh hot buns and a large crock of strawberry jam, which she placed on the table. As soon as the two men were seated, a bowl of porridge was placed in front of each one, accompanied by a stack of hot cakes, a large cruet of syrup, and a platter of butter. Brown raisins and apple bits, with the red skin still attached, poked out through the porridge and Daniel was sorely tempted to swirl them about with his spoon to make a funny face as he had done in his nursery days, with eyes and nose and a grinning mouth.

The tea was in a kettle hanging over the fire. Dinn-Dinn brought it over and, perhaps because he'd had a good night's sleep, managed to pour them each a large cup without spilling a drop. It was an herbal brew of some kind, surprisingly pleasing to the palate and with an aroma slightly reminiscent of the spirits they'd had after dinner. They enjoyed three mugs apiece before the meal was over.

The two men ate in silence, and it was with a full stomach and the promise of expectations to come that the Earl of Chantry rose and called for their hats and coats. "Well, shall we be off, Mr. Pettigrew?"

"As you say, my lord," Mr. Pettigrew said, letting some of Lord Chantry's elevated spirit color the tone of his own voice.

"Don't forget your ledger. I shall want a full accounting from you."

"Oh, do stop pushing, Mary! There is not enough room for both of us behind this feed rack," Margaret said, hunkering down in back of a stack of hay which she'd sequestered for her hiding place. "Besides Hennypen has made a nest in the manger and Cock-a-doodle-do has already let me know by ruffling his feathers that he thinks it is too crowded in here already."

Mary was about to disagree, as she usually did, when the hum of masculine voices sealed her mouth. She scurried out of the stall and made a dash for the six empty barrels stacked in a pyramid on the other side of the room, startling more chickens by sending them flapping and squawking into the rafters.

The other girls quickly found their own hiding places. Freddie scrambled up a ladder to what had once been the solid floor of a loft and now more resembled a fisherman's net which was torn and aged. Georgette clambered after her and elected to cover herself completely with hay to make sure she wasn't discovered.

Curiosity, however, forced Freddie to inch her way out onto one of the ancient hand-hewn beams which afforded a perfect window to view the floor below. Sticking her head down for a look around, Freddie called out in a husky whisper, "Hide quickly! I think I hear Lord Chantry and Mr. Pettigrew coming!"

The mishmash of farm equipment and the hodgepodge of broken furniture below her was in its usual disarray: slats from crates piled for kindling, thick hemp rope hanging from the rafters, a hoe and rake, an old stand-up pendulum clock which hadn't worked for years resting against the wall, as well as some broken wheels which had outlasted the vehicles to which they'd been attached. All was familiar except for the snorting and nickering, the clomping of heavy hooves, and the pungent odors of his lordship's cattle coming from the stalls at the stable end of the building.

"Aren't Ruth and Rebecca coming?" hissed Mary.

"They said if they joined us, they would walk into the barn like ladies and greet their brother with a dignified good morning," called Margaret from her hiding place in the unused stall.

Freddie gave a little snort. "That is no fun. We wouldn't get to overhear what your brother is about if we did that."

There were some giggles from under the canvas tarpaulin mysteriously shaped into two mounds at the back of the wagonette with a broken wheel.

"Hush!" Freddie warned. "I hear the men coming in from the carriage house. They will be in the stables in a few minutes." At the first sight of boots, she pulled her head up before she could be seen.

Lord Chantry walked down the right side of the long row of stalls. "I cannot understand it at all, Mr. Pettigrew. Where are the Knocktigh horses? All I see are my own."

Mr. Pettigrew did likewise, only on the opposite side. "I do believe that this is not one of yours, my lord."

Daniel crossed over to the other side and peered at the old brown draft horse, head down, eyes closed, right shoulder and thigh balanced against the side of the stall as if he'd put down a bumper too many and couldn't stand up without support. Farther down, past several empty stalls, the earl found his own Scots Grey helping himself to a full rack of fresh hay. He seemed contented enough, so Daniel did not attempt to gain his attention.

Besides, the great beast would respond only if he heard his name first, and since there was no way his owner was going to call *that* out for all the world to hear, Daniel proceeded on to the other larger area of the building which opened to the outside.

The carriage house had been just as disappointing. Daniel had expected to find at least enough vehicles to carry the young ladies, their maidservants, and their baggage to London. There was a pony cart with a broken shaft and only one carriage of a suitable size for a journey to London. He was going to have to find other equipage. Now to discover that there were no high-bred cattle as well was beyond all understanding.

"Where is everyone, Mr. Pettigrew? I didn't see either Hartshorn or Parks. They were supposed to have rooms over the carriage house, and I don't see a single Knocktigh stableman in here."

" 'Tis likely they are all in the kitchen having breakfast, my lord," Mr. Pettigrew said, glancing about apprehensively, hoping someone would pop up to give some explanation to his master. He certainly couldn't.

"Surely my father would have had more than one vehicle worthy of travel. A pony cart with a broken shaft is not my idea of a suitable carriage to transport eight young ladies and their maids on a three-hundred-mile journey."

"Do you want me to write that down, my lord?"

Daniel marched on past the stalls toward the larger part of the building where equipment and stores would be kept. "No, I don't," he grumbled.

But Mr. Pettigrew knew his duty. He wrote *One pony cart with broken shaft* on the first line; *One traveling carriage* on the second; and *One old brown draft horse with white stockings and a wart on its nose* on the third. Then with a look of satisfaction, he followed the earl, pencil poised and ready for the next entry.

Daniel's eyes, ears, nose, and feet were keeping him so occupied with all the sensations they were experiencing that he had no time to take Mr. Pettigrew to task for his scribblings. His eyes sought to identify a conglomeration of shapes. His feet felt the unevenness of the floor. The odors of horse, oily leather, and musty hay were familiar enough, but there were strange whistlings and whirrings, thin pleading complaints, and *clickityclacks* from without the building, which were becoming louder by the minute.

For a day which had started with such promise, Daniel could not believe how badly things were turning out. The sharp descent had commenced the moment he'd stepped out into the rear courtyard and slipped on the rain-wet cobbles, to be catapulted into the mire of the kitchen garden which had softened overnight. Thank goodness, Mr. Pettigrew had caught him before he'd fallen to his knees and ruined his pantaloons. The mud did splatter his Hessians somewhat. Luckily, it had gone no further. Tilbury could clean the leather, but he would never have forgiven Daniel if he had ruined the little silver and gold bells which swung from the tops of his boots.

"Is there anything else, my lord?" the good secretary asked.

The earl's fists clenched and unclenched and clenched again. "Yes! I want you to find me the person who is responsible for this disaster."

The statement was no sooner made than a bearded monster loomed up in the arched doorway, casting a long shadow and blocking out much of the light coming into the barn. His deep gravelly voice rumbled in after it. "I be Loof MacLief. Ye wish ta see me, sir?"

A cap of snow white hair covered his head, spilled down the sides of his face, curled around his chin, and continued down his chest.

Daniel had to tilt back his head to be able to see the top of the giant. It did not improve his disposition. "I do indeed, sirrah," he barked. "I demand an explanation for the unacceptable condition of my father's equipage and the disappearance of his horses."

The man stayed where he was. "Ye're askin' me to cuim in there, then?"

"I am the present Earl of Chantry," Daniel said sternly. "I am not *asking* you anything. I am *ordering* you to come in."

The man took a wider stance and spread out his arms, blocking more of the wide double doorway than he had before. "As ye say, yir lairdship. But I think ye be a wise mon to step back a bit."

The noise outside was rising like a chorus of banshees, and Daniel began to wonder if a windstorm were sweeping into the hills. "Are you telling me what to do, Mr. MacLief?"

"Now why wud I do that?"

"Then you will come in and answer my questions."

"If ye say so, yir lairdship," Loof said good-naturedly, quickly stepping to the side and flattening himself against the wall.

Daniel would not have believed what transpired next except that it happened to him, and even then he would be heard to say later that it had to have been a wild dream—or more descriptively, a nightmare—only it had come in the day and not in the night.

A cloud of the evilest-looking creatures he'd ever seen, braying, nipping, flailing their heads from side to side, galloped roughshod over anything and everything in their path, and would have leveled his faithful secretary, Mr. James Pettigrew, to the ground had not that gentleman possessed the nimblest of feet and managed to leap to safety behind some wooden barrels. The donkeys—for that is what on closer observation they proved to be—seemed bent on vying like quarrelsome little children to squeeze all at one time through the narrow gate into a stall left open.

This hubbub was followed by ghostly creatures swooping from the rafters, hooting and cooing, their feathers exploding every which way. Black-winged bats flounced and fluttered about, hitting Daniel on the side of the head and sending his curly rimmed beaver flying. When he leaned over to retrieve his hat, something chewed on his pantaloons: he was butted from behind; his fingers were nibbled; and when he looked down to capture the culprit, it was just in time to see the last of Tilbury's pride and joy—the tiny silver and gold bells—disappearing into the mouth of a nimble-jawed little white goat.

As the cackling and crowing, hooting and bleating, spits and growls, braying and smacking of wings continued, Daniel glanced up toward the heavy overhanging beams to see a leg dangling. Even he could identify it as a lady's limb encased in black woolen hose and a half boot with a hole in its sole. This appendage was followed slowly by the emergence of an arm, a shoulder, a neck with a head attached, and then, with sudden acceleration, a little body swiveled round upside down and plopped onto the straw at his feet.

Freddie scrambled to her knees, and would have managed to get away had he not grabbed her by the elbow.

"Lady Winifred!" Daniel spoke severely, trying to bring whatever dignity he could to the situation. But what could one do when he'd just extracted a bat from his hair and he could still feel the knees of his trousers being chewed by a little creature who bleated at him? "You will stay. I wish to talk to you."

"I tried to warn hem, Mistress Freddie," the big man shouted over the din which had abated somewhat, but still made it necessary to raise one's voice to be heard.

Freddie patted the big man's arm. "Yes, I heard you, Loof. Indeed, I did. Do not blame yourself for his not listening."

"Lady Winifred!" Daniel said sharply, while looking with disapproval on the intimacy, "I want to speak to Mr. MacLief alone. You will wait for me over there," he concluded with a tilt of his head toward the stalls where his horses were stabled.

Freddie and the retainer both raised their eyebrows at each other before she did as she was told.

If Daniel had not known that Winifred was older, he would have guessed her to be no more than twelve years of age. She was that tiny. He waited until he thought her out of earshot before he spoke. "Mr. MacLief, I will have no disrespect shown in this house. From now on you will address my sister as *Lady Winifred*. Is that clear?"

"I meant no disrespect, yir lairdship. I wud never disrespect Mistress . . . Lady Winifred."

"I am glad to hear that. Now that I am master here I shall demand that the proper amenities be followed. Are you in charge here, Mr. MacLief?"

"Oh, no, yir lairdship. I jist take care of the wee craturs," he said with a sweep of his arm.

Daniel became aware of the vast audience which he had attracted: curious eyes stared, ears twitched, and noses sniffed. He tried to ignore them. "Who is the man my father appointed to manage Knocktigh?"

"Niver heard o' such a mon, yir lairdship. And tha's the truth. We jist dae as we alwa' dune."

Daniel frowned, then called over his shoulder, "Mr. Pettigrew. Come here, please."

The gentleman whom he'd addressed stepped from behind the stacked barrels, his eyebrows twitching delightedly and a beaming smile upon his face. "You wish me to do something, my lord?"

"Yes, I do. While I am speaking to Lady Winifred, I want you to return to the manor and question the servants. See if you can find out the man my father appointed steward, or if there was none, whom he engaged as trustee—" Daniel was interrupted by such a cacophony of loud brayings and squawkings being emitted from one of the stalls that he had to shout the remainder of his sentence, *"To oversee the management of Knocktigh."*

"I will do what I can!" Mr. Pettigrew shouted back. With one last look toward the barrels, he exited the building, whistling.

The noise within the barn subsided as quickly as it had begun. Daniel leaned down and pulled out from under his coat the little goat which was nibbling at the back of his knee. He now knew, without a doubt, that when they left London his coachman Hartshorn had taken a wrong turn and carried them straight into Bedlam.

Cocking his head toward the long-eared creatures which had now come out of the stall to form a circle around them, Daniel demanded, "Mr. MacLief, where did these bandits come from?"

"They be the wild donkeys o' the hills, yir lairdship. They cum in of a morning hoping for a tidbit or two."

"Well, that must be stopped. I will not have you encouraging them. They could be dangerous to my sisters."

"Aye," Loof said, running the back of his gloved hand under his nose and across his face so that his grin did not show. "Or t'other way round."

"What did you say, MacLief?"

"I said, aye, yir lairdship."

"Good! I'm glad you understand that it is my orders which are to be followed from now on. I shall be busy until after noon meal today, but I shall want to take my horse for a ride around the property this afternoon. Parks will be in to see to him. Now remove these beasts from the barn. I wish to speak to my sister."

He pushed the kid toward the big stableman, then, executing an about-face, he started toward Freddie. He did not see the bouncing ball of white following happily in his wake.

Freddie watched Lord Chantry coming and sent a warning look to her sisters to remain where they were. Mr. Pettigrew had to have discovered Mary hiding behind the barrels when he'd sought refuge there. Yet, he had not tattled on her. Did that mean they had an ally? She wondered what his lordship would think if he knew that every morning in the barnyard started as noisily as today had.

The donkeys, always hoping to have a fast morning race, came in from the hills the minute they saw Loof about. If they could snitch a free breakfast of hay and oats before the girls appeared, so much the better. But from what Freddie had observed from her hiding place in the hayloft, Hennypen had decided to lay an egg in one of the mangers, and Cock-a-doodle-doo was going to defend his wife's nest even if it meant sacrificing himself to do so.

Now as Lord Chantry and Tweedle-dee approached, she was surprised to see that his lordship had chosen to wear such fancy footwear into the barn. Tweedle-dee was obviously quite pleased that the earl had done so, for she showed her fascination by licking the shiny leather. It looked as though Lord Chantry was permanently attached whether he wished to be or not.

Daniel was having other thoughts. Now that he was facing the little brown mouse, he was not sure of what to say. His mind had been made up; he was not going to start off the day by showing disapproval of any of his sisters and thereby throwing them back into a fright of him. He had even decided he would address them by their Christian names in hopes of establishing a closer bond. But the minute he looked her over, really looked her over, he knew he could not condone her appearance or her behavior.

"Lady Winifred! You have hay in your hair." It was outside of enough that she had been found hanging from the rafters looking more like a country wench than the daughter of an earl. There were other flaws, too, such as a torn hem and mud on her shoes, but he thought himself quite generous in not mentioning those travesties to fashion.

"There is hay in your hair, too." She giggled, reaching up and pulling a long stem from over his ear without a bit of self-consciousness. "Have you finished with your inventory now so that we can leave for Londontown tomorrow?"

The question took him by surprise, but it did eliminate the embarrassment of having to provide a reason as to why he should criticize her when he must look as much a rustic as she. Practical matters were easier to handle. "I will have to find more carriages if we are to have all eight of you and your abigails carried to London."

She gave him a puzzled look.

"I have not seen any of your lady's maids. How many do you have?"

"We do very well by ourselves, thank you, my lord," Freddie answered.

"But that will not suffice," said Daniel. "Every lady needs her maid. Otherwise how can she be dressed or coiffed properly? When you are all settled at Terrace Palace, I shall have my housekeeper, Mrs. Vervaine, see to hiring suitable attendants from the registry office. We cannot have you going about alone in the city."

"Do you mean that we have to have a servant with us wherever we go?" That cumbersome possibility had never occurred to Freddie. *Oh, Piffle!*

"Of course, dear sister. Someone from the household or a reliable escort approved by me must accompany you. If not, people will talk . . . and a young girl's reputation can be ruined beyond repair. Didn't you know that?"

Freddie's mind raced about for a solution. "Oh, you mean someone like Flora."

"Flora?"

"Flora Doone. I forgot to mention her. She assists all of us."

"Then you do have a personal maid."

Freddie nodded hopefully. "Perhaps Flora would agree to come with us," she said. Heaven forbid if they were to be surrounded by tittletattlers who reported their every move to his lordship. Flora would stay loyal to her.

"How long has she been in service?" Daniel asked.

"Ever so long. She came to Knocktigh when she was very young. Since her mama came to cook for us." Freddie could imagine what Flora's wild reaction would be when told that she would accompany them to Londontown.

"Is she refined and trustworthy?" Daniel asked.

"The veriest, my lord," Freddie said. Flora would come in handy in London. She was always willing to fall in—and that was meant literally—with every madcap scheme she and the girls roiled up. She even knew how to ride a donkey. Yes, Flora might be very useful.

"Ah, good. Flora will come with us as well. Then I won't

have to see to hiring other attendants for you until we reach Town. That will cut down on the number of conveyances needed. Now, there is another matter I wish to ask about."

Freddie clasped her hands in front of her and gave him a reassuring smile. She had no doubt that she could think up a good answer to anything Lord Chantry asked.

Six

Daniel felt quite pleased with himself. How wrong Mr. Pettigrew and Tilbury had been to think that he could not readily gain the trust and cooperation of his sisters. It predisposed him to speak gently. "Did you ever hear our father speak of any gentleman . . . a solicitor . . . a close acquaintance he would trust . . . or a man of business, for instance, whom he might have given over the power of attorney for the running of Knocktigh?"

Freddie had no sooner formed a no with her lips when a loud blast—very like the belch of a blacksmith's bellows—exploded nearby. A tiny dormouse dashed out of the stall behind her, an orange and white tomcat close on its heels. The hunted and the hunter zigzagged this way and that, back and forth across the floor, skittered over a coil of rope, dashed under the three-wheeled wagonette and made for the wall. The chase would have ended then and there had not the little mouse dived into a tiny hole at the base of the old clock, leaped onto the pendulum, and vanished straight up into the works. The pendulum swung wildly. The clock struck one.

" 'Hickory, dickory, dock,' " Daniel and Freddie said as one.

In shocked silence they stared at each other.

Suddenly shy, and she didn't know why, Freddie turned away quickly to hide her blush and found herself staring over the half-door of the stall at a gray-white rump and tail. "What a big horse," she said, as if she'd never seen one before.

Daniel stared at the back of her head. She must think him

ridiculous. Whatever had made him blurt out a nursery rhyme? But perhaps she really hadn't noticed, since her interest seemed quite taken with his smoky mount. "Over sixteen and an half hands high," Daniel said, a bit of pride sneaking into his voice. "He's a Scots Grey. I brought him back from Belgium."

"My goodness!" Freddie said, still not daring to show her flaming face. She wished she were taller, because all she saw of the horse was its tail end and the long pink scar that slashed a long path down its entire left hip. "What is his name?"

Heaven help him! Daniel didn't want to get into that story, and fishing about for an excuse to leave, he thankfully remembered that he was to meet with Mr. Pettigrew. "You will excuse me, sister. My secretary is expecting me. I shall see you at noon meal."

Freddie still stared straight at the stall. The rump hadn't moved. Not one twitch of the tail since she'd first looked at it. Now truly interested in seeing all of the animal, Freddie didn't answer Daniel. Instead, she gripped the top of the gate, stuck the toe of her boot between the slats and pulled herself up for a better view. From what she saw of the languid creature, she was of the opinion that the Grey could not have been the source of the bullish sounds she'd heard. His head drooped to the floor.

At first she thought he was asleep until he snorted and curiously began to plow a furrow through the straw with his nose to the far corner of the stall. There he had to stop because he could go no further, so she continued to sniff and snort and stare at the mound he had made.

"Madam!" the earl's voice rang out sharply. Freddie felt strong hands grasp her firmly by the shoulders, lift her off the door, and plunk her on the floor. "Pray do not go near that horse!"

"Whyever not? He looks quite harmless," she argued, as the animal, seeming to pay not the least bit of attention to the earl's sharp command, began to repeat his odd behavior of rearranging the straw on the floor of the stall. Then she heard a nicker. A teeny-tiny nicker, almost like a squeak.

"His actions are erratic at the least, and I cannot answer for what may happen if you should get within his reach," the earl said. "My groom, Parks, is the only other person besides myself whom I allow to handle him." Besides, Daniel thought, he is the *only other person* who knows the secret word that will get the beast to obey. "Now, I must return to the manor to talk to Mr. Pettigrew. You will mind me and warn your sisters as well to stay away from him. He can be dangerous."

"Who would have ever thought it?" Freddie exclaimed, craning her neck to see into the stall without going nearer. "You still did not tell me his name. No, *don't* tell me . . . Let me guess. Thor? Thunder? Or, is it Storm?"

When there was no answer, Freddie turned round only to see his lordship pick up his crushed hat from the floor and, with head held high, stride toward the barn entrance with as much dignity as a man could be expected to muster when he had a seven-pound kid bouncing round him on stiff little stilts; first to the front of him, then to the back of him. *Click-clickety-click!* Round to the front again, bleating frantically, crying desperately, pleading with little bbbaaahhhs in ever-ascending tones. It was evident that Tweedle-dee believed she was being abandoned.

With a giggle, Freddie swung back only to find two huge eyes staring from a dizzying height above her, ears flicking back and forth like warning flags. She caught her breath and clinched her fists to her sides, but Freddie was not one to give even an inch of ground.

When the creature saw that her gaze met his, he shook out his mane wildly, then thrust his long quivering nose toward her so suddenly that the hot explosion of breath sent her leaping back just beyond his reach. One side of his mouth was drawn up as if he were smiling and a long stem stuck forward from his lips.

Freddie's hand flew to her throat. "Well, I never," she said. "Aren't you ashamed of yourself for being such a rogue? No, my big fellow. I am sorry to disappoint you, but I refuse to be your meal for today." She was quite persuaded that she detected a look of disappointment in the beast's eyes as she turned and walked away.

* * *

Whack! Whack! Daniel tried to slap some shape back into his hat before plopping it onto his head, then stomped across the stableyard, taking great care to watch where his boots were landing. He tried to ignore the *click-clickety-click* of tiny hooves on the cobbles behind him. It had turned colder, but the mud had not frozen. The moment he arrived at the back door of the manor house, Daniel was met by Ruth and Rebecca on their way out. They dropped him a quick curtsy and smiled sweetly. He nodded in recognition.

"Good morning, sisters."

"Good morning, brother," they said together, looking up shyly.

As he left them, Daniel let out a sigh of relief. One of them—was it Ruth or Rebecca?—had scooped up the little beggar before it could follow him into the house. At least his full sisters were all that refined young ladies should be. He then made his way to the Great Hall, and after handing his wraps to Dinn-Dinn, instructed the servant to find Mr. Pettigrew and request that he join him immediately.

As soon as the old butler had shuffled off on his errand, Daniel drew two of the straight-backed chairs over by the window overlooking the river. It was cold away from the fire, but he wished to be where no one would overhear their conversation.

Mr. Pettigrew arrived shortly thereafter and took a seat.

"I hope that you were able to gain more information than I, Mr. Pettigrew. What have you found out?"

The secretary shifted his weight about on the chair, first to one hip, then to the other. "I don't believe there is a steward, Lord Chantry."

"No steward? You mean . . . that the highest ranking servant in the house is . . . ?" Daniel could not finish.

Mr. Pettigrew's eyebrows began bouncing up and down, as he fought to keep his voice from squeaking. "Dinn-Dinn, my lord. But I did speak to him and Mrs. Ash," he continued in a rush of words, hoping his lordship would not ring a peal over his head for not uncovering more.

"And what did you find out?"

"Nothing."

"Nothing?"

Mr. Pettigrew now tried crossing his legs to gain his equilibrium. "The exact wording was more to the point that it was not their place to question how the Quality did things."

"Well then, aside from the butler, what are the duties of the other servants?"

"You just saw Mr. MacLief in the stables. Then there is Mrs. Ash, the housekeeper, whom you've met, and a couple of maids—one served supper last night. The cook, and the handyman, Gilby."

"Don't tell me," Daniel said. "He was the green leprechaun who masqueraded as footman last night?"

"Yes, my lord."

"Demme! It is worse than I thought. And no one knows the name of the man my father hired as trustee or who was to manage the property?"

"I cannot find a single person at Knocktigh who is very talkative when it comes to your father, my lord. They say only it is not their place to speak about the dead, nor would anyone expect that the earl would have confided in them."

"That is what everyone who was associated with my father seems to be saying here and in London. Well, someone must know who was entrusted with the account, and I intend to find out who that someone is."

"I don't think the staff trusts outsiders much."

"I am not an outsider, Mr. Pettigrew. At least not anymore. I am their new master," Daniel said, looking around the batten room. "I am certain that when they are used to the idea, they will accept me."

The secretary nodded encouragingly. "Oh, I am certain they will, my lord."

Daniel laughed. "It is strange, is it not, Mr. Pettigrew? Only last week I discovered that my father had acquired a six-hundred-acre farm in Sussex with a small manor house. A payment for a loss at the turn of a card in a game of whist at White's, I understand. Father had neglected to inform his man of business of that transaction also. The solicitor representing the loser, who had been cleaned out, appeared at Mr. Baumgartner's office to hand over the deed and ask where he was to send the tenants' rent, which his agent had collected.

"Now I find myself the owner of this grand old manor house, even if it has been stripped of its furnishings, and no one seems to know who is in charge of it. I may want to sell and let a new owner refurnish it, but I cannot until I find the papers. It may be entailed. It makes me wonder what other surprises I shall find that my father has neglected to inform anyone about."

Daniel remembered when he'd arrived in London from France, he had immediately contacted Mr. Pickins, his father's solicitor, even before he had spoken in depth with Mr. Pettigrew, only to find that the will was the same identical document which had been drawn up when Daniel was born.

"There have been no changes, my lord," Mr. Pickins had said. The family seat and all your father's holdings listed at the time of his death are entailed as they always have been for generations. You are the sole heir."

"What about my sisters, Ruth and Rebecca . . . and the others?" Daniel had asked hesitantly, realizing how little he knew about his father's subsequent wives and children. "Was there no provision made for them?"

"None, my lord. That is . . . not in his will. His lordship made it quite clear to me that his personal family finances were taken care of separately. I assumed that someone else had been appointed to oversee them."

Daniel had then contacted his father's man of business, but from Mr. Baumgartner he had received the same answer to his question. "I only tended to his lordship's business investments here in London. I would never have had the audacity to ask about his lordship's personal life."

It had not been until Daniel called Mr. Pettigrew into his presence and was handed his father's last letter, with its request that he give his sisters a Season in London, that he found out they were living near the Scottish border.

"It seems plausible that your sisters' affairs are being handled by someone near there, my lord," Mr. Pettigrew had said. "If not in Cornhill-on-Tweed, there is the possibility that your father could have hired a solicitor or given power of attorney to a personal friend in Edinburgh."

But now that they had arrived here in Knocktigh, Daniel found himself no nearer to solving the mystery. "Believe me, Mr. Pettigrew, I *will* find out who is responsible for this debacle. Either the trustee is a negligent fool, or worse, an unscrupulous gull; or my sisters have been so extravagant and undisciplined that they have squandered their living recklessly. It seems the house has been stripped of everything of value in only four years."

"Have you spoken to your sisters about it?"

"No, not directly. Under the circumstances I do not think it wise to make accusations which, if proven false, may only drive more of a wedge between us. Besides, I doubt that young ladies of their tender years would have any idea about the financial or practical matters of an estate."

"Is there nothing that we can do before we leave here?"

"Yes, there is, Mr. Pettigrew. This is what I want you to do. Tomorrow you will go into Cornhill-on-Tweed to inquire round to see what you can find out about my father's affairs. Discreetly, of course. Hartshorn and Parks will be taking in the coach we discovered today. It needs to be looked over by a wheelwright. Parks is to look into purchasing another team, and see to hiring a third driver and his hackney. We will need at least one more conveyance to transport all my sisters to London. Perhaps it is better that they only have one personal maid, for more would have necessitated another vehicle. I know that you would have been uncomfortable with such an arrangement, but I doubt Tilbury would protest being crowded into a carriage with several young maids," Daniel said with a grin.

Mr. Pettigrew suddenly bent his head over his note paper to keep his guilt from showing. Tilbury did comment often about his admiration for pretty ladies, but Mr. Pettigrew never joined in on the observations. He told the valet that he himself was too old to be thinking such thoughts, but Mr. Pettigrew did have them once in a while, nonetheless.

The earl didn't seem to notice his secretary's discomfiture, for he continued, "If we cannot find out here what we want to know, I will wait until I have my sisters settled at Terrace Palace in London. Then I shall engage an agent to come up here to ferret out who is supposed to be in charge of the estate."

Besides, there were other matters which took precedence in Daniel's opinion. Things were turning out to be a little more complicated than he had envisioned. The more he saw of the life his sisters had been leading, the more he wondered if they were ready for the big confrontation which lay ahead. Still, an army cannot turn up late on the battlefield or the battle is lost, so it was imperative that he get them to London before the Season began.

In May, Princess Charlotte was to be married to Prince Leopold of Saxe-Coburg-Saalfeld, and Daniel wished to be back in Town in time for all the galas. It would be a most auspicious time to present his sisters. Everybody who was anybody would be there.

Regardless of the fact that the girls had led an isolated life, it did not sit well with Daniel that they should have become so careless in their dress. It set a bad example for the servants and certainly wouldn't be tolerated among the *ton*. This made Daniel wonder about their education. He would ask them at the noon meal—quite casually, of course—to tell him what their tutoring had been.

Yes, the matter of an unscrupulous trustee would have to take a back seat to the more important issue of getting his sisters to London and outfitted with the proper gear for the Season.

"Mr. Pettigrew," Daniel said. "I believe I see the servants beginning to lay the table, and they will be needing our chairs." Just as he rose, Daniel cocked his head. "Listen! It sounds like . . . like the pounding of hooves."

Hooves?

After a moment, Daniel shook his head, and picking up his chair, he carried it back to the table. "It must be my imagination. Why would I hear a herd of horses galloping about in an isolated place like this? Let us retire to our rooms to refresh ourselves before lunch is announced, Mr. Pettigrew."

No sooner had the younger sisters come out of their hiding places than the two eldest entered the stables. Ruth held a wiggly Tweedle-dee in her arms.

"We just passed our brother as we were coming into the courtyard," Rebecca said. "What did you do to him to put him in such a pucker?"

"Baaaaahhh," Tweedle-dee bleated innocently, as she happily switched her nimble lips from tassels on Hessians to the fringe on Ruth's soft knitted scarf.

"He looked as if he'd been thrown off a hayer's wagon," Ruth added as she struggled to pull a strand of yarn from the little goat's mouth.

Shhlllooop. Tweedle-dee sucked happily.

Freddie's eyes twinkled. "His lordship has been getting acquainted with some of our pets. Tweedle-dee has chosen him for her playmate I'm afraid."

"Well that explains a lot," Ruth said. "Here you little rascal, there is Tweedle-dum. Go play with someone your own size." Setting the fidgety nanny goat on the floor, she pushed her toward the curly black lamb bouncing into the barn beside its more sedate mother.

"Is that why our sturdy steeds are up on the hillside looking quite put out?" Rebecca asked.

Freddie puckered her lips. "Your brother had them banished from the barn."

Ruth looked disappointed. "Won't we have time for a ride?"

Freddie's eyebrows flicked in a most delightful manner. "Of course, we will. Why should that signify? I reckon his lordship will be kept quite busy the remainder of the morning with Mr. Pettigrew, trying to straighten out matters. Georgette," she said, "come call them in."

Georgette quickly clambered to the top of the fence and, placing two fingers in her mouth, gave a piercing, *"Whhoooeeeeeettt!"* In seconds, the donkeys, flipping their heads wildly, braying and hee-hawing, thundered down the hill into the stableyard, and *clippety-clopped* across the cobbles. Babette and Antoinette came running from the tack room with long leather thongs and passed them out to their sisters. Deft fingers quickly knotted these around the don-keys' noses and tossed the loop up over their necks.

The animals danced and pranced and pounded their hooves on the stones, impatient to be off. Loof helped steady the ani-mals while each girl grabbed a fistful of mane and swung her-self onto her donkey's bare back.

Freddie was easily the first mounted and at the front. She raised her arm in the air. "Are ye bridled?"

"Aye!" they all answered.

"Are ye ready for the calf?"

"Aye! Aye! Aye!"

Freddie lowered her arm, pointing forward. "Then aff an' awa!" she cried, as her donkey stretched out its neck and shot off across the hills with her troops closing in behind her.

Loof raised his fist in the air and cheered them on. *"Buad-haich! Conquer!"* He shouted the old Scottish battle call, then turned to see Parks standing in his shadow. The giant stable-man's eyebrows shot up. The groom's mouth fell down to his chin. The two men stared at each other for an instant then ex-changed broad grins.

The noon meal consisted of simple country fare, but was more than satisfying. A hot thick soup with plenty of potatoes and vegetables, three kinds of bread with fresh butter and jams. The same spicy herb tea, steaming hot and welcome on such a cold day. The brief visit by the sun that morning had turned back to the usual bitter cloudy March weather of the north country.

The girls were dressed in fresh frocks, their faces aglow with a healthy pink, their hair neat and tidy. Even Lady Winifred had combed the hay from her tresses. Thank goodness his other sisters were not as prone to madcap tomfoolery as the tiniest one.

When all their appetites were satisfied, Daniel folded his napkin and cleared his throat. As he expected them to, the girls as well as Mr. Pettigrew put down their cutlery immediately and turned their attention his way.

"I was wondering who had taught you your lessons," he asked as casually as he could.

"Mama Gilliane," they all cried in unison.

Daniel had not expected so enthusiastic a response. He was pleased to see that his sisters did not look upon learning as a chore. He himself had embraced his education much more responsibly than most of his school chums, and he feared that many of his friends thought him odd for it.

"Mama had *The Book,* you see," Freddie explained. "She said that whenever we are not sure of what to do or how to go about, that is where we will find the answer," Freddie said. "When she went away we tutored each other."

"Ask us anything," Margaret said, finding it very hard to wait her turn. "Especially anything about *orthoptera*. That's grasshoppers and crickets," she explained.

"Oh, Maggie, his lordship is not interested in bugs," Mary exclaimed, turning red at her sister's boldness. "She just repeats what she hears Dr. MacDougal say."

"Ah, but I am interested in everything you have learned," Daniel said, thankful that he had found a way to encourage his sisters to talk. And taking the clue that since her sister had called her *Maggie* it must be Margaret who had just spoken. "And who is Dr. McDougal, Margaret?"

"He is a lepidopterist from the university in Edinburgh," she said, happily. "And *The Book* does too tell us about insects," she added with a knowing look at Mary.

"I am pleased to find that you have been exposed to such learned people. Now what else have you studied? Have you read any history?"

"Oh, yes," Freddie said. "All about ancient peoples and how we got here. All about the kings and queens."

"The Book also teaches us counting and our Roman Numerals," Mary said, her eagerness returning when she found she had something to add.

"It also tells us how to behave, said Ruth, nodding sweetly.

"And what happens to us if we are not nice to others," Rebecca added.

"We dance the dances that are in *The Book,*" Georgette said with a laugh, because she liked that part more than anything and was looking forward to going to the balls in Londontown.

They were all talking so rapidly now that Daniel was finding it hard to keep up with them. Only the two dark-haired twins remained silent, but their bright eyes and adorable red lips curving upward showed that they agreed with everything their sisters said.

"Antoinette and Babette are quite skilled with the needle, too," Ruth said kindly, not wanting to leave the silent sisters out of the conversation. "They are stitching the tapestry by the fireplace."

"That is an exemplary feminine skill," Daniel said.

Daniel was greatly relieved to find that his sisters were so accomplished, and the temptation to reply in kind to their enthusiasm actually caused one of his rare smiles to cross his face.

"Mama told us all about the law, too," Freddie added.

Daniel could not refrain from a low chuckle. "Well, I can assure you that you need not concern your pretty heads on legalities. Anything having to do with the law is for your brother to worry about from now on."

Then, turning serious, he added quietly to himself, "And I also assure you that if a wrong has been done, I shall hunt down the culprit. Our father may have been lax in his vigilance, but your brother will not be so trusting. For whoever wronged my sisters has wronged our father as well."

Seven

Daniel was as surprised as the rest of the household that things had gone so well during the rest of the week, and he told everybody at breakfast that they would be able to leave for London in two days.

The Knocktigh coach needed few repairs; Parks had found a fine team to pull it, and Hartshorn had been referred by the wheelwright to a hackney driver who said he'd be willing to carry them to London in his carriage.

The only disappointment—for Daniel had taken a day to go over into Coldstream to make inquiries by himself—was that neither Mr. Pettigrew nor he had been able to dig up any information on how his father had arranged for the upkeep of the estate. No agent, no solicitor, no papers were found. There was nothing that Daniel could do until he got to London. Therefore since his sisters seemed so eager to be off, he'd set the date of departure for the day after tomorrow.

Daniel hadn't thought it necessary to bring along any of his footmen, for he had not expected to find his sisters living in such grievous circumstances. Nor had he expected that he would be taking all the young ladies back to London with him. However, he saw no reason to hire someone now, for there would be no room in the carriages. If his sisters had been caring for each other's needs for four years, and Daniel found he had to admire them for that, they certainly could do so for another six or seven days until they reached London.

"Heaven only knows, I cannot ask any of the menservants whom I've seen at Knocktigh to come back with us, Mr. Pettigrew."

"I am sure that Tilbury and the drivers will be just as willing as I to help assist you with the young ladies, my lord. But how will the household run itself when their mistresses are gone?" Mr. Pettigrew asked.

"I left some money with Mrs. Ash, since she seems the most sensible and can read and write," Daniel said. "I told her that I had placed a draft at the small bank in Cornhill-on-Tweed for her to draw upon. I also gave her my addresses for both the Albany apartment and Terrace Palace off the Strand. She will be able to reach me at either place if need be."

Mr. Pettigrew nodded his approval. "That was very generous of you, my lord. I am sure your father would be very pleased with the honorable way in which you have chosen to resolve this perplexing situation."

"Thank you, Mr. Pettigrew. I, too, hope that I always conduct myself in a manner of which he would approve."

For all his father's dedication to the king—and numerous absences from home—Daniel thought of him as a kind and generous man to his family. Had he not supplied his wives with everything a woman could want?

Daniel's own mother had lived in the resplendent Durham Hall at their four-thousand-acre family seat, Chantry Park in Oxfordshire. For his second wife, his father had purchased Terrace Palace off the Strand, because she didn't like to rusticate in the country. And since he was away so much on government business, he had indulged his third wife, the woman who had raised the eight girls, by permitting her to live in the house she wished to occupy near the Scottish border. Yes, he had indeed indulged the women in his life regardless of his own desires.

His father had not been an outwardly affectionate man, but his occasional letters to Daniel acknowledging his pride in some achievement—an award of merit for scholarship or being made captain of the cricket team—showed that the earl kept close tabs on his only son's progress. Each word of praise had pushed Daniel to achieve higher goals. And Mr. Pettigrew's encouraging words made him realize that he now had to prove his worth once again, even if his father was no longer there to praise him. The honor of the Durham name was at stake.

The next day, Freddie and the other girls told Loof that they would be leaving. They had not had to stop their daily rides on the donkeys because the new earl, after so many years of having no choice of when he arose or where he slept, preferred to rise late and ride in the afternoon. This morning Mama's mare had come out of the hills and had followed them for quite a while. Then, finally, she had stopped, tossed her head, and whinnied. It was as if she knew they were departing and had come to say goodbye. She stood on the top of the hill glowing golden-red against the gray of the western sky and watched them until the path dipped and wound into a valley and they could see her no longer.

During the last week, when Freddie thought no one would see her, she would watch for her moment to sneak into the stables to study the big Scots Grey. He fascinated her.

His attention usually focused on the edges around the stall or on the feed box. Every once in a while, his ears would perk up, and nickering, he would stare straight at the rim of his feed rack or start routing about with his nose in the same peculiar way that he'd done before. Freddie began to suspect that the horse was deaf, daft, or both. When she'd turn to go away she'd catch him studying her as well from the corner of his eye, each time a little longer than the last. So she made sure that she kept her distance in case he should lunge out at her again, the way he had that first morning.

But this time as she stood practically with her nose touching the gate of the big Grey's stall, his lordship's groom came out unexpectedly from one of the stalls across the way and caught her.

Parks knew full well that Lady Winifred had been told to keep her distance from the horse, but she didn't seem the least embarrassed for being found disobeying the earl's orders. "Best you stay back," he said, preparing to enter the stall of the big Grey with its saddle. "Never know what the demon is going t'do. Once he attacked a stableman who came in with a rake to muck out his stall an' near to took his head off. Another time the ol' bugger went after a terrier that was sniffing around. So you best leave now, m'lady. The master plans to go riding this afternoon, and you don't want to have him find you here."

Freddie pretended to go away, but instead she slipped into the adjacent stall and peeked through a crack in the planking dividing them.

Parks immediately put his mouth up to the horse's ear and said something too softly for her to hear. The big horse lowered his head and meekly put it into the simple bridle, which consisted of not much more than the nose piece, brow band, and crown piece. The single rein was thrown up over his ears.

"Mr. Parks," Freddie whispered through the opening in the divider, "why do you not put a bit in his mouth?"

The groom didn't flinch, but acted as though he was used to the walls speaking to him. "His teeth were knocked out and his jaw hurt so fierce at Quatre Bras that he cain't take anything pressing on his face," Parks said. "Just before the final battle at Waterloo his master were killed, and Lord Chantry—he were Major Durham then—near stuck his spoon in the wall as well. He don't talk much about it, but his lordship said this horse and some Highlander fell on him and it was they that took the blows. When his lordship heard that the Grey were to be put down he said he wouldn't have any of it, and got permission to bring the big fellow back to England with him and nursed him back to health."

"What happened to the Scotsman?"

"He were killed. His lordship said his own batman found him under both horse and Highlander. That's where this big fella got the stripe down his thigh there."

"Well, he certainly acts peculiar. And his face is lopsided. It makes him look like he's smiling," Freddie said, finding a bigger crack to look through.

"He do seem a trifle off the latch," Parks agreed, trying not to show his amusement while speaking to the little faery voice floating in the air. "That's why the earl only allows me and him to tend the beast. We never know when he'll decide to take on one of his fits."

As if that were his cue, the horse stuck his nose into the opening in the wall, snuffled along the entire length of the board, snorted, nickered, turned the left side of his head to the crack, and was now studying Freddie's big brown eyes with a great deal of interest. Then, without warning, he thrust out his neck, butted his nose against the board—and *squeaked*.

"My goodness! He squeaks."

"That's because he got a front tooth knocked out too, and when he's excited the air just sort of whistles through. Now, I think it best you go on back to the house, Lady Winifred. He seems to be acting queer in the head with you here. When he starts sounding like a rusty hinge we never know what he'll do. If he decides to take off, I wudna be able to hold him."

Reluctantly, Freddie agreed and left the barn. But it gave her a new insight into the earl's character—a soft streak which he kept well hidden beneath all that stuffiness. However, she still didn't know the horse's name. And she'd just been about to ask Mr. Parks.

When there was but one more day to get things ready Maggie came bursting into Freddie's room, a fistful of papers in hand. "May I come in here to write my letter to Dr. MacDougal? Mary is giving me the fidgets with her teasing."

"Of course, you may, dear," Freddie said, laughing. "You will have the room all to yourself, because I am about to go visit Granny Eizel now to tell her we are leaving tomorrow. Use my writing desk. I have already removed everything from it except the ink pot. I believe there is a pen, too. I am sure we shall have ample supplies of writing materials in Londontown."

"Thank you," Maggie said, with a sigh. "I want to tell Dr. MacDougal that I shall be thinking of him always and will be looking about for new and exciting insects to preserve for him. You just cannot imagine how exasperating it is to have such a persnickety twin like Mary forever breathing down your neck. Just wait until she falls in love."

At the sight of her sister's soulful expression Freddie fought the inclination of her lips to turn upward. It was a fact that Dr. MacDougal was a man of extraordinary character and brilliance and indubitably encouraged Maggie to follow him about with her net, but Freddie doubted very seriously that he returned her affection. However, she was not going to inform her sister of her suspicions.

"Well, you take all the time you need to write your letter," Freddie said, sympathetically. Then, slipping out of the room, she closed the door behind her and hurried along the corridor to the back stairs leading to the upper stories. Round and round she climbed until finally she reached a long narrow passageway which led to the room in the garret.

Granny Eizel had been at Knocktigh for as long as Freddie could remember. She and Agnes, her mama's old nurse, had come with Mama upon her marriage to the Honorable Frederick Hendry, the fourth son of the Earl of Bellingham. Her papa's family lived somewhere in Northumberland. There had been a disagreement, and the couple had run off to be married. That was all that Freddie knew, because her mother refused to talk about her life before Knocktigh.

Mama only told her that her name was Mrs. Gilliane Hendry until Freddie's papa died and Mama caught the eye of the newly widowed Earl of Chantry and became his third countess. That was how, she said, she was given the gift of eight little girls to raise. She had told Freddie once that she hoped someday the Hendrys would acknowledge her as their son's daughter.

Now Freddie came to the low, arched wooden doorway and

raised her fist to knock. But before her knuckles touched the door a thin voice came from within. "Cum in, you rascal."

Freddie eased open the door. Since she and Agnes were the only two people allowed to visit Granny, Freddie knew she was the one the old lady meant, because Agnes was old and sweet and never got into mischief.

"So you've cum to say goodbye to Granny, have ye?"

The room was dark. Two pinpoints of red fire pulled Freddie across the room to the woman sitting calmly in her rocking chair; a knitted shawl covered her shoulders, and a thatch of frizzly white covered her head. The color which had drawn her was in Granny's eyes not in the fireplace, for the hearth was black. But the nearer Freddie came to the chair, the warmer the air became and the clearer appeared the outline of the beloved face.

"We did as you told us," Freddie said eagerly. "The earl believes me to be his sister."

"So," said the old lady, "what did ye think of this young man . . . Lord Chantry's son?"

Freddie tilted her head to one side as if thinking it over. "He is not one to be easily duped, Granny."

"Ye will be well advised to keep that in mind, lass, if ye are to see yir sisters happily wed. A person is like a book. Sometimes its cover does not tell the true story inside—so ye have to open the book and read it before the truth is revealed. Ye must do that with Lord Chantry."

"But what if he should find out that I am not his sister? Will he not send me back? What will the girls do without me if he does?"

"Fear not, lass. All will be revealed in time. The place for ye all to be at this time is Londontown. Just keep on yir toes. Now tell me, how do the other girls feel about their journey?"

"All of them are quite excited—except Maggie, perhaps. She fancies herself taken ever since Dr. MacDougal visited here three summers ago."

"Do not worry about Margaret's infatuation. She will be . . ." the old woman paused, and Freddie strained to see her in the darkness. "Londontown is where all of ye need to be right now. Just do as I say. Behave yirself, young lady, and all will go according to plan."

"I always behave myself, Granny. And the girls will follow my perfect example," she said with mock umbrage.

The old lady chuckled. "Ah, yes. Ye forget how well I know ye, lass."

"Mama said that we cannot cast off our roots. A carrot planted in a potato field will still grow up to be a carrot, and vice versa."

"Aye, but to get some recognition women usually have to do something totally outlandish to get men to take them seriously. Few men listen to a woman with more than one ear, lass. Remember that. Yir mother asked her second husband to promise that if anything happened to her he wud pledge that *all her girls* would be presented at court and have a Season in Londontown. Granny was there, and I made him swear that he wud do as she said . . . or . . ."

"Or what?"

"Or else I would cast a spell on him if he dinna."

Freddie guffawed. "Oh, Granny, you did not."

"Aye, Granny did. I told him he'd niver go to heaven unless he did as Gilliane asked and sent *all her girls* to Londontown. If he dinna he'd be turned into a hare and he'd niver leave this world, but wud be chased by snaggle-toothed hounds forever.

> *"Ye sall gang intill a hare,*
> *Wi' sorrow. sigh. and muckle care;*
> *And Ye sall gang in the devil's name,*
> *Ay while ye come back again."*

"Oh, I see what you mean, Granny. The new Lord Chantry said *sisters,* his father said *daughters,* and Mama said *all my girls.* You were wise to advise us to pretend that I was their sister."

"Which proves my point, lass. Men only listen with one ear."

"But what shall I do when you are not around to advise me?"

"You forget that Granny sees beyond these walls. Ye will be fine."

"Why do your eyes glow like embers, Granny?"

"Did ye not know that Eizel mean hot cinders, lass? Ye have yir two eyes, but Granny Eizel can see far more without them. Ye will do yir mither and father proud."

"Tell me about my mother's kin, Granny."

"Nae, yir mither took a vow to niver speak of them again, lass, and Granny Eizel respected her for't."

"But Mama is dead now. Can you not tell me who her mama and daddy were?"

"Au' in guid time, lass. Au' in guid time."

Freddie clasped her hands in front of her chest. "But what's to become of me after I get my sisters married?"

"Best ye jist do as Granny says. Off now to Londontown, 'rings on yir fingers, bells on yir toes.' "

Freddie raised her arms, then dropped them. " 'London Bridge is falling down, falling down. London Bridge is falling down, my fair lady.' "

"And don't forget, 'Ding, dong, bell.' And, 'Ride a cockhorse to Banbury Cross, to see a fine lady upon a white horse,' " the old woman sang.

"We are going to Londontown not Banbury, Granny. Just like Mama said we would if we wished hard enough," Freddie said, laughing.

"Aye, that ye are, but remember what I told ye. Ye must watch the young lord carefully, lass. Read him well. Learn his every move. Every habit. Know his moods and the things he cares for."

"Oh, I will, Granny Eizel. Don't you fret. The earl will not get the better of me, and I shall take good care of the girls. I won't let anything bad happen to them. Mrs. Ash told me that Lord Chantry is leaving money for them to stay here and take care of Knocktigh. He is going to send a man from Londontown for just as long as need be, until he can find out who is handling the estate," Freddie said, giggling.

"That is kind of hem, dunna you think, lass?"

"Oh, yes, I do, Granny. Do you have all of Mama's keep-sakes?"

"Granny has all yir mither's things tucked away in her special chest under the eaves."

"Agnes says she will take good care of you."

"She always has, my child. Ye need not worry about aul' Granny Eizel. Jest keep yir promise to watch the earl very carefully. Habits, likes, and dislikes. Then ye will know how t' handle him."

"I will. And I promise we will have so much fun in London-town."

The old lady chuckled. "Ah, that ye will, lass. That ye will. Now gang on with ye and enjoy yirsel."

Freddie kissed the soft velvety cheek. As she slipped out the door and into the passageway she could hear Granny's singsong incantations:

> *"He lifted her on a milk-white steed,*
> *   And hisself on a dapple gray,*
> *With a bugelet horn hung down by his side,*
> *   And slowly they baith rade away."*

Eight

On the day which Lord Chantry had designated for their departure, three conveyances stood ready at the rear of Knocktigh. The curved carriageway leading to the front of the manor was so overgrown with weeds, and the gravel road so long neglected, that they had to load both luggage and travelers from the kitchen courtyard.

First in line was the earl's gilded-gold and blue traveling coach and four with the highly lacquered Durham family crest upon the door, pulled by four fine bays. Being the largest it held five passengers: the Ladies Ruth and Rebecca, Antoinette, Babette, and the maid, Flora Doone. It also carried all of his lordship's luggage and two trunks for the four sisters on top and in the rumble.

The second coach, which they had found in the carriage house at Knocktigh, was not as big and grand as the earl's coach, but served them adequately to accommodate the other four young ladies and their two trunks outside on the platform where usually a footman or two would perch.

Ample space under the seats of both coaches held satchels, portmanteaux, or traveling bags of various shapes and sizes which carried their nightrails and combs and brushes for their stays at inns. The sisters had never used or purchased cosmetics or perfumes so their needs were few. Flora Doone had even less to declare, and carried her second dress and apron, as well as her nightclothes and an extra pair of woolen socks and house slippers, in a canvas bag which her mother had quickly made for her.

Hartshorn was up on the box of the Durham coach, Jerome Parks on the second, and the hired man had charge of his own hackney. Unless they encountered weather of unmentionable violence, Daniel expected to ride his Scots Grey back as he had done on his journey north, but if the need arose, he could just as well take the ribbons of any of the vehicles.

The skies did not look promising, and since his own coach had only two fur carriage robes, the earl ordered the servants to put more blankets in the other two vehicles. When he heard Margaret and Mary gaily chanting an old Scottish ditty, it did not tend to make him feel any cheerier.

> *"The first o' them was wind and weet;*
> *The second o' them was snaw and sleet;*
> *The third o' them was sic a freeze,*
> *It froze the birds' feet to the trees."*

Lord Chantry sat his big Scots Grey at the front of the small cavalcade and watched his breath vaporize into tiny particles of ice as it rose in the air. He pulled down his tall hat, wrapped his scarf tighter around his neck, and hunched his shoulders deeper into the collar of his greatcoat. Without looking back, he raised his arm, lowered it, and kneed his horse to go forward. Narry a muscle twitched in the powerful body beneath him. *Demmit!* What had he expected? A miracle? Gritting his teeth, he leaned over his horse's neck and drawled hoarsely, *"Pre— cious, forward!"*

The big horse's ears sprang to attention. His powerful hind legs tensed and smartly started stride. Then, hoisting one foreleg at a time, happiness written all over his crooked face—if such could be said of an animal's expression—the great smoky horse pranced proudly out of the courtyard and onto the winding gravelly road.

"By all the powers that be!" Daniel grumbled to himself.

"How was I so fortunate to become saddled with a stallion called Precious?"

Squeeeeek! breathed out the big Grey.

Jerome Parks sprang the mismatched pair pulling the second coach. He was glad he'd left the army behind him and returned to England after Napoleon had been defeated. Service under the Earl of Chantry, if not as dangerous, was proving to be far more colorful than fighting the Frenchies had ever been. And if circumstances continued as Parks had observed so far, the young lord was going to need all the loyal troops he could recruit to keep tabs on his eight lively sisters. One in particular came into the groom's mind.

Starting as a foot soldier in the Peninsula, Parks had done nothing much to distinguish himself from any other sandal-shod, hard-drinking, tattered, roustabout in the infantry until the day he'd helped pull a limber, one of the two-wheeled vehicles used to carry a caisson full of ammunition, out of a mire. He'd taken over calming and coaxing the frightened horse to lie still while they tugged the heavy wagon off the wounded soldier underneath.

Parks found he had a natural way with horses and was able to talk his commanding officer into letting him work moving the cannon and ammunition wagons. He built a reputation of not only getting the heavy artillery through to their troops, but the horses he drove had the least injuries of any others in his unit and were the best cared for in the stables. When he returned to England and heard that the new Earl of Chantry was looking for grooms for his stables, Parks applied. And the former Major Daniel Durham, remembering the soldier's way with horses, hired him.

The wounds of the big Scots Grey had healed quickly after Daniel had gotten him back to England, but the steed's unresponsiveness to any commands baffled everyone who tried to work with him.

With his jaw having been so bruised and several teeth

knocked out, he would never be able to wear a bit again. "But this shouldn't interfere with his responses to leg and voice commands, Parks," Daniel had said.

"Unless he's deaf, my lord," the groom replied.

Parks got along well with the big horse, but he, too, was puzzled by the beast's bizarre behavior. Whenever the Scots Grey was put in a new stall, he immediately looked all around, sniffing and snorting, then inspected the entire perimeter of the floor, running his nose around the base of the walls. If straw had been strewn about the floor, he would plow with his nose until it was all piled in a corner and then stand and stare at it. He also refused to eat anything from his food bin until he had inspected all around the rim.

He remained passive in his behavior toward humans, until the day he attacked a bold stable man who came in with a fork to muck out his stall. From that day on, Daniel let it be known that only he or Parks would tend the horse.

Precious would let them lead him about from one place to another well enough, but the big fellow wouldn't follow a verbal command, and they feared that he may have been rendered deaf with the cannon- and gunfire going off so near him; the fact that he'd been struck in the face with a projectile of some kind only added to this assumption. Yet the smallest noise, such as the squeak of a wheel, or the meow of a cat prowling about the stables, would bring the horse's ears to attention.

Now it was not unusual for an officer to pick a special name or word to prompt his horse to obey. In case it was captured by the enemy, it could not be made to charge against his former master unless that signal were discovered.

It was Parks who had been the one to discover, quite by accident, the only name to which the horse would respond.

He had been arguing with a newly hired stable worker who had insisted that he was quite capable of caring for any of the earl's cattle and had entered the Grey's stall only to find himself chased, bitten, kicked, and slobbered upon before he could escape the horse's cantankerous fury.

Parks, having some sympathy for the badgered fellow and thinking to explain about the horse's troubled past, told him its history and their hopes of a full recovery.

The groom would not be mollified; he curled his lip, shook his fist at the warlock on the other side of the stall door, and swore a streak of unmentionable obscenities. "Thet divil near to kick m'dayloights," he growled, gingerly fingering his blackening eye. "Purre-cious chance o' that un ever bein' wurth aught but hawg feed."

Parks had just balled up his own fist to give the cheeky fellow a good facer when he heard a whinny, and looked up to see the big Grey staring at them, ears cocked like two cannons ready to blast off. By then, the angry groom had stalked off, alternately cussing and chuckling; cussing at the horse, chuckling at his own impudent humor. Parks was too taken with the change in the Scots Grey to pursue the malcontent.

Soon after, Daniel had entered the stables to see if Parks had settled the horse comfortably, and when told the tale, he asked that every word which the two men had spoken to each other be repeated. It wasn't until the groom imitated the cockney drawl of the nasty fellow that the horse once again perked up. A process of elimination finally came down to one word.

"Od'sbodkins!" the earl espostulated. "No soldier would name a warhorse Prrre-e-e . . . I cannot say it, Parks."

"Purrrr—essshhhuss," teased the groom with a glint in his eye in the direction of the horse.

"Neeeiiighhh—nicker-nicker—wheeeeeettt!"

"Look, your lordship. The rogue's ears are perkin' up again. And ask yerself, who'd ever suspect such a hum?"

"But I cannot go about calling him Precious every time I wish him to move," Daniel whispered.

"But there 'tis, my lord. The rascal will respond to nothing else."

"Then you and I will have to be the only two who know of it. I will not have it bandied about that Major Durham calls his mount Purr-rrressh . . . By such a name. Am I understood? Why

I'd be a laughing stock with every army officer in his majesty's service if it were known that Captain Durham called his horse . . . by such a *nom de plume.*"

"Yes, m' lord. No, m' lord," Parks had said, pulling his forelock, trying to keep the corners of his mouth from curling upward.

Daniel finally forced himself to say it. "Prrr-eee-ci-ous."

"Neeeiiighhhh," came the eager answer from within, accompanied with appropriate stomping of hooves and two swift kicks, which nearly splintered the boards enclosing the stall.

"Hear him, Lord Chantry? Precious is the name all right!"

"Quietly, Parks! Say it quietly," Daniel ordered, looking about furtively to make certain no other human was within hearing distance.

"Nicker-nicker," whinnied Precious. "Squeeeek."

It took the small caravan a good three hours to wind in and out of the hills before they hit the post road which ran between Edinburgh and London. They stopped at an inn to rest the horses and let the girls refresh themselves before starting their journey south. The air had not warmed much, but Daniel still preferred riding alongside where he could keep his own counsel. Neither was the road as crowded as it would have been had the weather been more accommodating. Still there was the usual bustle of travelers; tradesmen and farmers, fine carriages and overloaded wagonettes, herdsmen prodding their sheep or hustling a gaggle of geese, and a mail coach racing along to make its appointed stop, horn blaring to announce its arrival.

Daniel let Precious have his head then and allowed him to fall back until he was abreast of the second coach. It would be well that his sisters be reassured that he was there to protect them.

"Oh, look Freddie," Georgette said. "Lord Chantry is riding beside us."

Freddie wiped a circle in the foggy glass with her gloved hand and pressed her nose against the windowpane to look out. It was not his lordship she saw, but a big brown eye staring back at her. The Grey's nose reached out and butted the glass. She screeched, then laughed. "Oh, that rogue," she cried.

"Our brother? A rogue?" said Mary from the seat opposite her in the coach. "Never."

By now, Daniel had kneed his horse farther away to keep him from tangling with the wheels, and Freddie looked up to see his lordship's aristocratic profile facing straight ahead. He looked so grand that she did not want to take her gaze off him.

"Not his lordship," Freddie said, leaning toward the window to see him better. "That horse of his is the rogue. It is not the first time he has tried to stick his nose in my face."

"Oh, do let me see him," Mary begged, scooting against Maggie who sat across from Freddie.

"Whyever do you want to see a horse?" Margaret chided, knowing full well what her twin meant.

"Make her stop, Freddie," Mary pouted. "She knows very well that I mean his lordship. I do not believe I have ever seen anyone so well-looking."

"Here," Freddie said, trading places with her younger sister. "You may have a turn to look if you wish it so much." Besides, she thought, the less attention she called to herself the freer she would be to observe the man who thought he was her brother.

Mary scooted over and happily wiped away at the window to peer out. "Now he is riding forward again," she sighed, disappointment showing in her voice. "I do hope that all the young men of Londontown are as handsome. Do you think when we get there our brother will make them line up so that we may have our pick?"

"Do not be so foolish, you ninny," Margaret scolded. "We have to be introduced to the queen first, and then go to balls and parties before we make our selection."

Georgette pulled away from the window and spoke for the first time. "Do you have Mama's Gilliane's maps of Londontown, Freddie?"

Freddie pulled out the large traveling bag from under the seat and got out the folder of maps, but the carriage lanterns had not been lit and the day was so overcast that the light was too dim to read by. She stuffed them back in and tightened the cord.

"And *The Book*," she said. "So if we forget how to go about things, or cannot remember what to say, we can always refer to it."

Mama had not only told them about all the splendors of the big city, but she'd drawn maps of every shop, every museum, and the royal palaces which she could remember. She showed them where she had lived for a while in the lovely Terrace Palace off the Strand, and she had even made floor plans of the rooms inside. There was also a map of the magnificent Vauxhall Gardens where concerts were played and fireworks lighted up the skies. She had pointed out the big parks to walk in and even places on the River Thames where they could hire a boat to ferry them across the river to the other side. And the girls planned on seeing it all.

Mama Gilliane did love to tell a story, and the tales she had spun for them of the palaces and parks and gardens had grown bigger and better with the years; and the more laughs and claps and oohs and ahhs she could get from her little fairy princesses, the bigger and more outlandish the stories became. But the girls did not seem to mind, for they were all of a belief that everything Mama Gilliane told them was just as grand as she said it was.

"I am certain our brother will take us to all the places Mama Gilliane talked about if we ask him," Mary said.

"If he does not, I shall see that you get to them anyway," said Freddie with a nod of her head. "After all, I have Mama's maps. We do not need anyone to direct us."

The other three girls nodded in agreement because Freddie always did everything she said she would.

Georgette began to sing, "To London, to London," and the others joined in, but for some reason Granny Eizel's ditty kept ringing in Freddie's ears.

Ride a cock-horse to Banbury Cross
To see a fine lady upon a white horse.

For some unknown reason Precious had veered toward the middle carriage—even put his nose to the window—and Daniel had seen those chocolate eyes staring back at him. Had the little mouse done something naughty to tease the horse? From what he'd observed of Lady Winifred so far, he supposed that she had. He kneed his mount forward and rode up to take the lead once more, and although he did not acknowledge them, he was fully aware of the interest he engendered and of the faces pressed to the windows as he passed.

The previous week when Daniel and Mr. Pettigrew had ridden together into Cornhill-on-Tweed to see if they could ferret out any further information about Knocktigh's trusteeship, he had questioned his secretary further about life at the manor. After all, it had been Mr. Pettigrew who'd provided the information which gave Daniel a clue as to the whereabouts of his twin sisters, Ruth and Rebecca . . . and his other siblings of whom he had little memory.

"To tell the truth, my lord, your father never discussed his family with me," Mr. Pettigrew had said. "The only times I recall his lordship bringing up the subject were when he would inform me that we were going to Edinburgh. As his secretary, I always accompanied him, of course. Except for his last visit after the countess's death.

"We would have a stay-over at Knocktigh on our way up, and then we stopped again on the way back to London. I never knew what transpired between his lady and himself, but I assumed . . . that is . . ." Mr. Pettigrew stumbled over his words, wrung his gloved hands together, and made a great display of tucking in his carriage robe around his knees. "It is not my place to assume anything, my lord. Forgive me."

"Pray go on, Mr. Pettigrew. What kind of a reception did my

father receive from the countess?" Daniel asked, holding up his hands when he saw that Mr. Pettigrew was reluctant to comment. "I will not hold you to blame for plain speaking. I am just trying to cipher this puzzle of destitution which I have been witnessing. Believe me when I assure you that an astute officer always seeks counsel of his aides."

This view of his status was a new one to Mr. Pettigrew, and it took him a moment to digest it. Then, suddenly hit with the surprising revelation that his opinion was being sought, he blinked three times, raised his eyebrows so high that it appeared he had no forehead at all, and, sitting considerably straighter, cleared his throat and spoke. "Lady Chantry always seemed to welcome her husband with genuine pleasure, my lord. After she passed on, he returned once that I know of. I did not accompany him at that time and I again . . . I again assumed that he had come here to make arrangements for the young ladies. I cannot believe that he did not. The earl never mentioned his daughters to me until that . . . that last night . . . when he gave up this mortal coil." Mr. Pettigrew made a little choking sound. "I am sorry, my lord. I was in the earl's employ for nearly half my life. There was never a more distinguished figure of a man."

"Take your time, Mr. Pettigrew," Daniel said, feeling an unexpected twinge of camaraderie with this nervous, fuddy-duddy secretary. "You say he never mentioned my sisters until the night of his passing?"

"No, my lord," Mr. Pettigrew said. Then recovering from his melancholy somewhat, he smiled wanly. "He mentioned you though. Quite often," he added with a wee note of envy. There had been so many brothers in Mr. Pettigrew's family, and his father—so addicted to the bottle as he was—never did quite get the right of it when it came to his sons' names.

Daniel's mind also was wandering off into what could have been. He had believed that once he got to Knocktigh, it would be but a simple matter to meet his sisters and arrange for their care. He, of course, now knew that he'd been sadly mistaken on that score. Surely his father had left them supplied handsomely enough to carry them through. But where then had the funds been left, and who was in charge of dispensing them? Something was havey-cavey about the whole affair.

"So, Mr. Pettigrew, what you are saying is that there was no discord in my father's household. Could it have been that my father was thinking of closing down the house and was selling off its contents to create a living for his daughters, and that he was more generous than he should have been? That would mean that my sisters have been either very spoiled or very foolish or both to have squandered their money in such a short time. It only shows that women—especially green girls right out of the classroom—are incapable of taking care of their own financial matters, and English lawmakers were wise to place a woman's money in the hands of a male guardian."

If Daniel found that this were the case, and not the fault of a conniving agent, it was more than evident that he should have to teach his sisters thrift. He had not counted on being their schoolmaster as well. "And would you elaborate more on the condition of the manor and the estate at that time?"

"As I told you before, the house was magnificently furnished, my lord. A number of servants were about and the stables and outbuildings were bursting with activity. The land was rocky and did not appear to be favorable to crops, but I do believe they raised a number of sheep. I do remember this coach, but it was in much better condition. Oh, everything was much grander in those days. I cannot imagine how it could have run down so. The Great Hall was filled with bright banners and ancient tapestries of battles covered the walls, and his lordship had given the countess a beautiful chestnut mare. They rode out every day when he was here."

"A chestnut mare, you say?" Daniel asked. "Why that must be the horse I saw when I was out riding in the Cheviots. She was a beauty. I saw Arabian blood in the lines of her face, though she was much smaller than that breed. I did not mention it because I did not connect it with the estate. I wish I had known that the mare belonged to Knocktigh. She should not be running wild like that. I wonder why she was not sold off as the other cattle must have been. Well, when I have my sisters safely settled in London, I shall have the mare roped and brought in. If I do not keep her, she will most likely fetch a good price at Tattersalls."

Daniel sat back for a minute with a puzzled look. "But if my father was selling his possessions to create some sort of living for the girls, why did he not mention any of this when he knew he was dying?"

"Perhaps he tried, my lord. He was so weak and shaken with ague that it was all I could do to hear what he said. Doctors and nurses running in and out . . . out and in. He called for me several times, I hear, before they let me attend him. He seemed to be terrified that some unspeakable curse would come upon him because he had not carried out a promise he had made to his late wife. He kept complaining that her red eyes were burning holes straight through him."

"The countess had red eyes?"

"Oh, no, my lord. Lady Chantry's eyes were as blue as cornflowers in summer. If I remember correctly, his words were that he had sworn an oath to the witch that when his daughters reached the proper age, he would see that they each had her Season in London. But he claimed the she-devil put a hex on him because he did not carry out his promise. He grasped my hand when he said that, and pleaded with me to make you swear on the Durham name to fulfill that pledge."

Daniel looked incredulous. "Witches and goblins, my foot! My father was not a man who would be intimidated by such balderdash. It was the fever."

"I said as much too," said Mr. Pettigrew, not sounding the least bit convinced.

Nine

"I am going blind, Mr. Hefflewicker! I told you if you took me out in this weather it would be the death of me."

"Now, now, Mrs. Hefflewicker. We have just come in from the out-of-doors into a darkened room."

Indeed the comfortably fixed country squire and his hoity-toity wife had only that minute blown in from the courtyard of the Crown and Hare, a familiar stopover for them when they were in and about County Durham.

"Your eyes will adjust in a few minutes. You are not going blind."

It had been but ten minutes earlier that the young Earl of Chantry led his little party into the same inn, a well-recommended establishment along the post road, though not as pretentious as some would expect those of the Fashionable World to patronize; but the stables were of goodly size and spacious enough for those who could afford to keep extra cattle. Daniel had chosen the Crown and Hare to accommodate him with another team of coach horses for his return journey to London.

They had been on the road for two days now. When they entered the inn Flora Doone and a serving maid took the girls' wraps. Tilbury removed his masters outer garments and started off to see to their rooms. Instead of following the proprietor's wife as Mr. Pettigrew, her sisters, and his lordship did, Freddie ran after the valet to whisper her request that all the girls would like to be together as best as he could arrange it. "Please, Mr. Tilbury?" she said, her lovely brown eyes looking up at him.

Now Daniel's gentleman's gentleman was the sort of man who, if a pretty lady with a sweet smile on her face should ask him for the Tower of London, would move heaven and earth to get it for her. "I shall do my best, Lady Winifred," he said, his round little cheeks growing pinker by the second.

The others had already been ushered into the one private parlor off the common room when the Hefflewickers also tried to make their entrance.

Tried—it is best explained—because they became wedged in the doorway, attempting to make their entry into the parlor at the same precise moment. Both appeared to be as wide as they were tall, and did not succeed. The tall part of their stature came from the mister's tall beaver and her high-crowned blue velvet bonnet; the wider and most hindering factors to their predicament were their thick woolen coats, several capes, muffs, and mufflers.

"I will decide whether or not I am going blind, Mr. Hefflewicker," she said, giving a wiggle while he did a twist. It took a bit of maneuvering before they at last wriggled free of each other and popped into the room.

The commotion had served to make the sisters turn from the fireplace, and upon spying them, Mrs. Hefflewicker shrieked, "See, I told you! My sight has gone. Everything is double, I tell you . . . and triple!"

The seven girls had been lined up facing the fireplace, holding their hands out to the flames for warmth. The commotion so startled them that Antoinette twirled around and bumped into Babette, who flung her arms around Georgette's neck to keep her balance. Georgette let out a gasp, Rebecca clasped her hands to her cheeks, Ruth threw out her arms to keep the younger girls from falling backward into the fire, while Mary squealed and grabbed Margaret who had taken up the poker from its stand and was holding it over her head.

Mrs. Hefflewicker stared at the jumble of jostling bodies, dancing feet, and flailing arms. Then pressing the back of her hand to her forehead in a most dramatic gesture, she closed her eyes and screamed.

Freddie was behind the couple when she heard Mrs. Hefflewicker's cry of alarm, and so did not find out the reason for it until she stepped into the room.

Mr. Pettigrew rushed to the side of the distressed lady. "May I be of some help, madam?" he said, taking her arm as her husband struggled to keep her upright.

Daniel found the sturdiest chair in the room and pushed it in front of the fireplace.

Fanning her face with her hand, her gaze still suspiciously on the girls, Mrs. Hefflewicker sank into the chair.

"The room is too hot," she said, casting an accusing look at Daniel, for she surmised anyone dressed so somberly to be a servant. "Fetch me something to drink."

Georgette snickered, Margaret snorted, and Freddie felt the giggles coming on.

Mrs. Hefflewicker looked from one girl to the other. "I was right, Mr. Hefflewicker! I am seeing everything double."

"You are not seeing double, madam," Daniel said, stepping from the shadows.

"Young man," she replied, raising her many chins and sighting over her bulbous nose to peruse Daniel. "Are you disputing what I say I see?"

"No, madam. I am not questioning what you *think* you saw. What you *are* seeing are four sets of twins," he said, not taking that much notice of Freddie in the doorway. "Might I introduce myself? I am the Earl of Chantry."

"You cannot be, sir," said Mrs. Hefflewicker, with so much conviction that for a moment Daniel almost questioned his own identity.

It was at that time that he really became fully conscious of his sisters' plain threadbare apparel, and his own somber clothing. Never was he made more aware of the importance of costume.

"We may live in the country for the most part of the year, young man, but we do keep up. My sister is Lady Lisbone. She lives in London and posts me a letter every Wednesday—without fail—informing me of all the goings-on. I know for a fact that Lord Chantry is dead."

Daniel pulled himself up stiffly. "She was correct, madam, but I am his son, now the seventh Earl of Chantry. These are my sisters. I am taking them to London for the Season."

The matron's eyes grew wide. "Ohhhh, Mr. Hefflewicker!" she cried, fluttering her handkerchief in the air, looking very like a goose about to take flight, "I do believe I am going to have one of my spells."

"My dear Mrs. Hefflewicker," pleaded her distressed husband, "I beg you, do not have one of those." He looked imploringly at Daniel. "They are most dreadful to witness, my lord," he said, grabbing his wife's handkerchief and swiping away at his forehead. "I hope you will excuse our boldness. Had we known . . ."

The poor man looked as if he were going to have his own version of a fit, and Daniel, not wanting that on his hands, quickly took over expediting the situation. In fact, he and Mr. Pettigrew themselves assisted the woman out of the chair and to the door, where her husband called their own footman, then the proprietor. Between the five men they bore her up the stairs to her room.

Half an hour later Daniel was touchingly aware of his sisters' silence throughout the meal. He hoped that the upsetting experience which they had just been put through had not been so frightening as to cause them to revert to the painful shyness he had witnessed at their first meeting. With luck, they would not have another encounter with the likes of Mrs. Hefflewicker—ever again.

While Daniel and his party were eating in the parlor below, Mr. Hefflewicker was hovering over his wife as she lay prostrate on the large four-postered bed in their bedroom.

"Are they gone, Mr. Hefflewicker?" she asked, opening one eye.

"Yes, my dearest. Do you wish to turn back for home tomorrow?"

"Of course not, Mr. Hefflewicker," she said, swatting away her husband's hand and sitting up. "I told Thessalonia that we would come to London for the Season, and we will do so. Did you think for a moment that I would miss being in Town for all the hullabaloo and goings-on over the royal marriage?"

"No, my dear Mrs. Hefflewicker, I did not think you would," said her husband with a jovial smile. "Shall I call to have supper sent up?"

"That is a splendid idea, Mr. Hefflewicker," she agreed, already clearing a space on the bedside table for the anticipated repast. "While you are ordering, tell them to pack a hamper for us in the morning, to carry in the carriage. I want to get an early start for London. My sister always thinks she knows all the latest tittle-tattle, but this year I shall get the march on her and bring her an *on-dit* that shall have the *ton's* ears standing on end."

"*Hair,* my dear."

"Ears hear, Mr. Hefflewicker. Hair does not."

"You are right as always, my love."

Over the next four days, while he was riding Precious alongside the coaches, Daniel had a good deal of time to think long and hard about Mr. Pettigrew's tales of his father's strange delusions; and he wondered if perhaps nightmares were hereditary.

"Devil take it!" Daniel knew that he had strange dreams of his own. Although the stories themselves would often take different turns and twists, they always started the same way.

He would hear pounding hooves and see a riderless horse coming toward him, a wild red-haired, howling, smiling madman clinging to the stirrup and being carried along on the momentum. Other times he'd see bayonets poised over his head. No matter how the dreams began, they always ended with the red-haired man grinning at him.

Edgar Buttons had found Major Durham in a field in Belgium

more dead than alive. If Buttons hadn't known that Daniel was dispatched on a secret mission to an area south of Quatre Bras two days before the Duchess of Richmond's ball in Brussels, and therefore was aware of where he had been sent, his story would have been far different.

Disguised as a peasant, Major Durham was on his way back to Wellington's headquarters at Waterloo to report, when he'd fallen into the center of a surprise attack by Boney's army. He'd tried to make his way around the enemy forces but his horse was shot from under him, and he'd received a ball in his shoulder.

As he tried to rise he saw a bayonet raised above his head. Through the confusion Daniel remembered hearing the galloping of horses and a great orange cloud coming at him through the haze. Then an arm grabbed him around his waist and carried him away.

The next thing Daniel remembered was awakening three days later in a barn, which had been converted into a makeshift field hospital, to find that the war was over, Bonaparte defeated.

Buttons told him that he'd found him half under a kilted warrior and a great gray horse. The horse had struggled to rise and then stood nearby, its head hanging and bloody and a slash down the length of its hip. The Celtic warrior had taken the brunt of the blow meant for Daniel.

His batman stayed with him there. When Daniel told him that he wished he could have thanked his rescuer who came out of nowhere, hanging onto the great Scots Grey, Buttons told him that the fields and woods were already being cleared of the thousands of dead, the bodies buried quickly in shallow graves. But he said the big Grey still remained near where Daniel had fallen. Daniel sent Buttons out immediately to bring in the horse.

Daniel was lucky; he was soon in a better hospital at Wellington's headquarters at Waterloo and was waiting to be transported back to England when word came of his father's death.

Daniel learned later that it had been the 2nd Dragoons of the Royal Scots Greys who had charged wildly through the ranks of the 92nd Highlander Company. Some of the Scotsmen had grabbed the stirrups of the charging horses and gotten a free ride

into the battle. Who the soldier was who had saved his life he
probably would never know.

A blast of cold air awakened Daniel from his daydreams, and
pulling his muffler tighter, he thought for the first time about
seeking the shelter of the coach. Ironically, instead of getting
warmer as they neared London, it seemed to be growing colder.
He wondered if Margaret and Mary's little incantation—*It froze
the birds' feet to the trees*—was an omen of any kind.

The skies were gray and foreboding, which made the days
seem shorter than usual. By early afternoon of the fifth day a
chill wind began to swoosh and swirl in from the fallow fields
and meadows bordering the post road. Bullets of rain now pelted
the little caravan forcing Daniel, after one of their stops, to tie
the big Scots Grey to the hackney and climb in with Mr. Pettigrew
and Tilbury.

The two servants scooted over to the far side, where they sat
facing each other, to give Lord Chantry more room. Once they
were upon the road again they knew enough not to interrupt their
young master's thoughts as he sat brooding for some time over
a sheet of paper he had withdrawn from the inside of his coat.

Finally he spoke. "How could this have come to pass, Mr.
Pettigrew?"

The question popped so unexpectedly into the silence that it
took a moment for the secretary to realize he'd been addressed.
"Everyone must go to meet his Maker someday, my lord," Mr.
Pettigrew said, assuming his lordship was thinking of the late
earl.

"I do not refer to my father's passing. I mean how could my
father have accomplished so much good for his countrymen and
have done so badly when it came to his own daughters?"

"I do not think his lordship intentionally neglected the young
ladies, my lord. It is only that they lived so far away . . . and they
were . . . they were . . ." Pettigrew hesitated, exchanging glances
with Tilbury who was not doing at all well in trying to hide his
profound interest in the conversation.

Daniel raised an eyebrow. ". . . Females?" he finished.

"Exactly so, my lord," the secretary said with a sign of relief at his young master's understanding.

"Even if my father were too sick to recall my sisters' names, could you not?"

"I never really heard them, my lord."

"Hmmmm," the earl murmured while contemplating some invisible spot on the torn leather back of the empty seat across from him. "But you said that you had accompanied my father to the Scottish border on numerous occasions."

"His lordship only made half a dozen journeys there in the last ten years that the countess was alive and only one after that. None in the last four years after she passed on."

"Didn't you see the girls when you were there?"

Mr. Pettigrew's eyes grew large as if he were picturing some horror. "I only remember, my lord, that the huge house seemed overrun with their girlish activities every time we visited. There did not seem to be a piece of furniture or a banister which did not have a little girl behind it or peeking through it. A person had to bolt his door to escape their pranks."

Daniel hooted and slapped his knee. "Ho! Well, we can be thankful that they are beyond that age now, can't we?" Still chuckling, he referred back to his sheet of paper. All except one, he said to himself.

"Yes, indeed, my lord, we can be thankful for that," Mr. Pettigrew agreed, wondering why the mere mention of his sisters should suddenly be a source of amusement for his lordship when only a few moments before he'd been in a brown study about their situation.

"What was the third countess like, Mr. Pettigrew? She must have been an exemplary woman."

"And very pretty . . . as all his wives were," Mr. Pettigrew said. Then as he realized the presumptuousness of his observations, he blushed so warmly he was certain that his face glowed brighter than the carriage lights.

The secretary's discomfiture seemed to skip his lordship's notice altogether. "I only want the best for my sisters, Mr. Pettigrew." It seemed to Daniel that his father had done no better in recalling the number of his daughters than he himself had the number of his sisters, but at least Daniel felt he had made an earnest effort to learn their names—attaching each to the right twin was another matter, however, because one looked so much like another.

Except perhaps for his brown-haired sister. The hint of a smile once more turned up the corners of Daniel's mouth, and for some reason he was sorely tempted to laugh aloud. Poor unique sister Winifred. She would always be as conspicuous as a little brown mouse trying to hide in a meadow of colorful flowers. For her there would be no passing the blame for any mischief on to another, because she had no look-alike twin to hide behind.

Daniel was just about to say *Ho!* again when his smile disappeared as quickly as it had come and he shook his head sorrowfully. The challenge his father had so recently thrust upon him was beyond all reason, but like it or not it now fell on him to carry out the old earl's wishes.

The young earl, however was a practical man. He could see no reason why he should not make good use of the time spent doing the pretty for his sisters in London. Even though he fully expected to be strictly observing his full year of mourning, there would be no reason why he couldn't be surreptitiously looking over the available young ladies for himself while he escorted his sisters about Town.

"Mr. Pettigrew," Daniel said after several minutes of contemplation.

"Yes, your lordship?"

"I have an assignment for you."

Eyebrows flicked knowingly. "I am here and ready to assist you in any way that I can, your lordship," Pettigrew whispered.

Tilbury, too, leaned forward as much as his roly-poly body would permit. Far be it for him to be left out if any conspiracy was afoot.

"First, it is necessary that I have some idea of what your battle plans are," Daniel said.

Mr. Pettigrew felt his Adam's apple climbing up and down in

his throat. "My plans, your lordship? You wish to know what they are?"

"Yes. I am sorry that I have not asked before this, but I had not realized how much time it would take getting my sisters billeted in the inns."

"Billeted, my lord?"

"Yes," Daniel said, missing the point altogether. "So much confusion getting them all assigned to rooms. It never occurred to me how much of a hullabaloo it would cause escorting so many sets of look-alikes.

"There was that matter two nights ago when we were in the Crown and Hare and Mrs. Hefflewicker started to scream that she was losing her sight because she was seeing double. In fact we seem to be causing some sort of bubble everywhere we stay. I had not realized how unusual it was to have so many sets of twins in a family."

"No, my lord," Mr. Pettigrew said, hoping his lordship had forgotten the original question about hearing his battle plans."

Unfortunately for the secretary, the earl had not. "Yes, well, that is not to excuse my neglect or interest in what you have come up with for our campaign. As soon as I have my sisters settled and under the competent care of Mrs. Vervaine at Terrace Palace, I shall want to hear your suggestions on how we should proceed."

Mr. Pettigrew was beginning to come to the conclusion that his true nature did not tend toward secret tactics and skirmishes. But now he sighed with some sense of relief at not having to admit it to Lord Chantry immediately. "Yes, your lordship. I wouldn't want to bother you with my plans until the young ladies are situated. I know you have had other things on your mind—the Knocktigh mystery and all."

"That is very thoughtful of you, Mr. Pettigrew. Yes, we shall have to set aside our concerns for my father's northern properties and ready ourselves for the big battle here in London. Soften up the enemy first, so to speak. Little skirmishes first."

"I had not been thinking exactly of the young men as our enemies, your lordship. Or balls and parties as skirmishes."

"Well, no, of course not. Didn't mean it quite like that. How does this sound? *Concentrating on our victory.*"

"Very good, your lordship. I agree with that wholeheartedly," Mr. Pettigrew said.

Tilbury, whose head had disappeared further and farther into his coat so that only his plump little nose and two berry eyes showed above his plum-colored muffler nodded his compliance as well. Even though he hadn't been asked for his opinion, he did not intend to be left out of the fray. After all, he considered himself a master connoiterer, and he could see that those two were going to need all the help they could get, or face disaster with this venture.

Daniel took one last look at the list in his hand, then stuffed it back inside his coat. "Well, I'm glad I have you in my camp, Mr. Pettigrew. I am sure my father felt the same way and consulted with you many times over the years."

Mr. Pettigrew let out a little gasp and wondered how anyone could think such an impossibility had ever occurred, but he managed to come through the shock of his lordship's assumption very well without making an utter fool of himself by choking or letting his mouth fall open.

"Thank goodness, the Hefflewickers had already departed the Crown and Hare by the time I had my troops assembled the next morning. But perhaps their meeting was just a warning to us. What if we had met someone who was going to be in London? I am afraid to think of what our reception would be if everybody knew what we were about—when I don't even know myself what it is we are going to do. The whole escapade could have turned into a circus."

Mr. Pettigrew nodded. "Indeed, your lordship. I agree. It could herald a complete disaster."

Daniel rested his chin in his gloved hand and, looking out the window, contemplated the landscape. "On the other hand, I am persuaded that our encounter with the Hefflewickers was a harbinger of things to come and a warning to us of what our reception might well have been in London had we not been forewarned. Perhaps we should rethink our entrance."

Mr. Pettigrew puckered his lips for a moment. "Perhaps you could consider introducing them two at a time instead of all at once, my lord."

Daniel looked at his secretary in amazement. "Yes! yes! That is a splendid idea. Delaying tactics. Good thinking, Mr. Pettigrew. I shall let it be known that I have brought my sisters back to London with me for the Season. I will not designate right away how many I have. Then I will introduce them two at a time until the *ton* is used to seeing double."

Tilbury nibbled his tongue, trying to keep silent until he could stand it no longer. "My lord," he said.

"Yes, Tilbury?"

"There is a matter of their wardrobes, your lordship. From what I have observed so far there are not enough frocks for even two of the young ladies to appear in public at one time."

Daniel had been so worried, contemplating their introductions to *le beau monde,* that he had forgotten about their apparel momentarily, but what his valet said was all too painfully true. Only five of his sisters wore bonnets and those were rather floppy affairs with lack of ribbons or any other decorations, which, of course, would be appropriate for their mourning period. But, aside from that, none of the hats appeared to have seen the light of day for some time and two were sadly out of shape. Three of the girls—the dark-haired ones—wore no hats at all, only knitted shawls over their heads.

They had shown little variety in their apparel in the two weeks that he had been at Knocktigh either, and he'd seen only one change of dress since they had started their journey to London.

"Of course, of course," Daniel said. "Thank you for reminding me. You will have to help me with that one, Tilbury. I don't suppose Meyer or Weston will do."

"No, I do not believe so, my lord."

"That is what I thought," Daniel said, feeling that this idea of introducing young ladies to Society was getting to be more and more complicated all the time, especially since he was only familiar with the gentlemen tailors.

Tilbury's eyes widened as he saw his lordship's gaze settle on him. Remembering a former conversation they had held back at Knocktigh, the valet knew he had better get in his two pence worth quickly before his lordship decided to dump the whole rigmarole on his shoulders. However, the prospect of having to advise the eight sisters on what to wear left him with an open mouth, but no words.

"I . . . I am certain Mrs. Vervaine will know what to do, my lord," Mr. Pettigrew interjected quickly, taking pity on the valet who was becoming more of a compatriot to him in devious schemes than just a fellow employee.

On the other hand, Daniel was centering all his concentration on the talents of his housekeeper. "By Jove! You are right, Mr. Pettigrew."

"Quite so, my lord!"

"Although I did not specify my exact intentions," Daniel said, "I did send word ahead for her to hire a full staff and to open all the west wing bedrooms."

"Mrs. Vervaine should know everything about young ladies," Tilbury sputtered, finally finding his tongue.

"Of course, she should. After all she was one herself at one time, wasn't she?" Mr. Pettigrew said, with a bit of hesitation.

Hearing the doubtful tone in his voice, Daniel cocked an eyebrow in his secretary's direction. "Does my housekeeper put you in a tremble, Mr. Pettigrew?"

"Does she not put everyone in a tremble, my lord?"

"Aye, I suppose she does," the earl said.

Tilbury nodded his considerable agreement.

Daniel settled back and folded his arms across his chest. "Well, that is just the sort of commander we need if we are to be successful in our bold venture. Is it not? The British would not have won the war if Wellington had been a timid soul."

Ten

On the last morning of their journey the sun actually peeked through the clouds to give the little party some promise of a more pleasant introduction to the city than at first expected. As he saddled Precious in the stables of the Purple Hound Inn, Daniel decided that today he would leave witches, goblins, and even mice running up clocks to fairy tales and nursery rhymes. Eventually he quit trying to get the stubborn horse to give up the piece of straw, which protruded like some long, thin cigarillo from his lips, and led him out into the courtyard.

Daniel mounted, rode out in front of the three coaches, then dropped back to give his sisters the reassurance of his presence, before proceeding to the front again. He dipped his head slightly to them as he came abreast of their carriages. The glimpse he had of their smiling faces pressed against the glass sent a wave of confidence through him that all was going well. Indeed, quite well. There would not be many men who could resist such beauty—such sweet countenances—such biddable natures as those possessed by his eight sisters. Of course, too, there were the large dowries which he was offering to sweeten the pot.

As soon as he had passed the lead horses, Daniel settled back in the saddle and relaxed. It took no more than a mere tightening of a knee or a click of his tongue to turn the big Grey to the left . . . slow his pace . . . or stop altogether. So well trained was he for war that the reins were no more than adornment.

Precious danced along, grinning down at the other travelers, lipping his straw, quite content to make his way without any further directions from the man on his back.

"Only one more day until we begin our last campaign, ol' boy," Daniel said. "When that is over we can call our lives our own again."

"Londontown! Londontown! Freddie, we are in Londontown!" Mary cried, flattening her nose against the window of the coach to see out.

" 'London bridge is broken down, broken down,' " sang Margaret. " 'London bridge is broken down . . .' "

"Freddie, make her stop!" cried her sister. "Maggie always spoils everything."

It was Georgette who spoke out, for Freddie seemed strangely preoccupied. "Do shush, girls. It is not the time to be pestering each other. Especially when we know that when Freddie is in her otherworld she is thinking up some escapade for us. Let us rejoice! 'Gay go up and gay go down, To ring the bells of London Town.' "

"Indeed you are right, girls. We are there," said Freddie, suddenly aware that her sisters had been speaking to her.

Then all four became silent as they entered the outskirts of the city. The traffic thickened as the streets grew narrower; grand coaches, wagonettes, and pushcarts, vied for space. People afoot bundled in their warm clothing—some silent, some hailing friends—went about on foot. There were men, too, of every size, age, and rank on horseback, zigzagging in and out among the slower travelers.

The farms and houses on large plots of land became fewer and the buildings began to crowd in upon themselves as they grew taller. This was the magical city Mama had told them about. The very place Granny Eizel said they should be; and riding beside them at that moment was his lordship, looking so very splendid upon his big smoky horse. As Freddie studied

Daniel through the carriage window, she forgot to look at anything else for several minutes.

After all, Granny Eizel's words to her had been, "Ye must watch the young lord carefully, lass. Learn his every move. Every habit. Know his moods and the things he cares for."

Since Freddie was always a dutiful girl, she was doing only as she had been told, she thought with a smile and a sigh. In this case, it was not difficult to do her duty. Her sisters' brother was indeed a magnificent specimen.

The night before at the Purple Hound, a crowded wayside inn, Lord Chantry had waited until after they'd had a warm supper and were ready to retire before he'd told them that they were only a half-day away from London. It was all that Freddie and the other girls could do to contain their excitement until they retired to their rooms.

When they had informed Flora Doone that their journey was almost ended and their adventures were about to begin, the silly goose screamed, "Oh, my goodness! Oh, my goodness!" so loudly that they had to jump on her. Freddie tried to put a hand across her mouth to keep her squeals from alarming the other guests. Consequently, Mary got the hiccups, which only sent them all into more fits of merriment, making the girls forget altogether about being quiet.

The sisters barely slept a wink that night and were up and ready a full twenty minutes before Mr. Pettigrew knocked on their doors to tell them breakfast was set in the private parlor and the coachmen had come to carry their luggage down. They made quick work of breaking their fast and were now about to see the house where Mama Gilliane had lived near the great River Thames.

"Ohhhh!" The cry went up from both coaches as they approached the front columned portico. It was all that they had hoped it to be and more.

Terrace Palace was a grand sprawling edifice off the extreme western end of the Strand. Mr. Pettigrew had informed them that there were over one hundred rooms and that it was one of a few elegant houses owned by the more affluent aristocrats of which the Durham family was one of the wealthiest. The sixth Earl of Chantry had bought it as a wedding present for his second wife: Georgette's, Babette's, and Antoinette's mother. It was where Mama Gilliane had stayed too for a short time before moving to the northern border of England.

Ruth and Rebecca lived there, too, as infants, having been brought in from Durham Hall in Oxfordshire when they were no more than one year old, but of course they had no recollection of that.

It had been maintained by a small staff for many years while the late earl was so much away on government business.

In the last coach, Mr. Pettigrew also readied himself to disembark.

Tilbury would continue on with Lord Chantry's luggage to the Albany apartment, where be would wait until his lordship had settled the young ladies. "Has Lord Chantry told his sisters about Mrs. Vervaine?" Tilbury asked.

The secretary remained silent for a minute. "He has," Mr. Pettigrew finally said, with just the slightest quaver in his voice. "I heard him tell them that they will be placed in her unexceptionable care and that they are to obey any direction she gives them."

"Do you think that was wise of him? After all there are Butterworth's sensibilities and Williams's authority to be considered."

"But whom do *those* gentlemen obey, Tilbury?"

The valet said no more.

Today Mr. Pettigrew would enter by the front door, as he had done since his young master had come into the earldom. It had been quite a different story during his service to the former Lord Chantry.

Mr. Pettigrew had been assigned a small back room on the third floor of the east wing of Terrace Palace. He would enter by the servants rear entrance at the kitchen level and climb up the four flights of narrow stairs to his room. There he kept his modest wardrobe and his collection of painted eggshells and the few books he owned. When he was not in attendance to the earl he was permitted the use of the large library, or he spent time in his room contentedly painting his shells.

More often than not, Daniel's father stayed at Albany, the former residence of the Duke of Albany, Frederick, also Duke of York, the second son of the king. It had been divided into sets of select bachelor apartments and, being just north of Piccadilly, was nearer his clubs. He had used his apartments at Terrace Palace only on occasion, when he gave a state dinner or hosted a gala ball of some sort. When he was in residence, the late earl had tended to his affairs in the study which adjoined the large library on the ground floor. Here he would receive his solicitor, Mr. Pickins; his man of business, Mr. Baumgartner; or any member of the government who needed assistance. It was very convenient for Mr. Pettigrew to have his lodgings in the same edifice, because his lordship's requests often required the secretary to work long hours.

If the late earl chose to stay at the smaller set of rooms at Albany instead of Terrace Palace, his secretary was expected to be ready on the mark to come at a moment's notice if his lordship needed him. Of course, being the tidy, efficient, and punctual employee that he was, Mr. Pettigrew always appeared on the dot.

When Major Daniel Durham had come home to step into his father's shoes, Mr. Pettigrew had told him that he was quite satisfied with this living arrangement.

"Then I see no reason to discontinue the practice," his lordship had said, "even though I have no wish to rattle around in that vast mansion myself and prefer to stay at Albany. You may keep your same accommodations if you wish. However, I insist you avail yourself of the adjoining room. Surely you must be very crowded."

"Thank you, my lord," Mr. Pettigrew had said. His collection of eggshells was becoming quite extensive, and he had decided that he would like to practice more on his watercolors. There was a nice window in the next room which would provide him with adequate light for his painting. Yes, the new lord of the manor was not nearly as demanding as his father had been, which did make life a tad easier for a hardworking employee.

Now Mr. Pettigrew was not so sure that even though he would be living in another wing altogether his hithertofore peaceful existence might be in danger of being disturbed with the arrival of eight young ladies at Terrace Palace. But where else could he go unless he found a room to let? That would cost more than Mr. Pettigrew could afford. With things as they were now, he was able to contribute a large share of his income—as did all his siblings who were able—to their mother in Sussex, to keep that sweet, long-suffering lady from losing the small property which was all that had been left to her.

As soon as the doors of their coaches were opened by the lavishly liveried footmen already awaiting them at the curb, the occupants of the three coaches disembarked, varying thoughts and expectations reflected on their faces.

Daniel had dismounted and stood at the ready to lead them up the steps to the front door of the mansion.

"Welcome back to London, my lord," said the tall slender young man standing to his left, just inside the door. He was dressed in the impeccable black ensemble of a proper butler and did his best not to stare over the earl's shoulder at the string of young ladies behind him, rather drolly frocked.

"Thank you, Beetleworth," Daniel said, looking up at the stringbean who had been but a swift-footed houseboy running errands for the family only six years ago.

"We are honored that you have seen fit to bring your family back to London," added the shorter, middle-aged mustachioed gentleman to his right, who, too, was trying to decipher which of the young ladies were noblewomen and which were servants.

"Thank you, Williams," Daniel said to his groom of the chambers. " 'Tis good to be back."

While Beetleworth divested his lordship of his hat and greatcoat, the girls filed in. Serving maids in freshly starched aprons and caps rushed forward to take their wraps. Flora Doone refused to give hers over, however, and, eyeing the servants suspiciously, hugged her cape tighter about her. The maids looked at her imposing figure, dipped, and backed away.

The grand entry hall with its black and white tiled floors and marbled pillars was also lined with servants, many of whom were new to Daniel. Mrs. Vervaine had produced a miracle to have staffed the grand mansion so quickly, he thought, only verifying his faith in her abilities to lead his sisters to victory.

As the girls followed Daniel down the long hallway, Ruth took Rebecca's hand. Rebecca reached out behind her and felt a hand take hers. In turn Freddie clasped Georgette's hand, and on down the line.

Freddie heard a little cry of "Whoops-a-me!" in back of her and turned just in time to see Mary grab Flora's hand to keep her from falling. "Well done, Mary," Freddie whispered. Flora flushed and gave a weak grin.

Once again like a string of paper dolls, the girls continued to march behind their brother to the end of the hallway and then to the base of a divided stairs, where Freddie spied a figure of amazing proportions awaiting them.

The woman, of whom they were supposed to be in awe, was so short that even Freddie didn't have to look up to her, which, of course, was a surprise because it seldom happened that she found anyone in the adult world who was any shorter than she. However, Freddie suspected that being on eye level with Mrs. Vervaine did not have as many advantages as one would expect. The housekeeper's violet eyes and Freddie's brown ones met, and both knew from the start that there would be no lies between them.

Freddie could not imagine anybody ever accusing Mrs. Vervaine of being young at any time in her life. Her face resembled an acorn topped with a stiffly starched mobcap which stretched over her brow, covered her ears, and was pulled so far down in back that not one strand of hair escaped at the nape of her neck.

Her body was thin as a twig, rigid as an oak, and clothed with a deep blue-grey bombazine dress. A chatelaine of keys and a variety of chiseling gadgets hung on chains round her waist, and because of her short stature, the lower tools came dangerously near to scraping the floor. She jingled even when she stood in one place.

Freddie quickly assessed the housekeeper to be the sort who would be said to keep a stiff upper lip, but upon second glance . . . the housekeeper didn't seem to have any lips at all.

"Mrs. Vervaine," the earl said, speaking much louder than was necessary. "May I present my sisters to you." As he called their names they stepped forward, eyes modestly cast downward, hands clasped in front of them.

Flora stood behind still clinging to the edge of Mary's dress. Daniel frowned, but decided to let the maid be, for now. He was more interested in Mrs. Vervaine's response. Not once had her eyes blinked as he'd called out eight names. She curtsied to each girl politely, but her snapping eyes told another story. Just what he'd hoped for—a stern taskmaster. A lieutenant worthy of the task set before them.

"Where are your ladies' maids?" the housekeeper asked, without moving her lips at all.

All eyes turned to Flora Doone who still clutched Mary's gown.

"Miss Doone, come forward," Daniel said.

The quaking girl took two steps, caught her boot in the torn hem of her skirt and fell flat on her face at Mary's feet.

Mary clasped her hands to her cheeks and cried out, "Oh, my, she's done it again!"

Margaret leaned over and tugged at Flora's arm. Antoinette, Babette, and Georgette ran round and grasped any part of the maid's anatomy which was handy to get a grip on, while Freddie heaved on her other arm. Between them all, they pulled the weeping girl to her feet.

"Oh, miss," Flora said to Freddie. "I am just a clumsy dodo."

"No, you are not," Freddie said, as Ruth pulled out her hand-kerchief to wipe the scullery maid's tears away.

"You just had an accident, dear," said Rebecca, giving Flora a hug.

The girl would not be mollified. "Oh, I know they'll send me home. I just know they will."

Only Mrs. Vervaine dared speak. Hoisting her pointy little nose in the air she intuitively addressed her words to the one introduced as Lady Winifred. "Is this the only servant that you brought with you?"

"She is my maid," said Freddie boldly, thrusting her chin forward and staring Mrs. Vervaine straight in the eye; which was not a difficult thing to do, since they were nose to nose.

Mrs. Vervaine wasn't the least intimidated. Oh, she will be a hard nut to crack, Freddie thought.

By now Daniel had put up with all the foolishness he could tolerate. "Attention!" he said sharply, zeroing in his gaze on Freddie more than anyone else. A profound silence pervaded the grand hallway. "Mrs. Vervaine, I am sure that my sisters are tired after their long journey. If you would be so good as to show them to their rooms I will see you in my study afterward."

The housekeeper dipped; her keys jingled; her gadgets jan-gled. "As you say, Lord Chantry. Now if you will follow me, my ladies," she said and, with more clinking and clanking, picked up her skirts and starting climbing the steps to the second-floor west wing.

Daniel headed for the study. Mr. Pettigrew hurried to catch up. "May I speak to you, your lordship?"

"What is it, Mr. Pettigrew? Can't it wait until I get this matter with Mrs. Vervaine and the girls taken care of?"

"I'm afraid not, my lord. Beetleworth just handed me this letter addressed to you and your sisters. He said it came yes-terday." The secretary handed Daniel a folded paper.

Frowning, Daniel wedged lose the seal and unfolded the mis-sive. Holding it up to window to study by the fading afternoon light, he roared, "Good lord! It is an invitation for me and my eight sisters to come to dinner Friday week, Mr. Pettigrew. How can this be?"

"I don't know, my lord."

"No one knew I was bringing all of my sisters back with me—even Mrs. Vervaine was not told the full number." Daniel looked at it once again. "It is from the countess of Lisbone. I don't even know the countess."

"If I may jog your memory, my lord . . . at the Crown and Hare in Durhamshire—"

"The Hefflewicker woman!"

"Just so, my lord. She mentioned that the countess was her sister."

"That means she must be in Town also. What are we to do, Mr. Pettigrew? Mrs. Hefflewicker was foolish enough to think she was seeing double and triple and will blow the circumstance out of all proportion. I know her type. She'll make a regular Banbury cock-and-bull out of it."

Mr. Pettigrew felt an unusual foolishness come over him. "You should know better than anyone, my lord."

Daniel looked askance at his secretary. "That is unlike you, Mr. Pettigrew."

Mr. Pettigrew's face turned scarlet. "I don't know what has come over me of late, my lord."

Daniel experienced a sense of fraternity with Mr. Pettigrew at that moment, for he, too, had been feeling completely unbalanced by circumstances beyond his control. "I think we are all a little rattled by the sudden changes in our lives."

"That is it, I am sure, your lordship."

"All I can say is that my sisters are not ready . . . *we* are not ready . . . to begin the Season. So I want you to find out what I can do to decline the invitation from the countess of Lisbone without getting us in a hobble before we're out of the stables. It will not do if it is bandied about that I have eight sisters with me—not before I have them trained and armed properly."

Mr. Pettigrew's brows began to bounce noticeably. "Yes, my lord. Is there anything else?"

Daniel mentally checked off the list of things he wished Mr. Pettigrew to do. "Only that sometime this week I will need to find a responsible agent to send to Cornhill-on-Tweed to inquire into my father's estate. It would be best if I had more than one name to choose from. See to that, will you?"

"Yes, my lord."

Daniel was pleased with the way matters were going. "Well, that's about it then. I am going to make a round of the clubs tonight. Hope to get the lay of the land. We want to do this properly, don't we?"

Before Mr. Pettigrew could gather his wits to respond, there was a knock on the door. Beetleworth admitted Mrs. Vervaine—herself sounding like the bells of St. Mary's and looking as if she had just returned from the battlefront.

Eleven

"You wished to speak to me, your lordship?" Mrs. Vervaine said firmly.

"Mrs. Vervaine, do come in," Daniel said with a sense of relief as he rose from his chair. The woman made her way tch-tching and jingle-jangling across the room toward him.

The diminutive housekeeper always clicked her tongue in such a way that Daniel could never interpret whether she was annoyed or being agreeable. Either way, he knew it best if he didn't interrupt.

"You did not tell me that you had so many sisters, Lord Chantry." She made it sound like an accusation.

"I did not know how many I would have accompanying me, Mrs. Vervaine," Daniel prevaricated.

"Where are their companions?"

"They said that they companion each other."

"I mean their abigails."

"You have already met Flora Doone."

"I doubt that silly gel knows one thing about dressing a lady, but the termagant put up such a hue and cry when I tried to send her off to the servants' quarters that I decided to have a cot set up for her in Lady Winifred's dressing room. I don't want her disturbing the other maids."

Daniel suspected it was Winifred's idea to put the cot in her chambers. How did the little brown mouse make the housekeeper think it was her own? "That was kind of you, Mrs. Vervaine."

"Humph," was all she answered.

"Perhaps you would—" Daniel started.

Mrs. Vervaine continued as if he hadn't even spoken. "I shall notify the registry first thing in the morning to send over some qualified young women to interview for the positions, Lord Chantry."

"Thank you, Mrs. Vervaine. And I apologize for not informing you more thoroughly of our plans. It was Mr. Pettigrew who recommended that I submit to your superior knowledge of what a lady needs." When Daniel's keen eye caught the slight nod of the housekeeper's head, he breathed easier. Mrs. Vervaine clearly agreed with that decision.

"When I received your message that your sisters would be in want of some new frocks, I made inquiries and found that the better dressmakers of the most prestigious establishments were already booked months ahead because of the Royal Wedding. However," she said, stopping him from saying anything with a look of censure, "I did manage to obtain an appointment with a certain Madame Lautrec who has only this year opened rooms off Oxford Street."

Things were going better than Daniel could have anticipated. The one thing he would admit was that he knew nothing about ladies' fashions. "I say! She sounds French enough, Mrs. Vervaine." He hoped that was a good response, because what did he know of women's dressmakers?

It did not seem to matter one way or another to the housekeeper. "She told me that she had been associated with the House of Fleur in New Bond Street for seven years—one of the most prestigious of the couturieres. She now wishes to establish her own business."

"You checked her references, of course."

"Under the pressing circumstances, Lord Chantry, there was no time to do so. I have made an appointment for eight o'clock tomorrow morning."

"Impossible, madam!" said Daniel. "No ladies of quality would be up at such an unfashionable hour."

"That is exactly what I am counting on, Lord Chantry. Your sisters can go in and out of Madame Lautrec's without attracting notice. No one of any consequence will be about in the streets of London to see the condition of your sisters' . . . costumes."

Daniel saw the wisdom of that. "Mrs. Vervaine, you are a diamond of the first water."

Flattery did not soften Mrs. Vervaine. "It still remains, Lord Chantry, that you only said you were returning for the Season. You did not inform me that you had eight sisters."

"Well, at first Mr. Pettigrew and I agreed that we would only need to introduce them two at a time, but there has been a new wrinkle added. It seems that already word has gotten out and an invitation has come in. My sisters need to be outfitted sooner than expected. How many young ladies did you tell Madame Lautrec were coming?"

"If I was not informed, I could not specify. Could I, Lord Chantry?"

"Well, there you are then. If you didn't tell her we can just march in the whole troop at one time."

When his lordship referred to his sisters as troops, Mr. Pettigrew looked to the ceiling and began to pray.

Mrs. Vervaine didn't give a hoot what he called them. She had her mind on things other than semantics. "Lord Chantry, have you any idea how many gowns and other accessories just one young debutante needs for the Season?"

"I would have to ask Tilbury how many changes I have."

"What you have in your wardrobe does not signify, Lord Chantry. Any lady of quality needs a different dress for each occasion."

"Can't the girls trade around with each other? You know, one would wear a dress one night, another could wear it the next?"

"Never, Lord Chantry!" she scolded. "Even if it were good *ton,* have you not noticed that each set of twins is in no way of a size as another? One set is not even like each other."

"Hmmm. I had not thought of it in quite that way," Daniel said, reviewing his sisters in his mind's eye. When he came to the images of the red-haired Margaret and Mary and considered all their other attributes, he concluded that his housekeeper was right. Their dresses would hang on Ruth or Rebecca, and the little brown mouse would disappear altogether in any of her sisters' frocks.

Mrs. Vervaine's mouth had now become no wider than a pencil line drawn taut across her face. "From what I have just seen of the state of their wardrobes it is fortunate that I *was not* able to book them at one of the better known mantua-makers. It would have been spread all over London in a trice that Lord Chantry's sisters are sadly countrified."

"Good lord! We cannot let that happen, Mrs. Vervaine. Whatever it takes to have them clothed quickly, pay it. I am certain that for the right price the job can be done with none of the *ton* the wiser."

"You wrote also that you will still be maintaining your residency at Albany. Is that correct Lord Chantry? You will not be staying here at Terrace Palace?"

"Yes, I plan on staying at Albany. I should be going there, for I had planned on dining at one of my clubs tonight. No, I shall not be here, but I will have both carriages sent around tomorrow to fetch the ladies at seven-thirty."

Mr. Pettigrew cleared his throat.

Daniel was beginning to take his secretary's sudden afflictions seriously enough to heed them immediately. "Yes, Mr. Pettigrew, what is it?"

"Beg pardon, your lordship. The coach and four of the Earl of Chantry is well known throughout London. Wouldn't its presence parked at the entrance of a side street bring a great deal of attention?"

"You are right again, Mr. Pettigrew. Subterfuge is what we need. I have it! To conceal what we are about, I shall keep the hackney and driver from Cornhill-on-Tweed for as long as we need them. The carriage we brought from Knocktigh has no identifiable connection to my family either. Those two conveyances should be sufficient to transport my sisters."

"But won't anyone in your livery or your coachman Mr. Hartshorn be recognized?"

"There is no need of an army escort when Mrs. Vervaine is accompanying them, Mr. Pettigrew. I shall have Mr. Hartshorn assign another coachman, and I shall tell Beetleworth to place a footman in plain livery on each equipage. That should be sufficient."

The housekeeper nodded her approval.

Daniel was relieved to see that she agreed. "So, Mrs. Vervaine, I will leave all in your capable hands. I have done my part. Now it is your turn."

Her brows rose almost imperceptibly. "For what, my lord?"

"Why to see that my sisters are outfitted properly for their debut into Society. Good day, Mrs. Vervaine," he said gesturing toward the exit.

"Tch-tch-tch," clicked the tiny woman as she jingled-jangled her way out of the room.

Daniel raised an eyebrow, then turned to his secretary. "Ah, Mr. Pettigrew. You are fortunate that you are already at your destination and have no more duties for the day. Get a good night's sleep tonight."

"Thank you, my lord. I shall try."

"Tomorrow you and I must put our heads together to consolidate our plans. Thank goodness, we do not have to worry about my sisters for several days."

"You do not think so, my lord?"

"Of course not. Mrs. Vervaine will keep them so busy they will have no time to get into any trouble."

"Aren't you all excited about going to the dressmaker's?" Mary said, finding it hard to sit still in the crowded carriage the next morning.

As Lord Chantry had promised, the two coaches had arrived

at Terrace Palace to fetch the girls just as the haze of dawn was striking the streets of Londontown.

"You would think you had never been to one," Margaret answered in her most worldly tone, while trying her best to act as though she went to town every day. "Mama Gilliane took us to Mrs. Flippit's in Cornhill-on-Tweed several times."

"Yes, but that was only a house," Mary said, "and it was over four years ago. Mrs. Vervaine said we are going to Madame Lautrec's *establishment*. That sounds ever so much more *tony*, don't you think?"

"Shush, girls," Freddie admonished. "You are missing the sights with your squabbling. We have now turned up Haymarket. See the marker on the corner of that building? Watch for the statue at Piccadilly Circus."

Georgette, Margaret, and Mary, all strained to peer out the windows.

What Freddie did not want to admit was that she missed the figure of Lord Chantry riding beside them. She missed the big Grey too, sticking his nose up to the carriage window to stare at her. It seemed strange that his lordship insisted the horse was dangerous, for she could not dismiss the notion that it was trying to communicate something to her. Freddie supposed now that they were in London she would see much less of them. She could not dictate to the earl when he should come see them, but there would be nothing to prevent her from visiting the stables to see the horse, she thought smugly. It was, after all, at the rear of the Terrace Palace property. Mama had marked it on her map of the mansion.

"Did you remember to bring Mama Gilliane's maps, Freddie?" Georgette asked, interrupting her thoughts.

Freddie reached down and pulled out the large traveling bag from under the seat of the hired carriage. Thank goodness she'd persuaded Mrs. Vervaine into thinking her place was in the better and more spacious coach with Ruth and Rebecca, Antoinette and Babette. She didn't want the housekeeper questioning their motives for carrying detailed outlines of Londontown.

Late last night, after the household was asleep, the girls had snuck into Freddie's and Georgette's room to go over the maps. They had pinpointed the places they wanted to see and marked each with an *X*. Then Ruth read to them for awhile from *The Book* like Mama used to do before they went to bed.

Freddie chuckled at the comical picture Mrs. Vervaine had made earlier that morning when she'd struggled desperately to keep her surprise from showing when she'd come to their rooms to awaken them—only to find all eight sisters dressed and fed and ready to start their journey to the dressmaker's. Mrs. Vervaine had no way of knowing, of course, that at Knocktigh they would have been riding into the Cheviots on their donkeys at that hour.

For a while the carriage continued up Regent Street then zig-zagged in such a way that it seemed to Freddie the coachmen were trying to escape being noticed. Mama hadn't noted these little side streets, so it was not until they came upon Oxford Street that she realized they were near their destination.

The coaches turned once more down a side street before coming to a stop at a narrow alley not wide enough for a carriage to enter. The two footmen jumped off to open the doors and hand down the women to the cobbles. They entered the rear of what had once been a family residence and climbed up three flights of stairs. There they were confronted by a newly painted blue door which did not quite conceal the dents in the layers of chipped wood underneath.

Mrs. Vervaine stood on tiptoe to reach the brass doorknocker and gave it a hefty bang. The door opened almost immediately. The reception room of the saloon held only three straight-backed chairs and was barely large enough to accommodate the nine women let alone the young lady who greeted them.

She could not have been much older than the sisters. "I am Madame Lautrec," she said a little self-consciously, looking from one to the other, her gaze coming back to rest on Mrs. Vervaine.

"And these are the sisters of the Earl of Chantry," Mrs. Vervaine said in a scolding voice.

Madame Lautrec swallowed hard and dipped a curtsy. Her

eyes revealed she did not believe a word of what her ears heard. But after all, *her* name was really Molly Jones, and if their procuress wanted to call them ladies it made no difference to her, as long as the woman had the blunt to pay. Her heart went out to the poor girls in their faded threadbare clothing. They were pretty things, and if Molly could make them look smart enough to attract protectors with deep pockets, she would do it. She knew what it was like to be born and raised in the dirty little streets and alleys of Tothill Fields. Not for nothing had she slaved for seven years, working her fingers to the bone for pennies in the back rooms of the House of Fleur, studying the ways and speech of the Fashionable World. She was owner of her own shop now. No matter that she'd had only two customers so far and owed the drapers and the seamstresses who had put their trust in her to give them a living.

She signaled the women to follow her through a gaslit workroom where a cutter snipped at fabrics spread out on a worktable and four other employees bent over their needles. Shelves along the walls were stacked with fabrics. At the back of the room a low triangular-shaped door opened into a niche under the eaves. There a glass panel in the roof allowed a stream of light to fall on a small rectangular table with three lady's fashion magazines on top, a folding screen, and a small wooden platform for a client to stand on.

"Had I known that there were so many ladies," Madame Lautrec said nervously, "I would have warmed up the larger fitting room.

Freddie eyed the iron brazier behind the platform. She was quite certain there was no such thing as a larger room. "This seems fine to me," she said cheerily. "We only plan to be here long enough to be measured."

Mrs. Vervaine clucked her tongue and added a sniff to her repertoire of sounds of disapproval. "We will look through your magazines first," she said, picking up a copy of *La Belle Assemblée* from the table. "Why this is two years old."

Madame Lautrec sucked in her breath. "My . . . my seam-

stresses have the latest plates in the other room," she answered.
"I am sure madam wants original designs for her young ladies.
She needs only to tell me what she has in mind."

"Can we tell her what we want?" Georgette asked eagerly.

"I would like that above all else," agreed Margaret, as the
others began to add their wishes.

"Girls," said Ruth. "Let us act like ladies."

The room fell silent.

"Humph!" said Mrs. Vervaine, turning to Madame Lautrec.
"Of course, I want . . . that is Lord Chantry will want original
designs for his sisters."

The girls all exchanged quick looks of satisfaction.

"Then may we start with the measurements?" asked Madame
Lautrec, relaxing her shoulders. "If you all would prefer you
may sit in the entry room or watch my seamstresses while I
measure each lady. You may wish to look over my selection of
fabrics in the other room."

Mrs. Vervaine marched immediately to the front of the shop,
wriggled up onto one of the straight-backed chairs until her feet
dangled two inches off the floor, folded her arms across her
chest, and never took her gaze off the door into the workroom.

Every one of the sisters said she wanted to be in the fitting
room with her twin. Ruth and Rebecca chose to go first. Georgette sat down on the floor and said she would look through
the magazines whether they were old or not. Mary joined her.
Antoinette and Babette elected to watch what the seamstresses
were doing until their turn came, because they liked to sew.
Margaret saw a little black speck skitter underneath a shelf and
forgot about dresses altogether to take pursuit while Freddie,
who wanted to check the lay of the land, wandered in and out
of all three rooms.

To her disappointment she saw that there was no other way
out of the building except past Mrs. Vervaine. They were
trapped inside as long as the housekeeper kept guard.

* * *

"What is the weather like this morning, Tilbury?"

"Very pleasant, my lord," the valet said, flicking a speck of lint from the sleeve of his master's morning coat.

"Ah, then I believe I shall walk over to Terrace Palace."

Tilbury was surprised to hear that. Had not his lordship vehemently expressed only hours ago that he was up to his ears in females and looked forward to going to one of his clubs where he could find the peace and quiet of an all-male environment? Now he was going back to the same house he'd been so glad to escape from the night before.

"You will be having lunch with your sisters?"

"No, no, no, Tilbury. Mrs. Vervaine has taken them to a seamstress to be measured for some new frocks. She said that the only time available was at eight o'clock this morning. Can you believe it? With the royal wedding coming up, the dressmakers and tailors must be raking in a fortune this Season."

"That is if their clients pay their bills, my lord."

"Yes, I suppose there is that, but the earls of Chantry are known for paying punctually and well. Because of that I believe any dressmaker can be persuaded to finish the job for me in record-breaking time. And that should mean that my sisters will be gone most of the day, I am sure. The mansion should be quiet as a tomb," he said cheerfully.

The valet did not think that a very pleasant analogy. Besides, he rather liked to hear the gay chattering of the young ladies. His lordship's chambers were quite somber when no one was about. Tilbury had enjoyed his travels to and from northern England with Mr. Pettigrew for company. The secretary was a fountain of all sorts on information of things he'd seen and read. Quite a pleasant fellow to be around actually.

"I posted ahead to both my solicitor and my man of business to attend me at Terrace Palace this afternoon," Daniel said. "Mr. Pettigrew and I also have much to go over. An invitation to a dinner party has already come for Friday week, but I don't think my sisters will be ready by that time. I told Mr. Pettigrew to find some way to get us out of the situation. I do not want it known yet that I plan on launching eight young ladies at one time. I only hope that the countess of Lisbone will not let the word out beforehand."

"It is Mrs. Hefflewicker you need worry about, my lord."

Daniel puzzled over how his valet had connected the two ladies when he had not been in the room with them at the Crown and Hare. "I sometimes believe that you have a sixth sense, Tilbury."

The servant did not want Lord Chantry to dwell on the subject too long. Besides, he was still dying to find out why his lordship had come in whistling this morning. "You had a good evening at your club then, my lord?"

"What? Oh, that. Actually I did not even get to Waitier's as planned. When I was on my way a former acquaintance—Captain Woods—hailed me as he was coming out of the Guard's Club. He said several of the chappies that we'd known were back in London. He was heading to Grillon's to meet one of them—Captain Oakley—and invited me to join them for dinner. We spent the entire evening catching up."

"I'm sure that was very exciting, my lord," the valet said, not much interested in hearing anything so mundane as old war stories. Tilbury was too romantic for that.

"So," Daniel said, as his valet helped him into his coat, "I shall be spending most of the day at Terrace Palace. After that I may take a canter through Hyde Park. Captain Woods said that several officers take their exercise there of an afternoon, and my big Grey is restless as am I when hobbled inside for too long a stretch. Now that my sisters will be kept suitably occupied for several days I shall be able to get back to my normal routine. So you do not need to expect me until early evening. I may get to a club or two yet."

"Very good, my lord," Tilbury answered, his mind already running ahead as to how he would dress his young master for the evening. Not that he was given much leeway for creativity when his nibs whole wardrobe was black. After the disaster at Knocktigh with the pretty little silver and gold tassels, he doubted he could ever again get Lord Chantry to try anything so decorative.

"You have been in the social whirl of the Fashionable World

for some time, Tilbury. What do you suggest would be the first invitations for me to accept for my sisters to have them favored by the best families?"

The valet did not consider that the world in which his late employer, Colonel Dell—an octogenarian and an irascible old curmudgeon at that—could be considered to be whirling, but Tilbury did know a thing or two about protocol.

"I do believe that young ladies who have been presented to the queen tend to be placed at the top of the deck, my lord."

"That is probably why my father mentioned it. It shows he was thinking of what was best for his daughters. Well then, that is what we shall do. I will tell Mr. Pettigrew to arrange it immediately. No sense in dragging our rifles in the dust on this business."

Tilbury hoped it would be as easy as that, but he did not think it his place to discourage his lordship, especially when the young master was in such high spirits. "No, my lord. Musn't drag our rifles," he said, handing the earl his hat.

"How long does it take to make a dress, Tilbury? Surely there is not as much work as goes into a tailor-made jacket for a man. After all there is a lot more territory to cover on a male. Is there not?"

Tilbury's eyes disappeared into the folds of his cheeks. "There are a lot more laces and pleats and things like that to be considered, my lord. Then there is more to it than just the gown. There are all the accessories to be purchased. Bonnets, capes, gloves, slippers, and the like."

"That is true," Daniel said happily. "That should mean my sisters will be out of the house for another week, don't you agree?"

"More than that, I should think, my lord."

"Really? That is a most welcome thought," Daniel said, twirling his walking stick. "Mr. Pettigrew and I should be able to lay out our whole battle plan by then."

Twelve

Freddie began to think she would never break free of Mrs. Vervaine's eagle-eyed surveillance and get to see Londontown. For four days they had traveled to Madame Lautrec's for measurements and fittings—each time by a different route. It was not as though the coachman was trying to show them the nicest parts of the city because for the most part they took side streets. Only a few appeared on Mama's map.

"Hold your arms out, please, my lady. Turn around, my lady. My, what a tiny waist you have, my lady," Madame Lautrec would croon in her soft voice.

Soon Freddie found that she could obey the requests automatically and at the same time let her mind wander to more venturesome occupations, such as going to see a ferocious tiger at the Tower Zoo or learning to drive one of those high two-wheeled carriages she had seen a lady of fashion guiding along Regent Street. She wondered if Lord Chantry had one in the Terrace Palace carriage house. She would have to find out.

In the last few days Mrs. Vervaine interviewed a number of women sent from the registry. She selected three young girls, each to be an abigail to a set of twins, making certain they were competent and knew their place. That is, they said little and did as she told them. They were given rooms on another floor of the west wing and came only when they were summoned by the bells in the girls' rooms.

Freddie, by insisting that Flora would stay with her and Georgette, had been just as stubborn as the housekeeper had in stating that she would be the one to hire the women to fill the positions of lady's maids. If Georgette's and her hair did not look as fine as the other girls it made no never mind to the pair. In the meantime Flora had forged a strong bond with Sukey—a tweenie just hired in the kitchen and herself a shy and frightened kitten who needed a friend.

When Freddie was at the dressmaker's, Flora told her that she went belowstairs, where she felt more at home anyway, to help Sukey with her chores.

"Cook reminds me of Mither," the big girl said. "She didn't scold me when I broke the butter crock or when I tripped and spilled potato peelings all over the floor. She said it were an accident and she knew I didn't mean to. Cook says I'm a good influence on Sukey too, 'cause I keep the silly girl busy. Before I came Sukey just stood round gaping at the other maids 'stead of working."

Now when the sisters returned in the afternoons from Madame Lautrec's, Flora was much more in countenance and happily filled Freddie's and Georgette's ears with her chatter of the goings-on belowstairs.

Aside from Antoinette and Babette who enjoyed observing the seamstresses at work in the next room, the other five girls, as well as Freddie, had become resigned to watching each other try on the new dresses. Even Freddie stopped peeking out hopefully into the anteroom to see if perchance their jailor had disappeared so that she could escape for a while to the outside. But Mrs. Vervaine proved to be no fool and never took her gaze off the door to the inner room.

Perhaps Molly Jones did not have the breeding suggested by the *nom de plume* she'd assumed—Madame Lautrec—but that did not deprive her of a natural wit to match colors or to exhibit a certain flair for style. Mrs. Vervaine had told her the ladies would need at least one outfit as quickly as possible to replace their present apparel. The costume should do double duty—for shopping or, should they receive a sudden invitation, for a social call.

Molly had nodded knowingly. She had seen the two carriages waiting at the entrance to the alley when she'd run an errand and had not been impressed. The one even looked like a hired hackney, and the footmen appeared to be stout characters dressed in the most ordinary attire, not the splendid livery a nobleman's servants would wear. But if it was Mrs. Vervaine's intention to attract protectors of the Quality for her charges, she had come to the right person.

More than once when Molly worked at the House of Fleur she had been asked to model some of her own designs. Afterward she'd received offers from several of the attending gentlemen, but she had no wish to be handed from man to man. She'd seen the miserable life her mother had led plying her trade in streets like Cabbage Lane and Pickpocket Alley. That was the reason Molly left the House of Fleur, because she'd refused to accede to her employer's insistence that she become the mistress to one of the wealthy patrons.

Molly's—that is, Madame Lautrec's—magazines may have been sadly out of date, but she had a good eye for figures, and her designs were intuitively rendered to provoke the most sated of gentlemen to sit up and take notice while at the same time to attract fashionable ladies to inquire as to their designer. The resulting gowns and pelisses were finished for all eight girls in four days.

The dresses were very high waisted, with ruffles around the necks to make them appear modest; laces were sewn on the bodices to give the illusion of innocence; and alternating layers of flounces around the hems were guaranteed to bring attention to the enticing movements of the girls' hips and legs.

The gowns were ankle length, and Madame Lautrec told Mrs. Vervaine, "The footwear to complete their ensembles should be half boots of satin, with lacing at the side in the same color, but of a lighter or darker hue than their dresses. The gloves should closely match the silk linings of their wrap-around pelisses, and make sure that their bonnets are only slightly rimmed so as not to hide the girls' lovely faces—just enough to provoke curiosity."

The two tallest girls, the ones their procuress called Lady Ruth and Lady Rebecca, were so fair and elegant that Madame dressed them in identical delicate pastel blue fabrics.

For the three dark-haired girls she chose primrose, daffodil, and violet.

The carrottops she put in sea green, with a little less lace on their bodices—which may not have been an attribute to their profession but which would not attract undo attention from any of the high-nosed ladies of the *haut ton*.

When Madame Lautrec came to the odd one out, the little brown-haired fidget, she knew that nothing else would do but a deep, deep, forest-green fabric with a touch of shimmering silver thread running through it. The girl had the quality of a woodland nymph, but from the way she kept darting in and out of the room, Molly wondered how she would be able to accommodate a gentleman for any length of time without provoking him beyond measure.

Molly handed them their old clothing rolled into bundles, then escorted them down to the alley so that she could watch how the fabrics flowed on the girls as they hurried to where their carriages were parked in the street. The pelisses looked lovely, but, "Oh," she cried, clapping her hand over her mouth, "those terrible shoes!" She hoped that the first thing Mrs. Vervaine did on the morrow was get her charges to the shoemakers.

Already the sky was growing dark and the tall buildings cut off what light there was. When Molly turned to go back up the stairs to her shop she saw a big hulk of a man with no trousers—was it a kilt?—and a blanket thrown over his head, edge out of a shadowed doorway across the cobbled yard, and lumber after the girls. Thank goodness there were so many of them and their carriages and manservants only a few yards away. There was Mrs. Vervaine too. Molly nearly laughed. The wild-looking creature running in and out of the doorways didn't know the danger he was in if he so much as dared come near the sharp-tongued little procuress.

Molly ran up the narrow stairway and slammed the door shut behind her. "Someday," she vowed, "I shall make enough money to move from this miserable alley into a proper shop in a proper street."

Mrs. Vervaine had other things on her mind, and these she voiced as she herded her charges to the coaches. "Madame Lautrec assured me that her employees will work around the clock to make two more dresses apiece by the end of the week. Therefore, since you each have one presentable outfit now, I shall take you shopping in Oxford Street tomorrow. Madame gave me a list of accessories: hats, shoes, gloves, and other personal items, which you will need to complete your ensembles."

After the two footmen had handed them up into the carriages, the girls sank back into their seats, ready for the ride back to Terrace Palace. The day was nearly over and the yards and yards of draped fabrics, racks of laces, ropes of cords, and cards of buttons finally had been transformed into eight beautiful dresses.

Freddie ran a hand down over her fine new skirt and watched the slender silver threads sparkle in the yellow light of the carriage lamp. Since Mary's and Margaret's outfits were identical all those two had to do was look at each other to admire their new clothes.

"Thank goodness," said Georgette as they settled back in the coach for the ride home, "we are finally going to get to see some of Londontown."

"How long do you think it will take us to buy the things we need tomorrow, Freddie," Margaret asked.

"It should not take long," Freddie said assuringly. "I plan to buy the first bonnet I see, the first shoes, the first pair of hose, and the first gloves I see. Then my shopping will be over."

"Make sure that you bring Mama's maps," said Mary. "I should hate to get lost."

Freddie laughed. "You need not fear, dear. It has become a habit to push the bag under the seat every day. I'm not about to forget now."

"We will finally get to use Mama's maps for something other than sneaking about the house after dark," Georgette said.

Margaret quit accessing the high collar which framed Mary's face. "I thought we were going to explore the third floor in the east wing tonight."

"We can still do that," Freddie said.

Since the maps had been of little use to them during the day while they were at Madame Lautrec's, the girls had been sneaking out of the their rooms after midnight, when the rest of the household was asleep. By candlelight they had followed Mama's drawings of the inside of Terrace Palace, exploring their own side of the mansion first, being careful when they wound their way through the narrow hallways off which the upper female servants had rooms, and avoiding the quarters of the housekeeper altogether. Yet Freddie was still wary and warned them, "I am sure Mrs. Vervaine has the ears and eyes of an owl in the dark, so be quiet as you can."

They even found the nursery, where all of the girls except Freddie, Margaret, and Mary had lived. It was still filled with their toys, and they said they would come back later in the daytime to visit.

The lower public rooms had proven to be no problem at all, such as the library and the study, where Freddie and Margaret oohed and ahhed over the rows and rows of books; and the drawing room, where Antoinette, Babette, and Georgette were especially interested in the oil portrait of their mother, which hung over the marble fireplace. The second Countess of Chantry looked very much like her three beautiful daughters.

They even explored the kitchen. Since Flora was with them she insisted on waking Sukey, who slept on a cot in the pantry. "Polly put the kettle on. Sukey take it off again," she chanted in the sleeping girl's ear.

The tweenie jumped up immediately and begged to join in on their explorations. Her fingers were nimble, she said, and since she knew where Mrs. Vervaine hung her chatelaine, she could snitch any or all of the keys without the housekeeper being the wiser.

However, Freddie told her that her particular talents were impressive but not needed, because so far they had found no doors to be locked.

The upper floors in the east wing had mostly been elegant apartments, and even though most of the furniture was under holland covers, there was one apartment on the first floor where it was not. The four-poster bed was a good three feet off the floor and the dressing room alone was large enough to have ten people to dinner. The walls on three sides of it were closets and Freddie surmised it was the one kept ready in case the earl himself stayed over.

They knew that the earl's secretary had a room on that side of the house, but they were not quite sure where.

For Mr. Pettigrew, who was the only inhabitant in the east wing, it was a quiet existence. Most evenings he would go to the library and select a book, then say good night to Williams as the house steward made his way about the mansion to see that the front door was locked and that no one was left in any of the downstairs rooms before he snuffed out the candles. The rounds were a rather symbolic ritual, since Mr. Pettigrew was most likely to be the only other one about, and he would be in the earl's study or the library.

"I will snuff out the candles when I leave," the secretary would state, and the two men would say good night.

When he was finished with his paperwork Mr. Pettigrew would take his book, mount the front staircase—now that he had been given permission to use it—and go to his room. He did not bother locking his door or his window because there had never been a need. Now that April was upon them the windows would often be opened a crack during the day to air out the house from the long winter.

However, on the fourth night, after he had crawled into bed to read, Mr. Pettigrew heard *things*. He was not quite sure what those *things* were, but it so happened he'd found a book in the library titled *Ghosts of the Medieval Castles and Keeps of England,* and had made his way into the middle of it when the sounds began. *Bump!* "Ohhhhhh!" *Thump!* "Eeahhh!" *Bang!* "Shhhhhh." So astounding were the strange noises that he had not been about to go into the hall to investigate.

It was after some time had passed, and the night had once more turned silent, that he was able to fall asleep.

Back on the second day of their return to London, Mr. Pettigrew had in his usual efficient manner handed Lord Chantry a list of three well-recommended detective agencies.

It had taken no time at all for Daniel to narrow it down to one—Mr. Bowie Slipperson—who had his own business, and was not likely confide in others as he would have had he been associated with a larger organization.

Mr. Slipperson set off for the Scottish border immediately. Daniel was confident that the mystery surrounding his father's northern estate would soon be solved. Now all of his energies could be centered on his greatest campaign. The Season of his sisters' debut.

So on this afternoon when his siblings were at that very moment looking forward to a potential day of freedom, Daniel awaited Mr. Pettigrew at his desk in the study at Terrace Palace, expecting to hear that all had been taken care of for his sisters' Presentation to Queen Charlotte.

However, what he heard was far different than he'd expected. "What do you mean, *The queen is not receiving?*"

Mr. Pettigrew began apologizing immediately. "I am sorry,

my lord. Because of her age and poor health Her Majesty will not be holding any of her Drawing Rooms until after the marriage of Princess Charlotte."

"What are we to do then, Mr. Pettigrew? I promised my father—that is he promised the countess."

The secretary's eyebrows became uncontrollable. The feeling that he had failed his employer in his commission was overwhelming. "Surely your sisters can have a successful Season without a Presentation."

"But it is unthinkable that the daughters of the sixth Earl of Chantry will not be presented at court."

"We could reconsider Lady Lisbone's offer." Mr. Pettigrew was beginning to consider himself a partner in this affair.

"No, no, no. Besides you said you already sent her an excuse for not coming. Let me think," Daniel said, steepling his fingers and drawing his hands to his face.

Mr. Pettigrew was trying his best to come up with an alternative suggestion also, but he was having a hard time of it. The secretary was beginning to come to the conclusion that he was not cut out to be a co-conspirator.

Daniel, however, was still rolling different scenarios over in his mind. "Of course you did not let on whom you represented when you contacted the palace."

"No, your lordship. I was very discreet."

The earl's fist came down on the desk in an uncharacteristic show of exasperation. "Od'sbodkins, Mr. Pettigrew! The Presentation was to be the announcement that my sisters were here in London. I did not want anyone to take notice of them until they were correctly outfitted and prepared."

"Their manners at Knocktigh were all that was proper as far as I could see, my lord."

"Aye, but there the girls were in familiar surroundings. You remember how shy they were that first day we arrived at the manor. Especially the little . . ." he started to say the little mouse. "Lady Winifred," he said instead. "Remember she was shaking all over from fright. We can't know how they will fare among total strangers."

"Couldn't you start with something smaller?"

"No, no. First the Presentation. Then Almack's. That is what we said, wasn't it?"

"Many debutantes start with Almack's."

"Good lord. They are not even ready for Almack's yet. The disapproval from the Patronesses would be a disaster, and those ladies, I hear, would definitely be put out of sorts if they should find that they had been slighted for the primal introduction in favor of someone even as highly placed as the countess of Lisbone. No, it is out of the question that we accept Lady Lisbone's invitation."

"Yes, my lord."

"I shudder to think of the catastrophe it would cause if anyone in the Fashionable World should see them as they are in their present state. They look like daughters of a country bumpkin. Well, you are just going to have to take another survey of the situation and come up with other measures that we can take."

"I will set my mind to it immediately," Mr. Pettigrew said, trying desperately to suppress the yawn he felt coming. "Do you need me for anything else, my lord?"

"No, you may go. You do look tired, Mr. Pettigrew. I am not working you too hard, am I?"

"Oh, no, my lord. It is just that I did not sleep well last night."

"Well, get to bed early. I won't need you until noon tomorrow. I still have not found time to get to my clubs. When we were riding in Hyde Park, Captain Woods and I ran into more of the chappies from Wellington's staff—Hawksby and Byrd. We've been meeting every evening for dinner. But tonight I definitely will get to White's. I hope a quiet night of cards will relax me a bit."

Just as he rose from his desk sounds of female gaiety penetrated even the thick walls of the study.

"Listen," Daniel said. "I think I hear my sisters arriving now.

Perhaps I should go say hello. It has been, after all, three days since we have spoken." Daniel could not believe that he looked forward to seeing them.

Mr. Pettigrew, too, found that he was much revived. "I think I should go to greet them also, my lord. It is the polite thing to do."

The earl found himself hurrying toward the entry hall and entered it just as his sisters were starting up the stairs. They were not the girls he'd seen just a few days ago. They had been transformed into ladies. Beetleworth and several others of the staff were also on hand to admire them.

Daniel's gaze ran the gamut, but it was the sight of Ruth and Rebecca, already a few steps above the others, who stirred a long-ago memory in Daniel. He pictured another fair-haired lady much like them sitting in the garden. A young boy stood at her knee eagerly showing her a baby robin redbreast he'd found on the ground alongside the hedgerow. Much to his disappointment, she had told him he must put it back where its parents could find it. She had helped him look for the nest in the shrubs. After soothing his anxieties his mother assured him that the fledgling would be all right. "That's what parents are for—to comfort their young. Only when the baby bird is ready to fly on its own will its parents leave it."

A month later his mother had died. "Gone away to be with the angels in Heaven." That was the way it was explained to Daniel, a small frightened boy of six who could not understand why the only real companion he had had was taken away. Soon after that, he was sent to boarding school where he found he was surrounded by several other bewildered little gentlemen, all as confused as he. He had not been at all ready to fly on his own.

Daniel had never felt that same closeness with a woman since then, and he believed it was not possible that he ever would—nor that he wanted to. But the memory remained in the depth of his heart to be pulled out and savored when the world threatened to overwhelm him with its ugliness and cruelty.

Now with the sight of Ruth and Rebecca, those feelings once more surged to the surface.

"Lord Chantry?" came a voice somewhere near his elbow. Daniel looked down to see Mrs. Vervaine standing in front of him. When she saw that she had his attention she turned to the girls. "Come, ladies," she ordered. "Come show his lordship your new clothes."

They hurried to line up before him. That his sisters were lovely creatures was only going to make his mission that much easier. Then he looked at their feet. Daniel steeled himself not to react and quickly shifted his gaze to the little mouse. No! She was not a mouse any longer, but a fairy princess come out of the forest. Her hair was not done up as much in style as the others, but its looseness became her.

Without even looking into her eyes, Daniel knew that Winifred was studying him also. For what purpose he could not suppose, but from the harum-scarum behavior, which he'd already become embarrassingly aware of, such as, dangling from rafters, and attempting to climb into the stall of a dangerous horse, he reckoned that whatever she had on her mind could only lead to trouble.

Mrs. Vervaine had been speaking all this time, but Daniel hadn't attended a word that she'd said. He hoped it wasn't something that required an answer.

"Then if it is all right with you, Lord Chantry, I shall take them to the shops in Oxford Street to select the necessary accessories to complete their outfits?"

He found himself brought back to the present with a jerk. "Most certainly, Mrs. Vervaine. That would be fine," Daniel said trying to recall what they had been talking about.

All the girls stood, smiling, but looked as if they expected something more to be said.

Beetleworth appeared quite cheerful. "What time would you like dinner to be served, your lordship?"

Daniel blinked twice, then thrice.

"You just agreed that you would stay for dinner, my lord," Mr. Pettigrew whispered behind him.

"I did? Oh, yes, I did, didn't I?" Daniel said, trying not to show his confusion.

Mr. Pettigrew, never capable of fabrication before in his life—but being the superior secretary that he was—made up a clanker on the spot. "I believe you mentioned in the study that you would like to dine with your sisters early, my lord, because you are committed to another engagement later in the evening."

Daniel decided that he had underestimated his quiet employee. "Thank you, Mr. Pettigrew, for reminding me. Shall we say supper in an hour? Tell Cook that she does not have to labor over anything on my account. I can freshen up in my chambers here, and you, of course, must join my sisters and me at the table, Mr. Pettigrew."

"I already said that I would be honored, my lord. But I thank you for mentioning it again."

"Well, then, shall we say in an hour, sisters?" Daniel said, bowing. He was sure that he heard a giggle, but he could not tell exactly where it came from because the young ladies were all curtsying and he could not see their faces.

As soon as everyone had left the hall, except for his secretary and himself, Daniel said, "Mr. Pettigrew—have a small carriage sent over to Albany with a message for Tilbury to bring my evening clothes over. I shall have to dress here if I am ever to make it to any of the clubs tonight."

"Very good, my lord."

Daniel started up the stairs two at a time, then stopped midway and turned. "By the bye, Mr. Pettigrew. I thank you for agreeing to dine with my sisters and me."

"Oh, my lord . . . it was not—"

"I will hear no more about it, and that is an order, Mr. Pettigrew. The fact is I refuse to be the only male at a table full of women."

"As you say, Lord Chantry," the secretary said, bowing. He waited a few seconds until his employer had disappeared down the corridor toward his apartment, then Mr. Pettigrew easily jumped three steps at a time all the way to the third floor.

From the floor above Freddie unashamedly peered out from between the balustrades on the opposite side of the hall. She knew that his lordship hadn't been attending Mrs. Vervaine when asked whether or not he would be dining at Terrace Palace. She could tell his mind was wandering. Nor had he heard Ruth and Rebecca when they'd begged him to stay. He had been look-ing right at them, as though he were seeing them . . . but not really seeing them at all. Perhaps Granny's admonition that men listened to a woman with only one ear was not always right, but it certainly proved true of his lordship.

Now she watched Mr. Pettigrew hop, skip, and jump over the steps, while Lord Chantry headed down the corridor looking as though he would not be afraid one whit had a bear jumped out of the corner that very minute to attack him.

Neither of these performances gave Freddie cause to ponder, but what had surprised her most was his lordship's admission that the thought of dining alone with eight young ladies terrified him. She watched him now and contemplated the wonder of it, because it was something she would not have suspected of so brave and gallant a soldier. Was that what Granny meant when she said a cover of a book did not always reveal what was inside?

Freddie ran a hand over the soft fabric of her new green dress. Did the story change when you stepped into a new cover? she wondered. "It certainly feels better anyway," she said, laughing, as she ran toward her room to prepare for supper.

Thirteen

Daniel did not go to his club that evening after all. Cook insisted on creating a dinner which would have done honor to the most exalted of worthies. His sisters were so much more outgoing now than when he had met them just a few weeks ago that the change was a delight to behold. If the remainder of their wardrobes flattered them half as well as the pretty gowns Madame Lautrec had already made for them, he would be well pleased. Their excitement over their anticipated expedition to Oxford Street so intrigued him that he was reluctant to rush off.

An even greater surprise was in the almost comical flip-flop demeanor Mr. Pettigrew was displaying—from his characteristic shy smile and flushed countenance whenever he caught one of the ladies glancing his way to his becoming an out-and-out chatterbox. Daniel's keen observation linked the glasses of wine his secretary consumed to the man's ability to increase the amount of words he spoke without taking a breath. So every time Mr. Pettigrew's glass threatened to run dry, Daniel signaled Beetleworth to refill it. He was certain that his sisters found far more enjoyment in listening to Mr. Pettigrew's tales of London than those he'd have chosen, and was sure he'd have bored them to death.

This scenario suited the earl. His sisters were full of questions, and his secretary seemed to have all the answers concerning a London Daniel himself had never known.

"You will like Oxford Street," Mr. Pettigrew said. "It is over a mile-long stretch of shops. The sidewalks are so deep that six people can stand abreast on them and not be crowded. Did you know that it is so well lit people still stroll along looking in the windows at eleven o'clock at night?"

After the appropriate oohs and ahhhs, he proceeded to paint word pictures of all the clothing shops they should expect to see as well as perfumeries and druggists, tea and coffee merchants, book shops and jewelers. "Long ago these were large family homes, and now some of the storeowners live over their shops and let off the extra rooms."

"Like Madam Lautrec does?" Georgette said.

"Yes, and the shops extend into side alleyways and the length of Old Bond and New Bond Street too."

"All the way to Picadilly," said Mary brightly, then chewed her lower lip as Freddie gave her one of her looks to be careful in what she said. They had been warned not to let anyone know they had Mama Gilliane's maps.

"But it is not so crowded here off the Strand," Rebecca said quickly to cover for Mary's error in blurting out her knowledge of the area, which she was never supposed to have been in or about before.

"Why are there so few houses on the side of the river, Mr. Pettigrew?" Margaret asked.

"Perhaps, dear," Ruth said, "Mr. Pettigrew could answer if we did not ask him so many questions at once."

"Yes, do be quiet Maggie," Mary interrupted, and then proceeded to ask the same question before he could answer any of the others. "Why aren't there many houses on the side of the river?"

Mr. Pettigrew turned his head to face Mary. "Most of the mansions of medieval days are gone or, like the Savoy Palace, lie in ruins. There are a few left deserted, either waiting for a buyer or the wreckers."

Freddie had been silent because she was studying Lord Chantry, taking note that it was the same strand of hair on the right side which seemed to persist in falling out of place over his forehead. It took away some of the stuffiness from his appearance, and she liked him better that way. Then he caught her looking at his forehead and brushed the stray lock back up to where it should be. She quickly turned her attention away and joined in asking questions of Mr. Pettigrew. "When we headed west on the Strand on our way to the dressmakers we passed a tall iron gate on the river side. Beyond it, there were turrets sticking up above the trees, but the property is so overgrown it looks like a jungle. Who lives there?"

"You must be speaking of the Farley mansion. Dismal old place now, but at one time it was considered quite the pinnacle of luxurious living. The ballroom I hear is a hundred feet long, and there were extensive gardens with graveled paths which ran down to the river. Viscount Farley had a private water stairs built and his own wherry to transport himself or his guests across the river to Vauxhall Gardens. They say that the old river stairs are still used by certain people who tie up their wherries and sculls there. But the old house has been deserted for more years than I can recall—even haunted I hear."

A big smile lit up Freddie's face. Never for a minute had she thought to limit her explorations of Londontown to linen and china shops, and she knew her sisters did not either. They had poured over Mama's maps too many years to be confined to only civilized areas. "That reminds me. I want very much to see the wild animals at the Tower Menagerie."

A warning flag went up in Daniel's mind. There was something different about his brown-haired sister, other than coloring, which set him on edge, and he couldn't quite put a finger on what it was. The change in her since their first meeting was astounding. Aside from having the nerve to stand up to his unpredictable, noodle-headed stallion, she showed no fear of Mrs. Vervaine—a woman who even put Daniel in a quake. He was also aware that the minute she now realized he was looking at her the expression on the little termagant's face altered immediately, and she looked away. Lady Winifred would bear watching. On the other hand he was probably being foolishly cautious. How much trouble could one small girl get into?

Daniel sat back in his chair and observed the entire tableau through narrowed eyes. Had he not been holding his glass, he would have been rubbing his hands with glee. All in all the campaign was going as planned. His sisters were behaving. Aside from the disappointment of finding that they could not be presented at court, if all went as well as it had during the last few days the metamorphosis would be complete. Eight country misses turned almost overnight into beautiful butter-flies.

"Why did our father buy this house and not that one on the river if it were bigger?" Georgette asked.

Mr. Pettigrew politely gave all his attention to the eldest of the dark-haired sisters. "Actually his lordship did inquire into buying it, but it was in such disrepair that it would have taken months before they could have moved in. Then the Terrace Palace came up for purchase. It had already been remodeled by the Adams brothers, who were also building the Adelphi Terrace, and the countess wanted to start inviting guests in right away. She loved to entertain, you know. Oh, yes, indeed. There were some splendid parties held here then. Everyone danced until dawn."

Daniel was glad he had thought to ask Mr. Pettigrew to dinner. The man was an encyclopedia of information and seemed to know more about his father's life than he did. Before Daniel knew it, the time had slipped away and it was past ten o'clock before he managed to get up to his apartment.

Tilbury was waiting with his greatcoat and hat when there was a knock on the door.

Beetleworth stood in the hallway. "Mrs. Vervaine wished me to remind your lordship that you said you would meet her in your study before leaving."

"I said that, Beetleworth?"

"Not exactly in words, my lord. Mrs. Vervaine mentioned it just before you went into the dining room and you nodded."

"You are sure I didn't *shake* my head?"

"I am afraid not, Lord Chantry. It was definitely a nod."

"Hell's bells! If everyone is going to read something into every twitch and shake I make, I will have to stop moving altogether."

"Shall I tell Mrs. Vervaine that you will see her at another time, my lord?" the butler asked with a little shudder when he thought of being the bearer of bad tidings.

"Don't you dare, Beetleworth," the earl said. "Tell her I shall be there as quickly as I can. Take my coat and hat down with you. I shall see what she has to say and leave from there. And Tilbury, meet me back at Albany."

Mrs. Vervaine stood stiffly in the middle of the study, wearing her full armor of keys, chains, and all her other household weapons. Her gaze was fixed on the doorway where Beetleworth remained pinned to a spot at the entrance, too frightened to move after he'd relayed the earl's message.

When Daniel entered, the housekeeper bobbed a curtsy—jingling and jangling as she dipped, jingling and jangling back up again.

"Lord Chantry, I told you that I am taking the ladies shopping tomorrow."

"Yes, Mrs. Vervaine. They are very excited about it."

"How am I to expect the shopkeepers to part with their merchandise when I have not been instructed on how I am to pay them?"

"Why just tell them that everything is to be charged to the Earl of Chantry and have them delivered here."

"They do not know me; they do not know the young ladies; and you said you do not want it made public that you are going to introduce your eight sisters for the Season. They are not invisible, Lord Chantry."

"Don't tell them that the girls are my sisters. That is all. It is as simple as that."

"And who am I to say that they are? Your harem? What a fine scandalbroth that would boil up for those tender young ladies' first introduction into the Fashionable World."

Good lord! Daniel hadn't even thought of the consequences. "Beetleworth, find Mr. Pettigrew."

"I believe he is in the library now, picking out a book, my lord."

"Then send him in and go fetch Williams. We must have a staff meeting about this."

Ten minutes later, when his servants had convened in the study, Daniel went over the problems facing them.

It was decided that the house steward would give Mrs. Vervaine monies from the household account. She, of course, had to remind the earl that multiplied by eight, the sum would be substantial. The words she used were, "A small fortune, Lord Chantry."

That problem was solved when Daniel had the three footmen called in. This took fifteen minutes, for the men to dress and come to the study. Another closed carriage would be needed, he told Beetleworth. One footman was to accompany Mrs. Vervaine at all times. The other two would carry purchases back to the carriages. The coachmen were to stay with their vehicles to keep the packages from being stolen. Under no circumstances were they to turn the horses over to the care of little beggars trying to make a bob.

"What if the young ladies see some little trinket they wish to buy, Lord Chantry? Am I to let them have it?"

Why not? Daniel thought. A pleasant way for his sisters to experience his generosity.

The housekeeper was not as agreeable. "I cannot be dribbling out pennies here and there, Lord Chantry, if I am haggling with merchants."

"No, of course not, Mrs. Vervaine. Each shall carry her own spending money. Williams, see that my sisters have some coins of their own."

"How much, my lord?"

Daniel looked at Mr. Pettigrew.

Mr. Pettigrew did not know either.

Mrs. Vervaine complained that Lord Chantry had now kept them so late she would get only a few hours' sleep if she did not get to bed soon.

In his opinion Daniel did the wisest thing he could and told Mrs. Vervaine that he would leave the amount up to her, and bid them all good night. But by the time he had gathered up his hat and coat and his walking stick, and was about to tell Beetleworth to have his carriage brought round, he decided it was way too late for him to go to his club that night. He had an engagement for lunch with Woods and Oakley at White's. He might as well wait until then and have a few rounds of cards while he was there.

"Don't bother calling my carriage, Beetleworth. I believe I shall go out to the stables and tell them myself. I have not seen that rapscallion Scots Grey of mine for three days now and want to check to see if he has been behaving himself."

Freddie sat on the floor of the landing peering down into the hall. It had been so late when they had gone up to their bedrooms that the girls had decided they wouldn't do any exploring that night, so she had decided to run down to pick up a book instead. The hum of voices came from the hallway which led to the library and study. She couldn't imagine what all those people were doing up so long after dinner was over. Now she would have to wait until everyone left, because she couldn't let them see her in her nightdress with only her old cape thrown over her shoulders.

Upon first seeing the library when they had explored that side of the house, all eight of them had never believed there could be so many books in the whole world. She and Georgette had sneaked down the night before and selected a book each to take to their room. Freddie didn't believe that with so many anybody would miss one or two. She was about to fall asleep when she heard voices coming into the hallway.

Mrs. Vervaine crossed the hall and went to the back of the house. The footmen headed toward their quarters belowstairs. Then she watched as four more men came out together and his lordship said something to the other three.

Mr. Pettigrew went up the circular stairs to his room, while Williams and Beetleworth headed for their rooms at the back of the east wing. Which was strange, she thought, because Williams did not see the earl out the front.

Instead Lord Chantry headed toward the back of the house. Wondering where he was going, she ran along the corridor that led to a window overlooking the gardens. She saw his figure emerge from the French windows, cross the patio, and head down the path toward the stables.

Their long days at the dressmakers had given the girls little chance to explore the gardens, let alone the stables. They all missed their morning rides on the wild donkeys, and Ruth had suggested that if their brother had enough mounts perhaps he would allow them to go for a ride in one of the parks someday. Freddie was curious as anybody to find out how many horses he kept at Terrace Palace.

Without giving it another thought, she flew down the steps, wrapping her cape tighter around her. She stepped outside. Then, pulling the hood up over her head, she ran swiftly from bush to bush, her slippered feet making no sound at all.

Freddie peeked round the door into the building which his lordship had entered. Gas lanterns threw a soft yellow glow on the stalls. She heard his lordship's low voice. He was speaking to a man at the far end. The fellow murmured something in return and exited through a rear door.

While Lord Chantry was peering into one of the dark stalls, she slipped in. He evidently was not getting any response from the occupant inside.

Freddie hunkered down and watched. The earl said a very

naughty word. Finally she heard his exasperated command, *"Purrr-e-cious! Get over here!"*

There was a nicker-nicker, a clattering of hooves, another nicker and a neeeiiighhh!

"Precious, you are a pain. Do you know that? Here I was going to take you for a walk. Now I don't know whether I should humor you or not."

Freddie clapped a hand over her mouth. Oh, my! *Precious?* The stiff-necked, proper, pattern-saint, army officer—the Earl of Chantry—called his horse Precious? Could a soft heart be hiding under that stuffy manner? Freddie did not have time to dwell on that preposterous notion, for his lordship had opened the stall gate and was leading the horse out.

"So you think you deserve an outing?" Chantry said in a husky whisper.

Precious evidently thought he did because Freddie heard him nicker several times, blow out his cheeks, and bubble his lips. Heaven help her! They were coming her way and she had no-where to hide.

Quickly she fell to her knees, pulled her hood over her head, rolled herself into a ball, held her breath, and prayed that in the dim light she looked like a sack of oats. Footsteps thumped and hooves clomped close—then stopped. A soft nose butted her shoulder.

Squeeeak. Whistle.

Freddie rocked dangerously.

"Precious, leave that sack alone, you devil. The stableboys will not appreciate it if you make a mess for them to clean up."

The *clomp-clomp-clickity-clack* continued on down the aisle and out the door just as Freddie fell over. She lay still until she was sure they were completely out of the stables before she jumped up and, not bothering to clean the bits of straw clinging to her cloak, made a dash for the back of the house.

Freddie changed into a clean nightrail and crawled into bed beside the sleeping Georgette. It took her awhile to settle down because all she could think about was the earl's voice talking foolishness to a horse named Precious. "Oh, Granny," she said, "His lordship is not at all what he seems. I should never have studied him so closely. Now I have fallen in love with him." Finally she buried her head in her pillow and giggled herself to sleep.

Just as Mr. Pettigrew had told them, Oxford Street seemed to go on forever. "Can you imagine a street which takes over half an hour to walk from end to end?" Margaret said.

Mary peered out the opposite side of the coach. "That is if you don't stop to see anything. I plan on looking into every single shop."

They had left Terrace Palace early and already the avenue was filled with both vehicles and pedestrians. Handsomely lacquered coaches were beginning to line up in rows on either side of the street, and there was still room for two coaches to pass one another. The Durham coachmen soon found a space for their own vehicles, and the sisters and Mrs. Vervaine were handed down to the sidewalk which was inlaid with flagstones.

"You are not going to take that hideous sack with you," Mrs. Vervaine said, eyeing the large canvas bag Freddie dragged out of the coach.

"I have some things in it that I may need," said Freddie, having no intention of leaving the maps behind.

"We will be purchasing pretty reticules which will match your outfits. We may even find some stocking purses that will fit inside to carry the coins Lord Chantry left for you. Until we do you can keep them knotted in your handkerchiefs."

Freddie stubbornly held onto the bag. Brown eyes met violet.

"Very well then," said Mrs. Vervaine, being the first to look away. "You may keep it until we find the reticules. Then you can switch whatever you have with you into one and be rid of that odious sack." *Stubborn girl.* "Come, ladies. Do not dilly-dally."

Mrs. Vervaine did not need a whip to make it plain that she

would brook no arguments from her charges. She only needed her umbrella, and pointing it toward the sky, she marched them into the first shop on her list, a shoemaker's.

Freddie never dreamed there were so many kinds of footware. They even had shoes for dolls if a little girl wanted them made to match her own. There were ready-made leather or satin slippers for indoor use in a variety of colors, and each girl found a pair that matched her dress well enough that Mrs. Vervaine had them all set aside to be delivered to Terrace Palace. Mindful that Madame Lautrec had recommended satin half boots in the colors of their gowns or pelisses, all the girls had their feet measured and the specified shoes ordered. All but Ruth and Rebecca found nankeen half-boots for walking, so they said they would wear their new blue leather slippers right away.

The housekeeper would have had the shoemaker throw away all their old shoes had not Freddie told him beforehand to bundle them up and hand them to the footman.

"Whatever do you want those hideous boots for, Freddie?" Georgette whispered. "They are beyond repair."

"Freddie always has something in mind," said Margaret.

"Do you?" Mary said, her eyes wide.

Anticipation lit up Babette's and Antoinette's eyes.

"One never knows when old friends may come in handy, does one?" Freddie said, trying to look knowing. Actually she had no idea what she would do with the battered shoes. It was just that she'd had to be frugal for so long she could not believe the dream would last. She wasn't really Lord Chantry's sister. What if he found out and told her she had to give back all the new clothes he was buying her?

Ruth signaled from the doorway of the shop. "Come, girls," she said in a loud whisper. "Mrs. Vervaine is pursing her lips and clucking like Hennypen. You know that means she is getting impatient."

Next they stopped by a bonnet shop, then a linen shop, and a ribbon and lace shop. The list went on and on, it seemed to the girls.

"Mrs. Vervaine," Freddie said, "how long will it take us to be finished with our shopping?"

"Finished?" said the housekeeper, humphing and clacking her tongue. "Why, there is no finishing. Not until you are all taken and settled. I can tell you that. For some ladies it takes years. Each set of dresses will take an equal amount of accessories. There are your toiletries to purchase: perfumes, pomades, fans, and gloves. Your maids have informed me that you have no jewelry. I am aware there is the family collection. Of course those will be worn someday by the next Countess. What Lord Chantry plans to do about that is none of my business, but the responsibility for the remainder of your wardrobes has been placed in my hands," she said, sniffing meaningfully. "Now follow me ladies."

Mrs. Vervaine marched out of the store her pointy little nose in the air, looking neither to the right or to the left—not even looking to see if anyone was following her.

Mrs. Vervaine was quite aware of the impact the twins were having on males and females alike, and she made the most of the attention. Heads began to turn on the street as well. And the shopkeepers, when they realized that they had a potential for eight sales instead of one, well, there was nothing they were not willing to do to keep the little party in their stores as long as possible. But Mrs. Vervaine would not allow them to tarry for long. "No dillydallying, ladies," she'd announce, and point her parasol toward the door.

Except for the Cranberry Roost Confectioner and Sandwich shop. There Mrs. Vervaine found an excuse to try a plate of tiny cucumber sandwiches on buttered bread, a bowl of sugared fruit, potted meat sandwiches, and a sample of some with egg and watercress. Then, of course, there were the salmon pinwheels, which she had to try, topped off with delicious almond biscuits and just a taste of plum cake. She had drunk three cups of tea before she was satisfied and pointed her parasol toward the door.

"How are we going to see all the places we want to see if

we are going to be shopping all day long?" Mary complained, as soon as they were out of earshot of Mrs. Vervaine.

"I want to visit the museums," said Margaret.

"Someone gave me a handbill on the street announcing that there is a student watercolor show in an empty store in Bond Street. I should like ever so much to go to that," Georgette said. "How many bonnets do we have to buy today? We will not get to see anything but the inside of shops."

"Mmmm," Freddie mused. " 'Tis a problem I did not anticipate either, or how particular Mrs. Vervaine would be in picking out gloves that have no fingers. Why they wouldn't keep a kitten warm. And why do we need a dozen lace handkerchiefs when we only have one nose? I would have taken that first hat I tried on, but she had me try on four more before we were back at the first."

"You are so amusing, Freddie," Mary said, laughing. "I liked trying on the hats, and I think Babette and Antoinette did too. When Ruth and Rebecca could not make up their minds, Mrs. Vervaine told the shopkeeper that she would take all four that they liked. She said our brother insisted that she was to buy anything she thought we needed."

"Yes, but did you notice that Mrs. Vervaine is not keeping track to see that we are all trailing after her? In the last linen shop we left Ruth behind and she did not even know it. She thought Ruth was herself the first time she saw her. The next time she passed her she called her Lady Rebecca."

"Do you have an idea, Freddie?"

"Yes I do. I noticed also that Mrs. Vervaine does not pay much attention to colors. It is probably because she wears that same blue-gray dress every day and never adds another. Do you remember when we were in the shop with the two rooms of linens and Georgette stopped outside at the confectioners window to look at the pyramid of pineapples? We were in the linen shop for half an hour picking out petticoats and nightgowns before Georgette came in. Mrs. Vervaine didn't even notice because Antoinette and Babette were running about from room to room trying to decide what they wanted to buy, and I don't think she could tell them apart."

"So what does that have to do with anything, Freddie?"

"I think Mrs. Vervaine is getting tired. She was up very late last night. Now that we have bought our shoes and hats from the list that Madame Lautrec gave her, she is not really paying any attention to what we say we want, and she just tells the shopkeepers to wrap up eight of everything. I don't think she would really pay any mind if one or two of us separated from the rest and went off to do a little exploring on our own. Antoinette and Babette wanted to go into the china and glass shop which we passed."

Ruth added to the list. "I would like to visit the watchmaker's store, and the dancing doll display at the toy shop."

"Did you notice how much she liked the sandwich shop?" Rebecca asked. "I'm sure I could persuade her to linger over some strawberry tarts and a pot of tea.

Mary clapped her hands. "May we go to Piccadilly, Freddie? It's on Mama's map. I saw it," she said, and started to sing:

> *"Up at Piccadilly oh!*
> *The coachman takes his stand,*
> *And when he meets a pretty girl,*
> *He takes her by the hand;"*

"How romantic," mimicked Margaret, fluttering her lashes and retaliating with a ditty of her own:

> *"Daffy-down-dilly has come up to town,*
> *In a yellow petticoat and a green gown."*

"I am not daffy," said Mary. "You are the daffy-dilly. Writing every day to Dr. MacDougal. You know he will never write you back."

"Come, come," Ruth admonished. "I will accompany Mary down Bond Street. Mr. Pettigrew said there are ever so many fine stores to see all the way from Oxford Street. You look very pretty, Mary, I am sure you will attract any number of handsome young men."

Georgette voiced her desire to browse the china and glass shops, and Antoinette and Babette seconded her choice with twin nods and smiles. "We could take turns going."

"Then when two come back, another two can go out," Rebecca said, smiling at the thought. "It will be just like the time that Babette and I were seen by Mr. Gowdie when we raided his storage bin for flour. When he described us to the constable, the widow Burkette swore that he couldn't have seen girls like that, because two lassies looking just like the ones he'd described had brought her fresh baked bread at the very same time."

"Well, I for one am going to find some place more exciting than linen or china shops," Margaret said.

"I was thinking to visit Hatchard's bookstore in Piccadilly," said Freddie.

"Let me go with you," Margaret begged. "That would be so much more to my liking."

"We're *aff then an' away*, " said Freddie. "All we have to do is make certain that some of us are with Mrs. Vervaine at all times."

Fourteen

When Daniel arrived at White's the next afternoon he found that Mr. Hefflewicker had preceded him by two days to that hallowed male sanctuary as the guest of his wife's brother-in-law, Lord Lisbone.

Captains Oakley and Woods were already seated around a gaming table with Forrest, Byrd, and Lord Finch, also former staffers to the Duke of Wellington. All but Finch and Daniel wore their regimentals. Oakley dealt the cards. The others didn't say anything, but all five men had grins upon their faces and quizzical glints in their eyes.

Daniel soon found out why. His appearance set off about the room a buzz of discussions which were not difficult to overhear, considering that voices had a way of carrying in a hushed atmosphere.

Which of the pair—the squire or his wife—could be termed the greater tittle-tattler would probably always remain debatable, but it might be said that Mr. Hefflewicker's breezy comments had started quite a hum, which in turn created a most uncomfortable reception for Lord Chantry.

Whoever was to blame was of little import. From the *on-dits* which floated over to him it was evident that the rumors were already too widespread to be retrievable.

"Eight sisters you say?"

"Well, if that don't beat all."

"Can't say as I heard anything like that ever happening before," Lord Erskine shouted, holding his horn to his ear. "The man must be mad."

Although the reference was intended for Daniel in that instance, he could tell that much of the gossip was aimed at the late sixth Earl of Chantry as much as his son.

"Think of the expense. What we spent on our Elsbeth for her come-out near to bankrupted us," Sir Charles rasped.

His companion agreed. "We have two daughters to marry off ourselves."

Those who were fathers murmured in sympathy.

"M'wife said that if the son is as attractive a scoundrel as his father, it don't matter. The title will be well worth the sacrifice."

"Must admit he had something going for him. How many men can claim to have fathered four sets of twins in as many years?"

Daniel tried to concentrate on the hand he'd been dealt. He was being forced to see his father in a whole new dimension. He sat staring at his cards and steeled his face to mask the thoughts swirling in his head. The earl had always appeared so circumspect, so proper. He had never thought of his lordship in any other manner than fully clothed, dignified, always in control. To think of his father in any other circumstance had never crossed his mind.

The last time their paths crossed had been in August of 1814 at the victory celebrations in St. James's Park. One of the few times that Daniel had been in London. The earl was to accompany Lord Castlereagh's party to Vienna that August, so Daniel knew that his father was understandably distracted with important considerations of what his party was going to try to accomplish. On that occasion he told Daniel that he was looking well, and he expected he was conducting himself in a manner befitting a Durham. Of course, neither had any idea that it would be the last time they would see each other or that in less than a year the war would resume again. Perhaps if he had, his father would have spent a little more time with him.

But now Daniel's attention was brought to the table next to him.

"More to the point, gentlemen," the foppish young Lord Davenport was saying, taking a pinch of snuff, "are the gels antidotes or fetchers I want to know?"

"And what is he going to offer to be rid of them?"

"I hear that Captain Durham was a no-nonsense exacting officer. Do you think now that he is the earl he'll be as particular in the choice of husbands?"

"He's frugal, I hear."

"You mean cheese-paring?"

"Perhaps not as bad as that, but he is known to pull out of a game of cards when the stakes get too high. Plays for relaxation, he says."

"You don't say. What a strange fellow."

"Then you do not think there is much chance for a large dowry?"

"Haven't the foggiest. Could go either way. Depends on how anxious he is to be rid of them."

"With that many sisters I can't see how he can be too particular in his choice of husbands."

Daniel fumed. It seemed that half the members of the *haut ton* were wondering if he himself had plans to choose a countess, and the other half were speculating on the beauty and wealth of his eight sisters.

Captain Oakley cleared his throat. "There are bets already on why you are keeping your sisters under wraps, Chantry. Why won't you let us see them?"

Viscount Finch, who like Daniel had also just recently come into his title, leaned forward. "Confidentially, Chantry, is there something we should know about your sisters that you can't tell others?"

"Good lord, no, Finch! They are well-looking and biddable. They will make perfectly acceptable wives. 'Tis just that they have lived quietly in the country for most of their lives, and I felt that the move to Town might prove upsetting. I thought they needed time to adjust. You shall see them soon enough."

Daniel hoped that satisfied his friends. If he should be forced to thrust his sisters out among the throngs now they would surely faint dead away. They must first learn how to deal with civilization—and today was to be their first day on the streets of London. Thank goodness he had someone like Mrs. Vervaine to look out for them. Under her watchful eye he had nothing to worry about.

Aside from the annoying banter when he had first arrived, the afternoon did turn out to be a pleasant one for Daniel. Good friends, little conversation, several glasses of wine, and a few hands of whist. It seemed his life was finally settling back into his usual sensible routine. He was just about to recommend that they choose a good restaurant for dinner when he was handed a message.

"The devil take it!"

"What is it, Chantry?"

"This is from my secretary, Mr. Pettigrew He says that my sisters went shopping in Oxford Street this morning with my housekeeper, as planned. Now all eight have come up missing."

"I cannot believe you let eight innocents and an old woman go out alone, Chantry. It's already dark outside."

"Demme! They should have been home hours ago. I sent three coaches and drivers. A footman with each vehicle. One of them was not to let Mrs. Vervaine out of his sight. They evidently took me literally because Mrs. Vervaine is safe, but they cannot find one trace of the girls. They did not come back to the coaches, he says, and all available staff are out scouring the city for them." Daniel was already heading for the front of the establishment. "Now I must return immediately to Terrace Palace to see what needs to be done."

"Have they notified the authorities?"

"No, and I prefer that the police be kept out of this until I have looked into the situation. If you will excuse me gentlemen."

"I can have my carriage here in a minute, Major," Byrd said, wobbling a little as he stood.

"It will be faster to grab a hackney," Daniel said, placing his hat on his head and pulling on his gloves.

"Do let us help you search, my lord," Captain Woods said as all the men called for their hats and cloaks.

Daniel ran out the door, waved down one of the hacks that plied the street, and jumped in giving the driver his direction as he did so.

The five men dashed out after him, but the earl was already disappearing onto Piccadilly. They reconnoitered at the curb.

"Confound it all, gentlemen!" Captain Forrest said. "There ought to be something we can do to help the major."

"We could be looking for his sisters while he's going home to see what's what," Byrd suggested.

"Righto!" agreed Oakley.

"Where shall we start?" Forrest yelled into Byrd's ear.

"We'll spread out in Piccadilly and head north from there toward Oxford Street. One of you take Albemarle, I'll head up Old Bond. Finch, you take whatever is left."

"They wouldn't have headed off into Tothill Field would they now?"

"Don't even think it!"

"By the bye," Lord Finch said. "What do his sisters look like?"

Oakley stopped and scratched his head. "Haven't the foggiest," he said. "Never saw them before in my life. How many twins can there be in London?"

"There are four sets that we know of," said Byrd, harr-harring.

"It's not a laughing matter, Byrd."

"No, sir. It is not."

"That's it then, gentlemen," Oakley said. "There are five of us and four sets of them. We'll have Major Durham's sisters back before he knows it."

* * *

Daniel thought that of all his sisters the one least likely to get lost would be the little brown mouse. Babette and Antoinette were the first to be brought in. Williams had found them in the back of Trishee's Chinese House watching the Orientals paint china plates. The twins' rare beauty, and the fact that there were two of them looking so much alike enabled the house steward to find several merchants who pointed him in the direction the girls had gone. They had quite lost track of time, they said, and looked so contrite and pretty and remorseful as their little lips quivered that Daniel did not have the heart to do more than send them to their rooms with a scold.

Mary and Ruth were next to arrive. Just as the nursery rhyme said she would, Mary found herself a handsome coachman in Piccadilly—that is, he was a nice young man in a curricle with whom she accepted a ride to carry her and Ruth home after it had turned dark. If Daniel had caught the man he would have wrung his neck, but the fellow had enough sense to drive off as soon as he saw the girls lived in a grand house off the Strand and not a room in Drury Lane.

Mr. Pettigrew discovered Rebecca and Georgette in the little shop which was displaying student watercolors. He was not entirely to blame for delaying their departure, for after shyly admitting to Lady Georgette that the little landscape of the River Thames seen from over the treetops had been painted from his bedroom window, she insisted on staying to see the entire exhibit.

"Why, that is lovely," Georgette had said. "Do you have any others?"

No one except the gentleman who had organized the student exhibit had ever shown any interest in Mr. Pettigrew's paintings so he was quite overwhelmed that a fine lady such as Lady Georgette should praise them. This in turn brought such a great rush of emotion to the young man that he forgot his place and confided to her of his secret hobby of painting eggshells.

"Why I have never heard of anyone doing such a thing," said Georgette. "You must let me see them sometime."

Mr. Pettigrew knew that she was just being polite, and at the sight of the footman who had accompanied him, he realized that he did need to get the sisters back to Lord Chantry as quickly as possible, so with a sigh, he took the girls back to Terrace Palace.

Margaret was found by Jerome Parks in a plane tree in Green Park directly across from St. James' Palace. She had gathered quite an audience, the groom said. Daniel was too aghast to even listen to her excuse that she was trying to reach a crow's nest, and sent her to her room after the others.

It had been several hours now since Daniel had been summoned from White's and still no sign of Lady Winifred. Her sisters did not seem to be the least bit worried about her absence. Daniel had word sent over to Tilbury at Albany to come over to Terrace Palace. He would be spending the night there.

When another hour had passed and still no sign of Winifred, Daniel knew he must go out and join the search. He ran his fingers through his hair. "Where the hell can she be!" he growled. He could not wait any longer and had just reached for the bell cord to call Beetleworth when he heard a scraping sound in the library. Daniel blew out the candle on his desk and listened. There it was again, this time longer. Then a *thunk*. He slipped out of the study, and tried to avoid the path of the one candle left lit in the library. Slowly he made his way along the wall toward the noise.

There was no missing the silvery sheen running through the green pelisse. A ripped left sleeve hung limply at her side. "I thought I'd just come into the library to get a book." Freddie said.

"Through the window?" Daniel asked.

"I hoped you wouldn't notice."

"I noticed, Winifred."

"I was afraid you had."

"May I ask what you were doing coming into the library this late at night?" he said, folding his arms across his chest. Heaven help him! He wanted to hug her, but his sister had to be made aware that what she had done was inexcusable. "We were worried to death. At least you have not been abducted and carried away to be auctioned to some far eastern bey."

Freddie didn't want him to know that may well have happened. "Humph. I am not afraid of a boy."

"Bey—Winifred. *B-e-y*—not boy. Oh, never mind. You are trying to change the subject. I still want to know where you were."

"Would you believe me if I told you I was taking a walk through the garden?"

"No, I would not."

"Well, that is exactly what I was doing," she said. "We haven't had much time to see the grounds yet, and I thought I'd just take a turn around the house."

"Win—i—fred!"

"Well, I was," she said stubbornly.

Daniel was just thankful she had gotten all the way back without being approached. "Do you have any idea of how dangerous it is for you to be out alone this late at night?"

"Oh, pooh!" Freddie gave a bark of laughter. "Alone? Why the streets were filled with people shopping."

He was angry again. "You were still shopping? It is near midnight."

"But Mr. Pettigrew said that people shopped until eleven o'clock at night on Oxford Street, and it truly was a spectacle with the lamps lighting it up as if it were day."

"We are a long way from Oxford Street."

Freddie didn't mean to upset his lordship, but she thought it best not to tell him that after she had left Margaret outside Hatchard's, and told her to catch up with Mary and Rebecca, she had decided to go on a little farther to see the Farley mansion. Someone did come out of the overgrown entranceway and followed her. But she ran much faster than he and lost him.

Before that happened, however, she'd already explored the grounds, looked at the house, and found the steps to the river. More than one shallow boat was tied to the rings at the bottom of the steps, and two people were being handed into one of them. She supposed the boats to be for hire as Pettigrew had said. Then she'd heard a rustling in the bushes and had the feeling that someone was watching her. Since it now was getting dark, she thought it time she started back to find her sisters. As she exited the estate, she saw a dark shadow move in her direction, following her, but she zigzagged her way through the streets until she lost him. Freddie had played hide-and-seek with her sisters so many times that it was not difficult to elude the prankster.

When she got back to Oxford Street it was already late, and not finding her sisters or the coaches, she had to make her way back home on foot. It was a pleasant hike, with many fine carriages crowding the streets, but it did take her a little longer than she expected. Then, when she saw lights inside Terrace Palace, and so many people still milling around, she decided it might be best to come in a way other than by the front door. She climbed over the west wall into the garden and circled the house before she found an unlatched window so that she could crawl in. Her only bad luck was that Lord Chantry should happen to come into the library just as she was making her entrance.

Now she was really in the stew. "It is not really that far," she said. "I am used to walking for miles in the hills. Londontown is only two miles from top to bottom. Mr. Pettigrew said so."

Daniel's relief at seeing her safe made him want to tell her how happy he was to see her. And he nearly did, but giving in was a weakness. "Well, what you did was very wrong. It is never to happen again. Do you understand?"

Freddie didn't want him to be angry with her, and she didn't want him to ask any more questions. "My gracious!" she said. "Would you look at that?" she said pointing to something over his shoulder, trying to do anything to separate herself from the strange feelings which ran through her when he had come near.

"Who?" Daniel said, swinging about in an instant and reaching automatically for where his sword should have been. He saw nothing out of the ordinary.

"Not *who*," said Freddie, pointing to the shelf behind him. "That is just the book I was looking for."

Daniel took the book down from the shelf, perused the title, and handed it to her. *"Ancient Gods of Mythology?"*

Freddie smiled sweetly. "Exactly what I wanted."

"You are trying to divert my attention, aren't you, Winifred?"

Freddie snickered and hung her head. "Yes, I am."

His eyes turned ebony. "Aye, and your tactics did not work."

She bit her lip. She hadn't meant to make him angry with her.

Daniel knew that he was too upset over what his sisters had done to decide their punishment now. "Go to your room, Lady Winifred. 'Tis late. Tell your sisters that I want to see all of you in my study at noon tomorrow. I shall tell you then what discipline I have decided is necessary. Have you been reading from *The Book* every night as you said you did at Knocktigh?"

"We have not had time lately, my lord. We have had so much to do."

She was of such small stature compared to his other sisters that it was hard to believe she was nineteen years old. "Well, it might very well be a good time for you to return to doing so again don't you think?"

Freddie nodded contritely.

"Very well, then. You are dismissed."

The moment Freddie rounded the corner, she pressed back against the wall and took a deep breath. It was then that she realized she still held the book. Well, she'd just have to read it to prove to him that it was the one she'd wanted. Lord Chantry was not an easy man to fool. She knew that the first time she'd seen him. He was no ordinary man. His midnight eyes told her that. And he was kind. A man who called his horse Precious had to be. Perhaps he would have taken care of her from the beginning even if he wasn't her brother. But the deed was already done. Now she didn't want to be his sister anymore.

* * *

Lord Chantry did not wish to get up the next day, but he had no other choice. He was lord of the manor.

"Tilbury, if I were not pledged to stay in mourning, I would have you dress me in my regimentals this meeting. I must make an impression on my sisters on the importance of sticking to protocol."

"I shall make you look as sinister as I can, my lord," said his valet.

"I was thinking impressive, Tilbury, but perhaps sinister is nearer what I have in mind for my sisters. I also have to consult with Mrs. Vervaine."

The valet took out the usual black attire and shook his head. He would be very happy when his master's year of sorrow was over and he could put more dash into his wardrobe.

At that moment the earl would have preferred that after he'd dressed he could just strap a saddle to a fine horse and ride away. "Our only hope is that yesterday's fiasco will be overshadowed by the preparations already underway for the Royal Wedding. Princess Charlotte is to be married on May second. There is no chance that we will be invited to that now. The Court Presentations have been canceled, and the girls will never be able to get vouchers to Almack's. It has not been a good beginning, Tilbury."

The valet murmured sympathetically as he helped the earl into the riding coat, which was one of the few selections he'd thought to bring over from Albany. Then he gave his lordship's shoulder an extra little pat before pushing him out the door.

Daniel faced his housekeeper in the study. Her violet eyes had him firmly fixed in their sights. Her button nose pointed at him accusingly.

Mrs. Vervaine jingled her keys with purpose. There was no way that she was going to let him blame her for what had happened yesterday. "Quite frankly, Lord Chantry, your sisters cannot be trusted, and I cannot put leading strings on them at their ages."

"I quite agree, Mrs. Vervaine. But I cannot confine them to the house when they must have wardrobes made."

Mrs. Vervaine sniffed. "I have been giving that some thought. There is nothing on the third floor except the old nursery. For the right price I believe Madame Lautrec can be persuaded to bring her seamstresses here to Terrace Palace."

The earl pounded his fist into his palm, the relief in his eyes so genuine, the rare smile on his face so charming that the housekeeper felt an unaccustomed urge to smile in return.

"Mrs. Vervaine, I could not have asked for a better quartermaster," he said enthusiastically. "Take a coach immediately to Madame Lautrec's. Tell her that the Earl of Chantry wishes to sequester her entire company for the duration of our campaign."

Fifteen minutes later, the Earl of Chantry's sisters filed in and formed a straight line in front of him, their heads bowed, their hands clasped in front of them. Daniel felt as if they were back to the day he had first met them. He had brought them all the way to London to give them a chance for a better life, and what thanks had he received? They were the ones who had been disobedient so why was he feeling guilty? Everything was going wrong with his plans, and they had seemed so efficient—so reasonable.

"You are confined to the house and garden until I say elsewise. Mrs. Vervaine is, at this moment, on her way to Madame Lautrec's to see if the dressmaker can be persuaded to move into Terrace Palace until your wardrobes are completed."

"Not one of you will go out without a person I can trust to accompany you. No matter how many footmen or chaperones, maids or guard dogs it takes. Mrs. Vervaine has been instructed to hire them. Is that clear?"

Not one head moved. They were making him feel like the devil's own advocate, but something had to be done to bring them into line. It was probably already all over Town that the Earl of Chantry's sisters were a band of misfits. They were not to be presented at court. They would make willful wives. He'd never be rid of them.

Daniel was about to dismiss the girls when there was a knock on the door. "Yes?" he said.

Williams stuck his head in and spoke in a strange timbre which sounded halfway between that of a bullfrog and a canary. "There is a *man* in the entrance hall asking to see you personally, my lord."

"Tell him to give you the message, Williams. Can't you see that I am busy?"

"I believe it best that you receive him, Lord Chantry. He has just arrived in a coach with the royal crest on the door and is accompanied by two guards wearing the livery of Her Majesty the Queen."

The girls' heads popped up.

Lord! What have they done now? "Send him in immediately, Williams; then find Mr. Pettigrew. I may need him to get in touch with my solicitor."

But it was not as Daniel thought. Tales had already reached St. James's Palace that the four sets of twin daughters of the late Earl of Chantry were in Town for the Season. The late earl had been a personal friend of their sovereign, and her majesty was quite as curious as the rest of London to see what they looked like, the royal spokesman said. An exception was therefore being made, and his sisters were being granted a private audience to be held with the queen in seven days. Even though it was to be a private gathering and the prince would not be present, court dress would be required nonetheless.

The queen wanted to see his sisters! Daniel looked from the gilt-edged invitation to the girls, back to the invitation, then up again. He could have hugged every single one of them.

Daniel was whistling when he entered his room. "We did it, Tilbury! I will be able to keep my promise to my father after all."

"Did you look sinister enough, my lord?" the valet commented. He had never seen his master look anything near less frightening than he did now.

Daniel explained that the girls were going to meet the queen.

"That is all well and good, my lord, but whom do you have in mind to sponsor them?"

"Why, what do you mean? I am their guardian. I shall."

"I am afraid that will not do, my lord. An older respectable lady who is accepted at court, and usually one who knows their character, must vouch for the girls. That is protocol."

"But the queen herself asked to see them."

"It don't make any difference, my lord. You wanted to know how they go about it here in London. Having a lady of quality introduce them will give them consequence with the *ton*."

In half an hour Daniel had gone from despair to elation—from the pits to the mountain top—and now he was down in the dumps again.

"The only older woman in London who knows them is Mrs. Vervaine, and I don't believe that is what you have in mind."

"No, your lordship, it is not."

"There is a Mrs. Hefflewicker who met them, but that lady would at best hurry out of Town if I should as much as mention sponsoring the girls. It is her sister's invitation I turned down. I know of no one else."

"What are you going to do, my lord?"

"I am going to do what I wanted to do when I first got up this morning, Tilbury. I am going to take the biggest, fastest horse I have and ride as far away from London as I can get."

Fifteen

Freddie had taken the book of mythology out to the garden. She was glad to have something new to read, for she was getting a little tired of studying *The Book* all the time. She found a bench in the sun where it was warm, and where she was hidden from view of the house. Daffodils and primroses were here and there, but, all in all, it had been such a long winter that few flowers were yet blooming. She couldn't understand why Lord Chantry's face looked like a thunderstorm when she saw him leave the house and head for the stables. Especially after the queen had just asked them to her palace. He'd seemed so happy when he read the invitation, and Freddie wished she could see his smile more often. The earl didn't seem to have much fun. Perhaps he didn't know how.

Mrs. Vervaine had returned and told them that Madame Lautrec and her seamstresses were moving in this very day. She also said two more dresses were finished for each of them. Of course, the seamstress would have to mend the tear in Lady Margaret's dress from climbing a tree and the torn sleeve Freddie had gotten from crawling in the library window. That was why Freddie now wore her faded brown dress, which suited her just fine.

As the sun moved, so did she, and Freddie soon found herself at the rear of the garden near the stables. She had been reading for quite some time about a deity named Zeus, the god of thunder, when the silence was jolted by a clattering of hooves. The voices she heard were familiar, as was the *whistle-squeeeeek*.

Freddie climbed up on the bench and peered over the bushes to see what the ruckus was all about.

The Scots Grey was rearing up, shaking his head from side to side. Parks stood on one side holding the reins with his left hand, grabbing at the air with his right. The earl was on the other side slapping here and there as if trying to catch flies.

The stallion was still keeping his nose as high as he could in the air and swishing his mane this way and that, when Freddie noticed that pinched between his lips was a daffodil, a much used and very bedraggled daffodil. The groom snatched. The earl grabbed.

"The devil take it, Parks!" the earl said. "Let him be. He's not going to give it up."

The horse came down with a thud. Eyeing them warily, he bubbled his lips, but did not let go of his yellow posy.

"At least it do look prettier than a piece of straw," Parks said, grinning.

"He picked it out of a church graveyard near Fensbury Fields and carried it all the way back. You say he has been continuing his nodcock behavior in the stall?"

"Aye, he has. He still pushes all the straw up against the boards. I reckon he just likes to have a clear floor."

Daniel gave the horse a slap on the rear. "Well, take the big fellow in and rub him down, Parks," the earl said before starting up the garden path leading to the mansion.

The groom whispered into the horse's ear, and the Grey followed him like a puppy into the building, the limpid flower hanging from his lips. Freddie knew exactly what name Parks had used.

That evening Daniel's natural reluctance to reveal his personal feelings was greatly diminished by the time he'd taken his fourth drink. The depth of despair over the difficulty to comply with his father's wishes and now the desertion of all his chums to riper pastures of pleasure—with the exception of Captain Oakley—made him pour out his problems to that officer. However, the earl's voice carried farther than he realized to a set of men who stood apart from the others, and who were debating their own possibilities of where they could go next since their wives were too busy with their own social activities to be wanting them around.

Daniel took another drink and leaned forward. "Don't tell anyone, Oakley, but m'sisters have been asked to a private audience with the queen."

"Splendid!" said the captain. "That should solve your problem."

"No, it doesn't. Thing is, they have to have a sponsor—a female sponsor. You know any female sponsors? I don't, you see."

Oakley shook his head grimly. "I don't think the female I've been seeing of late would be acceptable for that position, Chantry."

"That's all right. Don't worry yourself about my troubles. I'll just go home and sleep on it."

"Let me see you back safely, my lord," Oakley said, helping Daniel to steady himself as he rose. "I'll hail a hackney."

Good friend that he was, Captain Oakley did just that, but not knowing Daniel preferred to stay at Albany most of the time he deposited him in front of Terrace Palace, then drove off toward Covent Gardens.

No one seemed to be up and not wanting to awaken the household Daniel felt his way around the perimeter of the estate for a ways until he found a strong vine, climbed over the wall, and, remembering the slipped latch on the library window, entered the same way Lady Winifred had. Then he crept up the stairs and was halfway down the corridor when he heard a voice—a feminine voice—coming from a room where he was sure his own apartment should be. He put his ear to the door.

> *'Twinkle, twinkle, little star.*
> *How I wonder what you are!*
> *Up above the world so high,*
> *Like a diamond in the sky.'*

What foolishness was this? Daniel thought. *Nursery rhymes coming from my bedroom.* Now this was sufficient enough of a jolt to make the earl realize that he was in the wrong wing and to cause him to turn about and start in the other direction. He stumbled, shushed his feet, and finally made it back to his own side of the house and his own chambers.

One candle burned in the sconce on the wall across from his door. Daniel stared at the little flame.

> *"As your bright and tiny spark.*
> *Lights the traveler in the dark.*
> *Though I know not what you are,*
> *Twinkle, twinkle, little star."*

Foolishness! He wasn't a little boy anymore at his mother's knee. But that was exactly the picture that shot across Daniel's mind. He opened the door and entered the room. Why wasn't Tilbury there to help him out of his clothes?

> *When the traveler in the dark,*
> *Thanks you for your tiny spark,*
> *He could not see which way to go,*
> *If you did not twinkle so.*

"I got foxed," he said, making his way toward the bed, "and it is no wonder. I have eight sisters, and they are more trouble than eight hundred men."

"Twinkle, twinkle, little star," Daniel mumbled as he groped about, found the bed, then crawled up onto it.

"I'll wait until morning to notify Tilbury as to my whereabouts," he said to the pillow as he pulled it out from under the coverlet and pounded it into shape. Another memory came back of a little boy climbing into bed to say his prayers. "Foolishness," he mumbled falling asleep. "All foolishness."

* * *

The next day when Daniel awakened he couldn't remember exactly where he was. He was a little boy and he recalled something about wishing on a star for a white pony. He'd gotten one for his birthday—only it turned out to be a little larger and rather smoky-colored, and some fool had named it Precious. He had wanted to name it something more swashbuckling like Dragon or even Pegasus, the great winged horse. He was trying to think what else he had wished for when he realized his shoulder was being brutalized. He rolled over and opened one bleary eye to discover his valet frowning down upon him.

" 'Tis enough that you have us all in fits as to your whereabouts, my lord," Tilbury said. He then proceeded to tell him that one of the upstairs maids had discovered him sprawled on his bed fully clothed when she came in to dust. She ran screaming to Mrs. Vervaine, who called for Mr. Pettigrew, who in turn sent word over immediately to Albany to come forthwith, saying that his missing master had turned up in his bed at Terrace Palace.

"This back and forth must stop, my lord," scolded Tilbury. "We never know where you are. Beetleworth has just been up for the third time since we found you to see how you fare. He said Williams is in a dither. Two liveried footmen came over an hour ago requesting an audience with you. He put them in the library to wait for you, but they started arguing and are about to come to fisticuffs with each other. Beetleworth said they cannot keep them apart much longer."

Daniel swung a leg over the side of the bed, then the other, pushed himself up on his elbows, sat up, and promptly fell back again pressing the heels of his hands to his temples.

Mr. Pettigrew arrived at that moment to report that the butler and house steward were not going to be able to keep the two footmen apart much longer.

Half an hour later Daniel was shaved but only half-dressed when Mr. Pettigrew arrived again to say that the footmen were calling each other names.

"Od'sbodkins! Tilbury, hand me my dressing gown. Mr. Pettigrew, have the men brought up to my sitting room. Perhaps I can get to the root of this matter and have some peace."

The first footman in his grand green and gray livery said he represented Lady Jersey.

"The queen of London society," Tilbury whispered over his master's shoulder.

The other in blue and white was footman to Madame de Lieven, the wife of the Russian Ambassador to the Court of St. James and personal friend of the late Earl of Chantry.

Both claimed their mistresses to be the undisputed leaders of Almack's patronesses; both had heard of the present earl's dilemma, his need of a sponsor for his eight lovely sisters; both were offering to fill that vacancy.

Daniel's head had been spinning when he got up, now there was a regular cyclone swirling around in it. He had Beetleworth and Williams escort the men back to the library where they were to stay—at opposite ends of the room—until he sent down his replies. In other words the earl had no idea of what to do.

He sank down on a cushioned ottoman in front of the fireplace and ran a hand over the back of his neck.

"Now what should I do?" he said, as soon as the footmen were out of earshot. "One minute I thought my sisters would be forever snubbed by the *ton* for not being accepted by any of the hostesses of upper society; now I am approached by two of the highest. But if I accept the one, I shall make an enemy of the other."

Tilbury and Mr. Pettigrew looked at their young master, then at each other. They knew the earl was in no state to make such an important decision which could jeopardize the futures of the playful young ladies. It was up to them to resolve the situation. So while his lordship stared into the fire, they put their heads together, and after a short discussion, came up with a solution.

"My lord," said Tilbury who was chosen to speak because he had the more commanding voice; besides he'd been the one who came up with the antidote. "What was the deciding factor in the Battle of Waterloo?"

Mr. Pettigrew always did enjoy a good riddle and flicked his eyebrows to encourage his lordship to come up with the right answer.

Daniel was sobering up quickly. In fact he was beginning to think he was the only sane one in this upside-down world.

Tilbury was not a military statistician, but he did love to hear the tales of battle from his former employer Colonel Dell. "Well, *one* of the deciding factors anyway," he said, requalifying his statement, then continued before his present employer should get off the track. "When Blücher joined up with our duke, Napoleon could not defeat the allies."

Mr. Pettigrew saw that Lord Chantry was not getting the point. "So Tilbury and I have come to the conclusion that if your lordship can persuade the two leaders of Upper Society to join forces and divide the responsibility—that is, for each of them to present four of your sisters—there will be no one who would dare bring up the subject of the young ladies' little faux pas two days ago."

Tilbury was beside himself that Mr. Pettigrew should include him in partnership with himself, and when his lordship agreed that there was, indeed, merit in their suggestion, the valet's happiness was complete.

Daniel told Mr. Pettigrew to accompany him down to his study and there he dictated letters to both Lady Jersey and Madame de Lieven, thanking them for their generous offers, and extending them his invitation to come visit his sisters. Once the footmen had been sent back to their prospective houses, all Daniel could do was wait.

Their replies came within the hour. Both Lady Jersey and Madame de Lieven were pleased by his request that each represent four of Lord Chantry's sisters. They asked when it would be convenient for them to call to meet the young ladies, then each lady stated the specific time she would be arriving at Terrace Palace the next afternoon. Luckily their arrivals would not be at the same hour.

The patronesses came. They approved: Lord Chantry's sisters were all they should be and their gowns were exquisite. They were going to be the envy of *le beau monde*. Both ladies privately gave a nod of appreciation to the handsome, blond brother as well. Then they left.

When all was over and the girls had gone back to their rooms, Daniel gave a bark of relief. "Thank the lord, Mr. Pettigrew! Our troubles are over."

"How is that, my lord?"

"My sisters will be presented to the queen; they have the backing of the two undisputed leaders of London Society, Lady Jersey and Madame de Lieven; their wardrobes are equal to none; and now they will appear at Almack's. They are as good as married."

"It will be right for you to get out into Society too, your lordship," Mr. Pettigrew said.

"I have no intention of doing that," Daniel said. "Of course, I suppose I must escort my sisters to their first functions to smooth their way and give them support. However, I shall watch from the sides of the ballrooms. I am in mourning do not forget. I will not be participating."

"My goodness. I am afraid you must, my lord. Since their father is not present it will fall to you to lead each sister out for at least one dance. It will not reflect on your respect for your parent. In fact, it is a matter of duty because it was he who made you promise to see that your sisters had their Season."

Daniel frowned. "I am afraid that my dancing skills rather rusticated during the war, Mr. Pettigrew. There was not much time to practice the fancy on the battlefields."

"It won't matter, my lord," Mr. Pettigrew assured him. "Everyone's attention will be on the young ladies."

"That is a relief," Daniel said. Although all young gentlemen of Oxford had learned the social amenities very early in their lives, Daniel had never felt at ease at assemblies, and had therefore avoided them as much as possible. When he had returned to London, after his father's death, he'd kept busy attending his estates, taking his seat at Lords, and joining his chums at the men's clubs when he was in Town. He would just have to rely upon the girls' graces to cover up his clumsiness.

They had only six days to prepare for the court appearance. Madame Lautrec outdid herself. Not only did her seamstresses work round the clock but Mrs. Vervaine assigned every maid in the house who could ply a needle to sew seams and buttons and seed pearls and lace; whatever was needed to finish the elaborate gowns. Babette and Antoinette happily joined in, and all the court costumes were finished a day beforehand.

Daniel had the two grandest Durham coaches polished and lacquered. He had to hire two more because it took one of them to accommodate each pair of girls in their elaborate hooped skirts. All the horses were curried until their coats shone as brightly as the gilt on their carriages, and the plumes on their headpieces rivaled those which towered above the girls' heads.

When the carriages of Lady Jersey and Madame de Lieven were added and the escort of the King's Cavalry joined the entourage they made a splendid sight.

His lordship, the seventh Earl of Chantry, proudly sat his Scots Grey alongside the coaches. Jerome Parks rode a dark bay with a white blaze behind the procession to be on hand to handle Precious while his lord was in the palace. Freddie joined her voice with the others when they exclaimed with delight and proclaimed how proud they were to have such a handsome and stalwart brother, but she knew that she viewed his lordship in an altogether different way than his sisters.

As they had all lined up in the entrance hall of Terrace Palace for Lord Chantry's inspection before entering the carriages, Freddie was sure that their hearts did not dance around in their chests, nor their mouths go dry as hers did. He looked so splendid . . . so proud . . . so serious. His black attire set off his crown of golden hair and turned his dark eyes to ebony. Freddie decided his was the most pleasant face to look upon that she had seen in all of Londontown. Perhaps she should have been ashamed of lying to the earl, but if she had not she would have had no chance to come to the city let alone St. James's Palace. Then what kind of a life would she have had? An orphan girl left behind in a run-down house on a hill.

Now she supposed that if she were found out she certainly would be arrested and accused of being presented to the queen under false pretenses, but instead of feeling guilty Freddie found she was enjoying herself immensely. She smiled and curtsied as nicely as the others and saw the sparkle appear in Queen Charlotte's eyes when the name of the late Earl of Chantry was mentioned.

Freddie was beginning to suspect there had been a bit of a rogue in her sisters' father, and that the girls had inherited more of his spirit than his only son.

All of London knew—if not by Word of mouth, certainly by the time they had read their *Morning Post*—that the eight sisters of the Earl of Chantry, had been asked by Her Majesty the Queen to a private audience. It was said that the queen, who had canceled most appearances until after the Royal Wedding, was so delighted with their performance that she smiled throughout and said that the afternoon had not tired her very much at all.

The sisters' first social appearance, the paper said, was to be at Almack's Assembly Hall in King Street. There was much ado made over the revelation that their sponsors had been none other than the patronesses of that auspicious establishment, Lady Jersey and Madame de Lieven. The scramble for vouchers for that evening was unprecedented.

The following day Daniel and his sisters received their engraved invitation to attend the Royal Wedding of Princess Charlotte and Prince Leopold. Daniel's confidence in the success of his campaign was now unquestionable.

Mrs. Vervaine, however, was of a more suspicious nature, and insisted that no matter how successful their introduction to the queen, Lord Chantry should keep to his original decision that the girls must not be released from their punishment of confinement until they had made their debut into Society at Almack's.

"Madame Lautrec says she will need the girls available all day every day for their fittings if they are to have a suitable amount of gowns for their initial engagements. We cannot take the chance that they will run off."

"I do believe my sisters have learned their lesson, Mrs. Vervaine. But you are right, of course," Daniel said. "Leniency can lead to insubordination in the ranks. They shall be told to stay within the Terrace Palace grounds until the night of the assembly."

Only two days had passed since the girls visited St. James' Palace and they were already beginning to get tired of their isolation.

"I do wish we could go see something that was on our list," Ruth sighed.

Freddie was reading aloud to Ruth and Antoinette from her book of myths as they sat upon the iron benches in the garden awaiting their twins to come tell them that it was their turn to go up for their fitting, but for one reason or another their minds could not stay on the story. Margaret was somewhere searching around in the bushes for a grasshopper she'd spotted earlier. The weather was beginning to relent its hold on a cold winter— flowers were beginning to unfold and in just one week crocuses, daffodils, and drifts of snowdrops were already plentiful; two cherry trees were blossoming.

"I wish we could get out for at least a little bit," said Ruth.

"It does seem that we've been here ever so long, doesn't it?" agreed Freddie, closing the book.

"Why are we being cooped up like chickens, though?" Ruth said.

Antoinette's wide angelic eyes looked up through thick black lashes. "You know why. We were naughty."

"Can't you think of something, Freddie?"

"Yes, you always have the cleverest ideas," Antoinette said quietly, casting an admiring look toward the only brown-haired one in the lot.

"I wish I could," Freddie said. "It is nearly a week before we are to attend the assembly at Almack's."

Just then there came a whoop and a "Halloo!" from the direction of a thick hedge of rhododendron, cedar, and ivy which hid the stone wall running around the garden. "What's this?"

Margaret's face, framed by a wreath of red hair, poked out of a hole in the bushes. "Come see what I've found!" she called just before her head disappeared again.

Curiosity was a characteristic the sisters shared. They rose immediately to investigate, pulling aside the branches of the hedge to peek in.

Margaret had uncovered an old postern gate completely hidden, perhaps for years, and long forgotten from the looks of it. She had already torn much of the ivy away to reveal the latch. With a little pulling and jiggling they finally tugged the door open.

Freddie laughed. "If I'd known that was there I wouldn't have had to climb over the wall the other night." Then her eyes narrowed.

"What's the matter?" Margaret asked.

"Shhh," said Antoinette, putting her dainty finger to her lips.

"She's thinking," said Ruth in a hushed voice. "We have just said that we wished we could find some way to go adventuring."

"But we can't do that," said Margaret. "We are scheduled all day long for our fittings. An hour or two on, an hour or two off. That is not enough time to see anything and be back before we are missed."

"There is a way," Freddie said.

When the four sisters who had been trying on their gowns came into the garden to tell the others it was their turn, she told them her scheme. All they had to do was to switch identities. To find out if her plan worked, she told Babette and Mary and Re-

becca, to return to Madame Lautrec. Freddie would be there to
see if any of the seamstresses were able to tell them apart. If they
could not tell the difference, she said, then every other day a twin
would be free to sneak out the postern gate and go into town,
while one from a pair would go for fittings for both of them that
day. Flora could join them as their abigail, and, if need be, one
of the twins could dress as a maid too. She was sure Flora would
be only too happy to loan them her extra uniform.

The conspiracy worked. Not once that afternoon did the
seamstresses question the identity of the twin who came to the
third-floor rooms.

"But, Freddie," Ruth said afterward, "Georgette could exchange with Babette or Antoinette, but how can you go out
when you have no one who looks like you?"

There was the rub and Freddie knew it. She was doomed to
miss out on the adventure. She could not get away without being
caught, and she didn't wish to make Lord Chantry any madder
at her, so she accepted the fact that she would have to stay home.
Besides, it wouldn't be so bad. "You can tell me about your
adventures when you come back. After all, it is not too long
until the Almack's ball. I can finish the book his lordship gave
me in the library. I have not nearly come to the end of it yet.
There is much more to learn than what we read in *The Book*.
Zeus had so many children that I haven't begun to find out what
happened to them all yet."

"Just like the little old woman who lived in a shoe, she had
so many children she didn't know what to do," said Mary.

So it was that while her sisters explored the open market in
Covent Garden, little booksellers off Fleet Street, and the silk
shops on Ludgate Hill; and while they viewed St. Paul's Cathe-
dral and found Rundell and Bridge's diamond merchant shop,
which Mama Gilliane had marked on her map, Freddie discovered something just as surprising, while not moving out of the
garden at all.

She was reading aloud to herself in the garden because none
of her sisters were there to hear her. Zeus, the god of thunder

and lightning, had a son named Perseus—a very handsome and heroic fellow—who cut off the head of the terribly wicked and frightening Gorgon Medusa. Then he rode away on a beautiful winged white horse named Pegasus, which had sprung from Medusa's neck. Now this set Freddie to substituting Lord Chantry riding off victoriously, and the only horse she could think of to fit the picture was his great Scots Grey—Precious. The more she said it, the more she began to hear the similarity to the name Perseus—if spoken in the slow British drawl—and that of *Precious*.

This persuaded Freddie to think and ponder and ask herself, "Why would anyone name a majestic-looking stallion such a silly name as Precious?" She did not have to think or ponder too long before she headed for the stables.

Along the way she stooped and picked a daffodil. After assuring one of the grooms that she only wished to look at his lordship's cattle, she hurried to the Scots Grey's stall. Her eyes only cleared the top board of the half-door, but she could see the big stallion in his usual stance, head hanging down, staring at the floor. "P-e-r-s-e-u-s," she whispered.

Up came the big gray head. "Nicker-nicker." He turned sideways to see her better.

Freddie waved the daffodil, and when the stallion trotted toward her, she steeled herself not to move. "Purr-ess-shus?"

"Nicker-nicker. Neeeiiigh." He took the stem of the flower in his lips.

Freddie's large chocolate eyes grew rounder. 'Twas the first syllable of sound to which the big Grey responded. Who would ever have thought it?

Perseus pushed his velvety nose gently against her forehead.

She had just lowered her hand when a yell and the pounding of boots from the far end of the stables startled her.

"Lady Winifred! Get away from there!"

The stallion reared and pawed the air.

Freddie sat down with a thud and twisted around to see

Jerome Parks sprinting toward her from the far end of the corridor.

"Good Gawd! 'Scuse me, my lady, but you did scare me half out of m'britches," the groom rasped, putting a hand under her elbow to help her up. "You know you ain't to go near that beast. He's dangerous."

Freddie doubted that very much, but she said she was sorry and that she'd just wanted to see the horses.

"Well, it's best you go now before you get yourself into real trouble. His lordship would have my head if he knew I let anything happen to you in here."

Parks didn't know how near the truth he was, Freddie thought, picturing the mighty Greek god with his curved sword.

As she hurried out of the stables a long plaintiff, Whistle-squeeeeeak, followed her, and she heard Parks say, "Well, will you take a gander at that. Where'd you find another posy?"

Sixteen

The previous evening at Almack's had not turned out as Daniel had expected. He swore to himself that no fortune-teller could have foretold the turn of events which followed after his party's entrance into the hallowed Assembly Rooms in King Street. Now he faced his secretary who had just been admitted to his bedchambers at the Albany apartment and was still a bit out of breath after a swift walk from Terrace Palace.

"I cannot believe it, Mr. Pettigrew. My sisters don't know how to dance!" Daniel blurted out as Tilbury tried to straighten his master's cravat. "If they did not know the steps they made up their own and flew about freely like so many uninhibited woodland nymphs."

Mr. Pettigrew chewed on this astounding revelation for a moment. He had wondered why Lord Chantry had not remained at Terrace Palace after he had brought his sisters back from Almack's at sometime around one o'clock this morning. Mr. Pettigrew had gone to the library to exchange a book when he'd heard them come in. It was early by *tonnish* standards. 'Tis hard for me to grasp, my lord. When you questioned your sisters I thought surely they said they knew a few country dances."

"Their definition of a *few* seems to consist of the minuet and a couple of the most basic square steps." The expression on Daniel's face went from incomprehension to exasperation. "When a waltz was played I forbid them to participate of course. I had seen it performed in Belgium but never tried it myself."

"They sat out the set with their partners?" asked Mr. Petti-grew.

"No, they didn't. They formed a circle of their own in a corner of the ballroom and before long their voices and laughter became so loud the other dancers could not hear the orchestra. If they wished to humiliate me they could not have chosen a better place and time."

"Whatever were they doing, my lord?"

"They were shaking all parts of their persons, and whirling around like dervishes, while singing twiddle-twaddle."

"Oh, my goodness! Surely you are mistaken, my lord. I can-not imagine your sweet sisters saying anything naughty."

"Well, not naughty perhaps. 'Twas more like: 'Now we dance looby, looby, looby.' "

"Is that all, my lord? That may sound a little strange but hardly something that would start a scandal."

Daniel started to run his fingers through his hair, but Tilbury slapped his hand away. "No, that was not all. They started chant-ing: 'Shake your right hand a little. Shake your left hand a little and turn yourself round about.' " Daniel shuddered. "Before long all the young bucks were twitching and twirling about and making cakes of themselves as though they were puppets on strings. There was young Bradley Twilby, heir to the Twilby fortune, Lord Deemster, the Earl of Whitt's son—can't remem-ber his Christian name—and others, but I'm afraid it was all a blur at that point. Everybody had stopped waltzing to watch them, and I feared my sisters were in danger of becoming a laughingstock."

Mr. Pettigrew's eyes blinked rapidly all through Lord Chan-try's recital. "Surely the patrons did not hold it against your sisters if the young men were acting like fools, my lord."

"But I have never seen anything like it, Mr. Pettigrew."

"Were the patrons angry that their dance had been inter-rupted?"

"I didn't wait to find out, Mr. Pettigrew. As quickly as I could call muster I made our excuses to the hostesses, and returned to Terrace Palace."

"Well, if I may say so, my lord, I don't believe you need worry about your sisters being accepted."

"How can you say that, Mr. Pettigrew, after all that I have told you? They will never be asked anywhere in polite Society again."

"That is what I have been trying to tell you, my lord. By the time I left Terrace Palace this morning, Beetleworth had to fetch three more silver bowls and a tray, to hold all the cards and invitations pouring in. The entrance hall was beginning to look like Kensington Gardens in summer, and it was all Williams could do to fend off the young men begging to be permitted to throw themselves at the feet of your sisters."

Daniel could not believe what he was hearing. "Have the gentlemen of London gone mad? The ladies you so casually excuse have a tendency toward mischief I fear. They do not follow rules—they do not even know how to dance. They will make terrible wives."

Tilbury gave his master's coat sleeve an extra heavy dusting. The fact that Daniel's arm was already in it brought the assault more readily to his attention. "Yes, what is it Tilbury?"

"It seems to me the simplest solution is to have someone teach the young ladies correct dance form and decorum. I don't think your sisters are slowtops, my lord. They will learn quickly."

"There is no time for that, Tilbury. The Season is too far underway. If I hire a dance instructor at this late date it will be all over Town that my sisters know nothing about the social graces. Hopefully, last night's fiasco will be overlooked and chalked off to the excitement of their first venture into Society."

"But you have a master of the dance right under your own roof, my lord. I have seen him practicing his skills. Mr. Pettigrew has been given the feet of a gazelle. The grace of a ballet dancer."

Mr. Pettigrew blushed, his eyebrows began to twitch, he cleared his throat, and then the toe of his shoe began to move this way and that, tracing the pattern in the Aubusson carpet.

Daniel stared, unbelieving. "You, Mr. Pettigrew?"

"I know a little about dancing, your lordship. If you will permit me, perhaps I could teach the ladies a step or two."

"I did not know that you attended dances, Mr. Pettigrew?"

"I used to observe from the balcony where the orchestra was seated when the earl entertained," the secretary stammered.

Daniel looked at his secretary in amazement. "If you can do this you are a godsend, Mr. Pettigrew."

During the next week at least a small part of every day was taken up with instruction in country dances and the cotillion. Lord Chantry was astonished to find himself profiting much by the exercises too.

The question of music was solved in the most surprising way. Mrs. Vervaine, it seemed, hid a secret as well. She played the piano. Quite well, as it turned out. A fondness for the instrument she had learned in the home for young ladies where she'd been raised and trained for domestic service. Throughout the years she had continued practicing in the music room of Terrace Palace since the house had been so seldom occupied. It was Sukey who told Flora that she had heard her, and Flora told Georgette, and Georgette told Mr. Pettigrew. In his own polite way, that gentleman prevailed upon the woman to assist them, and Mrs. Vervaine could not resist the opportunity to display her talents to advantage for the first time in her life.

As the housekeeper's fingers moved magically over the keys, a twinkle appeared in her eyes, and whether she was aware of it or not, the corners of her mouth curled upward for the first time in ever so long.

"Do you know how to waltz?" Daniel asked Mr. Pettigrew. "Or do the quadrille?"

"No, I am afraid that I am not familiar with those, my lord."

"A pity," Daniel said. "Madame de Lieven introduced the waltz, I understand, and Lady Jersey the quadrille. I think they would be impressed and more apt to forgive my sisters' havey-cavey behavior if the young ladies learned them."

"How is it that you dance so well, Mr. Pettigrew?" Georgette asked.

"By watching," he said simply.

Georgette's lovely eyes opened wide. "Have you never attended a dance yourself—at least a country assembly, Mr. Pettigrew?"

"No, my lady."

"But you were right here in my father's house. I was led to understand that there were entertainments up until the late Lord Chantry's death."

"I am, after all, only a humble secretary and was not thought worthy to mingle with the Quality."

"Well, I never!" Georgette replied, stopping where she was to place her hands on her hips and toss her lovely head. She seemed in deep thought for a moment, then turned to Daniel. "My lord, perhaps if Mr. Pettigrew accompanied us to the balls, and had a chance to observe the dances you just mentioned, he could then teach us the steps, don't you think?"

Daniel, who had not heard Georgette's exchange with his secretary, proclaimed it to be an excellent idea. "Of course! Why had I not thought of it before? You must quit being such a stick-in-the-mud and come with us, Mr. Pettigrew. I shall see that your name is added to any invitations which we receive."

"Do say you will join us, Mr. Pettigrew," said Georgette. "We should like that above anything."

The secretary's heart overflowed with happiness, and he was sure his feet had grown wings.

Freddie caught Georgette's innocent little smile and wondered.

So it was that Mr. Pettigrew, in accepting Lord Chantry's invitation to join them, gained entrance to some of the most elegant homes in London and soon knew the waltz and quadrille well enough to teach them all.

In the weeks which followed, Lord Chantry was filling more and more of Freddie's thoughts. He was with them nearly every day now, accompanying them to soirees, balls, and the theater. She had finished the book of Greek mythology and had gone to fetch another from the library, but instead of taking down one which interested her, she found herself wondering what the earl would pick out for himself.

Lord Chantry was with them for their dancing lessons, too. When he attempted to whirl her round, as they practiced the waltz, she laughed so hard that she stumbled, taking him down with her. The girls clapped their hands to applaud their clumsiness, and as he picked her up he burst out laughing, too. It was a deep and robust sound that came up from deep inside him, and Freddie knew that she loved him very much.

She found out that he had an inclination toward barley porridge and Banbury cakes, and that he was always trying hard never to make a mistake. She hoped that Granny Eizel knew how hard she was trying to learn more about the earl every day.

She had not told him yet about what she'd found in the book of Greek mythologies, that his Scots Grey's name might very well be Perseus instead of Precious. Whatever it was it definitely started with a *P.* That would be her secret. Besides it was far more entertaining to watch the earl put his mouth up to the horse's ear and whisper and hope that no one heard him.

Whenever she could she took Precious a daffodil, but their social schedule became so crowded with activities that she had little time to go to the stables.

She knew her first priority should be to look for a husband. After all, Lord Chantry could find out any day that she was not his sister. Then where would she be? He would probably throw her out because she was poor and had no title. But she could not find a man who really interested her—not after she'd been touched by Lord Chantry.

Three weeks had gone by, and Daniel began to feel as if he'd been burned to a socket. Although the Royal Wedding was now over, and Princess Charlotte was married to her prince, that did not end the galas. In a moment of weakness or in a softening of his conscience, Daniel had even accepted an invitation to the Countess of Lisbone's ball.

Beetleworth and Williams had all they could handle just to keep answering the door and ushering in guests. Tilbury complained of having to keep a separate set of clothes at each residence. The exasperated man said he would think he had removed the black velvet coat to Terrace Palace only to find he had left it at Albany. Some articles seemed to have disappeared altogether.

As yet Daniel hadn't even revealed to anyone that he had been planning to offer a twenty-thousand-pound dowry with each of his sisters. Perhaps, with all the requests he was getting to take his sisters off his hands, he could lower it a bit.

Now he shoved aside the stacks of letters on the desk in the study at Terrace Palace. "Well, will you look at this, Mr. Pettigrew," he said, unfolding the *Morning Post* which Beetleworth had just handed him. "There is mention of my sisters in the Society column. It says here that a new dance has been introduced at Almack's.

"Whereas Madame de Lieven has made the waltz popular and Lady Jersey showed us the quadrille, all the *beau monde* is talking about a new dance which the sisters of the Earl of Chantry introduced on the first night of their debut at Almack's assembly rooms in King Street. The new country dance is called the Looby-Looby. It seems that all the young people are asking for it.

"Well, what do you say to that? My sisters are a sensation."

Daniel started to put the paper down and, in doing so, knocked a trayload of letters onto the floor. "What is all this, Beetleworth?"

"Those are why I suggested that Mr. Pettigrew call you, my lord," Beetleworth said. "They are invitations, I suppose. They keep piling up at an alarming rate."

"Can't you take care of them, Mr. Pettigrew?" Daniel asked.

"I am afraid not, my lord. They are addressed to your sisters as well as you. I am only authorized to open your mail, but I cannot if your sisters' names are on them."

"I believe the young ladies need a social secretary, my lord. That is the way it is done," Beetleworth said.

"A social secretary? I never needed one. I don't overburden you in that line, do I, Mr. Pettigrew?"

"Oh, no, indeed, your lordship, but that is because you never made many social engagements. You have been most fair with my time, considering I must go back and forth between two residences and travel halfway across town to see your solicitor or your man of business."

"Good. I am sure then that you won't think it too burdensome if I ask you to take on this rigmarole of sorting out all these invitations"

Mr. Pettigrew looked helplessly at the mountain of mail. "Of course not, my lord."

"Then I will have time to work on my list of men I deem eligible mates for my sisters."

In his appointment book, Mr. Pettigrew dutifully jotted down, *Sort invitations and organize social activities for the Durham ladies*.

"Perhaps having one of your sisters assist Mr. Pettigrew, instead of having to consult with all eight, would facilitate matters, my lord," interjected Beetleworth.

Daniel thought that over. "That seems reasonable. Ruth or Rebecca perhaps. They are the oldest."

Mr. Pettigrew cleared his throat to give himself time to plump up his courage. "I was thinking that Lady Georgette would be a wise choice, my lord. I have noticed that the young lady tends to have a rather organized sense of things."

"Really? I had not noticed such a quality, but if you say so, I shall tell her to lend you her assistance."

All Mr. Pettigrew could do was blink and nod and hope that his heart was not pounding so loud that it gave away his joyous thoughts.

Later when she was consulted by her brother, Lady Georgette, of course, told him that she had no objections whatsoever, and in a great show of cooperation and goodwill suggested that she and Mr. Pettigrew set to their duties immediately. "In the garden, don't you think, Mr. Pettigrew? It is a pity to waste one of our few pleasant days cooped up inside. There is an iron bench under the weeping willow tree. We can sort the invitations there," she said, walking over to the window where she knew he would follow. "And if it is not too much trouble," she whispered, "perhaps you could bring one of those painted eggshells you promised to show me?"

That night Freddie remarked on the fragile delicately decorated, porcelain sculpture on the mantelpiece over the marble fireplace in their bedroom.

Georgette blushed. "Mr. Pettigrew gave it to me."

"Mrs. Vervaine says that a lady cannot accept an expensive piece from a gentleman until they are betrothed," Freddie said. "I am afraid you will have to give it back."

"It is an eggshell, Freddie. Do I have to give back an eggshell?" Georgette pleaded.

"My goodness! Is that what it is?" She guffawed. "We used to take plenty of eggs from the neighbors' hen houses when we were at Knocktigh, and we never gave them back. I suppose you don't have to do it here either."

"Thank you, Freddie," Georgette said, giving her a hug.

"You seem to like Mr. Pettigrew, and I think he likes you," Freddie said, with a tinge of envy.

"He is a very sweet man. And he is so intelligent. I do not believe that there is a subject he has not read about."

Freddie placed her hand on Georgette's. "Then keep the eggshell, dear. We just won't tell anyone about it."

If Daniel had thought it difficult to keep his sisters in line before their debut, he found it nearly impossible afterward, even with a social secretary.

In the beginning Daniel had thought a bevy of abigails for chaperones was a nuisance, and had told them to chose only one who could fetch and carry for them. That way they would only need two coaches. They chose the girl named Flora. The silly girl was nowhere around when she was needed, so he had added the other three abigails and another carriage to their entourage . . . with the same disappointing results. They could not keep track of their mistresses.

As if that were not enough, the girls could not agree on which functions to attend. Ruth and Rebecca preferred balls and dinners. Margaret wanted to visit the botanical gardens and parks. Mary liked musicals and the theater. Georgette wanted to see art exhibits, and Freddie expressed a desire to see the animals at the Tower or go horseback riding in the parks, which Daniel told them they could not do because he did not have the cattle. Antoinette and Babette had fun anywhere they went.

One place all the girls agreed they wanted to see was Vauxhall Gardens on the southside of the Thames. "Definitely not," Daniel said, and no amount of pleading could dissuade him. "It would take an army to keep track of them," he later told Mr. Pettigrew.

Daniel had hoped that his sisters would be a little more biddable, but for some reason or another he could not get them to stick to their schedule. He soon saw the impossibility of his accompanying each one to wherever she wished to go.

"They are outmaneuvering us, Mr. Pettigrew. What we need is reinforcements, and I know just where I can get them."

The five men, whom he'd been seeing in his clubs in St. James's Street, were already seated around the table when Daniel joined them. The captains: Oakley, Forrest, Byrd, Woods, and Finch.

Daniel had chosen a popular coffee-house near the Exchange because it was a favorite meeting place for businessmen, and one where they would be least likely to be overheard by someone who knew him.

Just as Daniel sat down the sixth man, Captain Hawksby—in full uniform and sporting a fierce brown mustache and sinister arched brows—walked in the door. "Good to see you again, Hawksby. Thank you for answering my call."

"Always happy to oblige, Major—or should I address you as Lord Chantry now?" he said with a deep laugh.

"Your summons sounded urgent. I thought the war was over?"

Daniel's fellow officers, Wellington's aide-de-camps, were mostly young captains of noble families. All had served under Daniel. "I have an assignment for you."

"I heard that you are thinking of selling out your commission," the young officer said.

"After I was wounded and my father died, I asked for leave to settle my estates. I have as yet not sold out."

"So Wellington seems not willing to give you much time. What can I do for you?"

" 'Tis not the duke who requires my services. Perhaps you have heard that I have eight sisters and that I am presenting all of them at once this Season."

Hawksby barked in reply, "Who has not heard? Or seen? They are hard to miss when eight pass at one time. What is it you need?"

"Escorts—or guards as it may be. The others here already volunteered their services. I cannot expect servants to keep tabs on all of my sisters at the same time. Servants cannot attend the social functions as you chaps can, and I cannot be in all places at all times."

"Why certainly, Major. Count me in. Which night do you need me?"

"It is not one particular event, Hawksby. What I have in mind will likely take the Season or until I have an acceptable offer."

"Dash it, Major!" the soldier sputtered. "I have this pretty little actress in Drury Lane who seems quite keen on me. She wouldn't wait that long for me to make her a bid."

"I can't wait either, Captain Hawksby. This is an order. I have already given the other men their schedules. Here is your assignment for next week. Each week I shall give you a new posting. You will report for duty tomorrow at four o'clock at Terrace Palace off the Strand. You are to be assigned to Lady Mary. She is the tender age of seventeen, and I do not want your attention to stray for a minute. The young ladies have a tendency to get lost."

Daniel heard a couple of snorts from the other chaps, but he ignored them.

"Seventeen! Good Gawd," Hawksby sputtered. "You are asking me to be a nursemaid to an infant?"

"Here, here!" said Finch. "That is not necessary, Hawksby. Chantry's sisters are quite fetching little things."

"We think we owe it to the Major," Oakley said.

"I seem to remember a certain instance around Salamanca," Woods interjected, "where if it weren't for his lordship you wouldn't be here."

"You are right," Hawksby said. "I'm sorry for my outburst, Major."

"All right then," Daniel replied. "Here is the situation. Keep your eyes on the targets as well as the men who approach them. If a young lady is taking a carriage ride in the park with a gentleman, or attending some function, I want one of you nearby. A little sword rattling will not be amiss if anyone steps out of line. Do you understand?"

They all nodded.

"Now you don't have to dance with my sisters unless one happens to have a space in her program. Then I will expect you to step in to fill the gap. I find it is better to keep them occupied or else they get into mischief. Mr. Pettigrew and I will fill in wherever replacements are needed. Is that understood?"

Again the men made no comment.

"Then I will see you tomorrow afternoon, gentlemen."

* * *

Just as Daniel began to relax with the knowledge that his sisters were safely in the hands of brave men who had proven their integrity and valor in combat, he received an unexpected but pleasant surprise. Edgar Buttons, his former batman during the close of the war, paid him a visit. He was on his way to visit his family before being reassigned, he said, and wanted to look the Major up to bring him a satchel he'd carried with him for a year. It contained Daniel's regimentals. The peasant clothes, which he'd been wearing when he was struck down, were wrapped in burlap and placed with the other things.

"I washed 'em best as I could, Major. Thought you'd like to have them as a souvenir."

Daniel picked up a folded piece of cloth. When he opened it a flat metal disc fell out. "What is this?" he asked turning it over.

"That were the rag I found wrapped around your head wound, pinned with that badge."

The strip of faded blue and green with a faint yellow stripe was a piece of Gordon plaid—a reminder of the tough 92nd Highlanders who had fought that day. The pin was scraped and scarred, but Daniel could make out a silver lion's head, and at the bottom the letters *nia Fort*. "Some kind of fort," he said, rolling it back up in the plaid and placing it in the box. He would keep it in memory of the brave lad who had saved his life.

Daniel could not persuade Buttons to stay. After they had said their goodbyes he packed the items back in the box, closed the lid, and placed it on the floor at the back of his armoire. All of six years in a box, he thought, and if all went as well as he expected with his sisters he should be able to start thinking of his own future very soon.

Seventeen

"I think it is very unfair of our brother not to let us go to Vauxhall Gardens," Margaret complained.

"Especially when his own friends are escorting us around Londontown," Mary added.

The eight sisters were gathered in Freddie's and Georgette's sitting room, where they could discuss what they were going to wear to the Lisbones' ball the following evening.

"It would be nice to see a fireworks display," Ruth put in. "Mama Gilliane said that they are so spectacular. There is to be a special display two weeks from now."

Babette and Antoinette nodded their agreement.

"You are looking very thoughtful, Freddie," Rebecca said.

Georgette pressed a finger to her lips. "I do believe I see the clockworks whirling in her head. Shhhh! If you are quiet you will hear them move."

Freddie bit her lip, furrowed her brow, then raised it. Finally a smile spread across her face.

Her sisters all sat waiting expectantly.

Pleased with her solution, Freddie said, "If Lord Chantry will not provide us with escorts to the Gardens then we will make do for ourselves—and this is how we will do it."

Freddie got out Mama Gilliane's maps, and while she traced the route they would take she laid out her plans. Three of them would dress as young men, she told them. Ruth and Rebecca being the tallest would pretend to be young men about town and would each partner two of their sisters. Since Freddie was so short, Georgette could easily pass as her escort. They could borrow the earl's clothes slowly over the next couple of weeks, a pair of trousers here, a shirt there. They had heard Tilbury say that he was losing track of where everything was, so perhaps no one would notice if a few items turned up missing.

Antoinette and Babette could make the necessary alterations on the earl's clothing. A stitch here, a tuck there, a little padding just so, and soon they would have enough for three young gentlemen. Hats would be a little more difficult to obtain, but the sisters were enterprising and thought if they couldn't *borrow* one from a young beaux, they could purchase some at a haberdasher's on the pretext of buying presents for their younger brothers. They would take masks in case they should see someone who might recognize them.

On the night of the special display they planned on making excuses to stay home, and Flora was told she'd have to keep Mrs. Vervaine from entering their rooms. They would sneak out through the postern gate.

To test their plan, Freddie with Georgette, who was dressed in pantaloons and a man's coat borrowed by Flora from the servant's quarters and quickly shortened by Babette, slipped out by way of the postern gate and made their way to the water stairs at the old Farley mansion. There Freddie found two boatmen who said they were always at the stairs every evening with their wherries for hire. The girls slipped back to Terrace Palace and announced to their sisters that the excursion had been successful.

"There were certainly a lot of strange characters lurking about the landing," Georgette remarked, her cheeks pink from the adventure. "But Freddie said it was that way before when she first found the water stairs. One fellow looked like a bear in kilts and kept staring at us from around the posts as if we couldn't see him. It was hard for us not to laugh."

* * *

As soon as he received Parks's urgent message, Daniel had Hartshorn take him directly to the carriage house instead of the entrance to Terrace Palace. "I came as quickly as I could, Parks. The boy said something is wrong with Precious. What has happened?"

"The big fella's been acting peculiar. Won't let anyone near for two days, your lordship, but it weren't until yesterday when a cat leaped up on the manger that he went plumb crazy—straight up over the hill. He won't even let me into his stall," Parks said, twisting his cap then retwisting it as he spoke.

Daniel stroked his chin and watched as the big Grey backed up until his rump hit the wall, charged the door, then backed up again. "Well, I'm not going to try again either," Daniel said after making his third attempt at soothing the horse. "I'd hate to have to put him down, Parks . . . but if he won't let anyone near him it's useless. The war has caught up with him as it has with so many old soldiers."

Parks wiped his sleeve across his mouth and cleared his throat before finding the nerve to speak. "I know you'll probably have my head for even suggesting it, your lordship, but . . ."

"But what? Out with it, Parks. If there is anything that may calm him, we'll try it.

"It isn't a thing, my lord. 'Tis a *she*. That is, Lady Winifred."

"Lady Winifred! Are you quizzing me, Parks?"

"When Mr. Pettigrew said they couldn't contact you at your other residence, I assumed you wouldn't be coming."

"In no way are you to send for her. That demon would trample her underfoot in a second."

"Fact is, I've already done so."

Daniel looked at Parks as if he were the one gone mad. "Why in the world . . . ?"

"Well, the lady do seem to have a way with the horse, my lord. She don't know that I see her, but she comes out and talks to him and brings him flowers."

That explains the yellow petals all over the floor, thought Daniel, but the rest of it had to be a hum. "You say Lady Winifred has been coming out here and you didn't tell me? I'll have your hide for this, Parks."

The groom crunched his cap to a final ruin. "I told you that was what you would say."

"Why didn't you tell me?"

"Well, I reckoned if I didn't let on that I saw her, then it was like I hadn't seen her at all. So I couldn't report something I hadn't seen. Besides, she hasn't been out here so much lately and I think he misses her."

Daniel shook his head, trying to make sense of what the man was saying. But one thing was sure, he couldn't have Winifred coming out here and was about to say so when a voice—a familiar female voice—called from the stable entrance.

"Mr. Parks? Did you wish to see me?"

"It's the Scots Grey, my lady," the groom called back.

"You aren't coming in here, Winifred," Daniel shouted.

Freddie kept coming. "I'm already in. What is the matter with him? The horse, that is," she said, with a toss of her head which reminded Daniel of Precious and his stubborn persistence in doing what he wished. She was only a few feet from them now, and he saw that she carried a freshly picked daffodil.

"Stop where you are! You aren't going any farther," Daniel ordered, stepping in front of her and raising his arms to block her way.

Freddie's forehead furrowed as she tried to peer around the earl, but he proved too big an obstacle for her to view the stall opening.

"I'm afraid he's ill," Daniel said. "He won't let anyone get within six feet of his stall." Daniel could see she was genuinely concerned, and he didn't want to worry her unnecessarily about the condition of the horse, but the stubborn girl ducked right under his arm and proceeded to go up to the half-door. She was so short that her eyes barely cleared the top.

The horse looked at her curiously. His ears raised in her direction. He blinked. Freddie didn't. Precious stood by the hay-rack, not eating anything. It was more as if he were trying to guard it. He pawed the floor and looked again at the two big brown eyes peering over the top of the half-door.

Lord Chantry and Parks both held their breath.

"Well, Perseus," she said in her usual what's-happening voice, "have you been naughty?"

The horse nicker-nickered and finished by bubbling his lips.

"What . . . what did you call him?" Daniel asked in a hoarse whisper.

Freddie didn't turn around. "I called him Perseus. That's a Greek god that went around chopping heads off the Gorgons," she said. "Though I think Precious is a far sweeter name."

"How did you know his name was Precious?" the voice behind her rasped.

"I heard you call him that."

Daniel decided not to lecture her at that moment on eavesdropping. "And how did you come to the conclusion that his name is Perseus?"

"I *don't* know for sure. It may be neither. I read about Perseus in the book you banded me in the library that night. I found out that your horse responded to a first sound, like the donkeys. The *P* or *Purr* sound followed by *shhh* after it. Personally, I prefer the name of Precious."

"Well, I don't," said Daniel with a hint of embarrassment in his voice. She stood there like a little pixie with a yellow daffodil dangling in her hand, her large chocolate brown eyes melting all the reserve he needed to be angry with her. One by one all of his sisters were capturing his heart. But he was also aware that she could be in danger. The Grey's docility could be only momentary. Then, to his horror, she lifted the latch and slipped into the enclosure.

She raised her hand and placed it on the horse's side. Precious did not move. "He is upset by something in here," she said.

It was all Daniel could do to stay calm. "How can you tell?"

"I can feel his skin quivering." She held up a hand for silence. "Shhh! Listen."

"I don't hear——" Daniel started.

"Shhh!" The authority in her voice stilled him. Freddie spotted a peculiarly familiar mound of straw and fluffs of cotton in the corner of the manger, then heard faint squeaking sounds. There were many such nests in the barn at Knocktigh. "Precious," she said, running her hand up his shoulder, "do you have a secret?"

Nicker-nicker, he replied bubbling his lips once more. Squeeek.

"This is demmed foolishness," muttered Daniel. "I'm coming in there."

"No, you're not!" came the reply from within the stall. Daniel didn't.

Freddie reached carefully into the manger and parted the straw. There was a *shooooosh,* then the sound of skittering, and a dark ball of fur scurried away into the recesses of the planking. All that was left were little pink and blind bodies rolling about together. Freddie kept one hand on the horse's neck and with the other covered the nest back up.

Freddie was out of view and by now both Parks and Daniel were ready to rush in. "What is it?" whispered the earl in exasperation.

"Precious is guarding a mouse's nest."

Complete silence. The minute Freddie stepped outside the stall, Parks leaped forward and slammed the half-door shut.

Daniel closed his eyes for a second and uttered up a prayer— something he hadn't done in years. But his reticence didn't last long. "Don't you ever do anything like that again!" he shouted, grabbing her by the shoulders. "Demme, Parks, was there ever so unfortunate a man as I to have such vexing sisters?"

"Precious was only trying to defend his family," Freddie said, slowly edging away from the earl. His hands upon her had done the same magic thing to her that they had when he'd waltzed with her. There was no similarity to a rhythmic dance and the concern she saw in his eyes, and yet they both had caused feelings of excitement to run rampant through her. "I believe Precious has developed a tendre for a mama mouse and her babies."

"I have never heard such nonsense," spouted Daniel. "Now go to the house."

Freddie was gazing back at the stall. "I dropped my daffodil."

"Don't you ever obey orders?"

"I have never been ordered about before, my lord."

Daniel shook his head and ran a hand over the back of his neck. "You would make a terrible soldier."

"But a good officer," Parks said under his breath.

They all three watched her go: Daniel, Parks, and the big horse with a daffodil hanging from his lips.

Parks rubbed his chin. "I know of horses what developed attachments for other animals. Once knew of a horse that liked a spotted goat. Wouldn't sleep or race unless that goat was nearby. Heard of another that took up with a stray cat in the Peninsula. Cat slept on his back at night, and his master finally had a special saddlebag made for it or his mount wouldn't go into battle. I suppose horses get lonely too."

"But a mouse, Parks? That is ridiculous."

"There were plenty of mice in the stables overseas. He may have had a family of mice in one of his stalls when the war was especially bad. Your Scots Grey ain't just an ordinary animal, my lord. He's special."

Daniel looked over at the stall door to where the huge beast stood, ears at full mast watching them while he rolled the stem of his flower from one side of his mouth to the other. "Well, I suppose that might account for his sweeping the straw off his floor."

Parks grinned. "You probably have the right of it, my lord. Precious wouldn't want to take the chance of stepping on one of his tiny friends. I reckon animals have hearts too."

Daniel shook his head. He was not about to try to understand animal behavior when he was having enough trouble trying to understand females. But one thing he did know. "From now on, Parks, I want you to call him Perseus."

* * *

The night of the Lisbones' ball was upon them. With as many galas as they'd attended, it amazed Daniel that there were many people he didn't know.

"Is that Lady Ruth or Lady Rebecca sitting in the corner with that young man?" Daniel asked Mr. Pettigrew.

"It is Lady Ruth, my lord."

It was amazing how his secretary could always tell the twins apart and he could not. Mr. Pettigrew had told him that you could always find some little difference, a distinguishing mark or a mannerism of some sort, if you looked hard enough.

"Do you know the man she is with?" Daniel asked. "There is something vaguely familiar about him, but I cannot place where I have seen him before." Of course, that could be said about half the people in the room. Daniel had not seen many of the older peers since he was a child.

Right now, trying to differentiate between his twin sisters was a problem he had put at the bottom of his list of most important concerns. Each sister of course was of equal concern to him—his mission, he told himself, was that he find a mate worthy of each. However, it seemed that no matter how many lists he made of eligible men, someone kept shuffling the deck faster than he could keep up. Therefore, he knew he had to thin out the ranks to only the fewest of acceptable candidates for alliances with the Durham family.

"I do not know who he is, my lord. Do you wish me to find out?" Mr. Pettigrew said.

At that moment Captain Woods, dutiful aide that he was, hurried across the floor to claim Lady Ruth's hand for the next dance. As the blond young man rose, Daniel saw that he was tall, stood militarily erect, had broad shoulders, and would most likely be considered very handsome by the female sex. It was also apparent to Daniel for the first time that the gentleman had but one leg. His kindhearted sister had sat out a reel with someone who could not possibly ask her to dance.

"No, Mr. Pettigrew. There will be no need. The poor chap has given a lot for his country and his countrymen. I am proud to see that one of my sisters has the kindness of heart to overlook a handicap."

"I believe you will find that all of your sisters harbor tender hearts, my lord," Mr. Pettigrew said, letting his gaze search for a certain one.

But Daniel was looking across at the blond giant when the man said something to his sister that made her blush. Daniel clenched his fists at his sides and was about to go over to give the cheeky fellow a reprimand when he saw that instead of looking down shyly and fluttering her lashes or hiding her face behind her fan, as any proper young lady who had been insulted would have done, Ruth looked him boldly in the eyes and said something in return which turned the fellow's face redder than hers. Then, taking Captain Woods's arm, she skipped off with a laugh.

The young man stood facing the dance floor with an intense expression on his face. Well, it served him right, Daniel thought with a grin. Where had he gotten the idea that his countrified sisters were going to need protection from young bucks?

"I do believe I see two of my dark-haired siblings heading our way with very exasperated looks upon their faces, Mr. Pettigrew," Daniel said. "I take it they are Babette and Antoinette. I swear I still cannot tell the difference."

Mr. Pettigrew only answered with the little smile turning up the corners of his mouth. The difference was very plain to him.

"We are probably late in claiming them for the cotillion." Daniel sighed in mock despair. "I swear, with all this dancing, I am more weary than I was after the Peninsular Campaign. How do the ladies do it?"

As Antoinette walked out on the arm of the earl, the shy secretary found himself gazing into the eyes of his beloved Georgette for the third time that evening.

She gave him a wink. "Babette said for me to take her place because she still must explain to Lord Finch how to count on his toes," she said. "Of course, she is only telling him. She says his education is terribly lacking in that he was not taught such lessons in the nursery."

"How do you count on your toes?" Mr. Pettigrew asked quite mystified. "Why, the same way that you count on your fingers," Georgette said, turning his hand over and pinching first the tip of his little finger.

> "One little pig went to market,
> Two little pigs stayed home,
> Three little pigs had roast beef,
> Four little pigs had none,
> Five little pigs cried, Wee-wee-wee
>   All the way home."

Mr. Pettigrew gave a little shiver of excitement. "Since I have met you and your sisters, my dear, I have found that my education has been sadly misdirected."

As soon as the cotillion was finished, Daniel looked about until he found the sister he sought. Or thought he did. "I only wish a minute of your time, Ruth," he said. "Who was that blond fellow you were talking to?"

"I am Rebecca," his sister said, trying not to show her amusement. "And I have danced with any number of blond men tonight."

"Oh, yes, of course you are Rebecca," Daniel said, studying her harder to see if he couldn't detect some little difference as Mr. Pettigrew had said there would be.

"Is it important?"

"Oh, no, no. Just that I thought he was someone I had known before. I probably saw him in uniform and now can't place him when he's out of it. He was not dancing," he said, trying to avoid making her feel uncomfortable by mentioning his disability.

"If you mean the tall man who has lost a leg, I think Ruth told me that his name is Sir Spencer. I'm not sure of his family name. He is Lady Lisbone's nephew."

"Then I was mistaken in his identity. Except for a chance encounter with the countess' sister, I am not acquainted with any of her family."

"Is there something that bothered you about him?" she asked with a little more interest than Daniel thought necessary.

"I just didn't like the way he stared at Ruth was all."

"My lord, he could not have done. Sir Spencer is blind."

"Blind?" Now Daniel felt the fool. "I did not know."

"Yes—in the war, Ruth told me. "And I do recall his full name now. It is Packard. Sir Spencer Packard."

Good lord! Spooney! It was Spooney Packard. The fat little boy who teased his own sisters. He was certainly not fat anymore. In fact, Daniel was sure women would think him quite attractive if it were not for the twist fate had dealt him—as it had so many young men who went to war.

Two days later Daniel called Mr. Pettigrew to his Albany residence. The earl, his face a study of deep concentration, was looking at the list of men he had thought so impressive only a few weeks before. "There are some people whom I wish to remove from the list of eligibles, Mr. Pettigrew. I want you to strike Lord Finch's name. He can be an escort, but that is all."

"Why is that, my lord?"

"He asked if he could make his addresses to Lady Rebecca."

"Isn't that what you hoped for when you chose these young comrades of yours? You said that every one of them was eligible in his own right."

"I have since changed my mind. I don't like the way he was looking at her."

"How was that?"

"Not like an officer should be looking at a sister of mine."

"May I remind you that Lady Rebecca is not *his* sister, my lord."

Daniel brooded over this awhile before saying he would think about it a bit longer. "Next," the earl said, "Mr. John Seymour. He has asked for Lady Georgette."

Mr. Pettigrew swallowed hard and tried not to let his hand shake as it hung poised over his ledger.

Daniel continued. "He is the son of the Honorable Julian Seymour. They have no money. Lady Georgette must marry much higher."

"Is that not up to the young lady to decide, my lord?"

"No, it is not. Strike him from the list."

Mr. Pettigrew drew a line through Mr. Seymour's name and, as he did so, mentally drew a line through his own.

"Next," Daniel said, "Captain Hawksby."

"For what, my lord?"

"Most unacceptable behavior. I observed him in the garden crawling about in the shrubbery with Lady Mary. I cannot imagine what possessed him. He has always been very particular about his uniform."

"Lady Margaret, your lordship."

"What has she to do with anything?"

"If any of your sisters was crawling about the shrubbery it would be Lady Margaret."

"I assigned Hawksby to watch Lady Mary. What would he be doing with Lady Margaret?"

"Lady Margaret collects insects and Captain Hawksby prefers the out-of-doors more than Captain Byrd. The girls do have a way of switching roles, my lord."

"You mean the men may not be following the assignments I gave them?"

"I am sure that your friends are acting with the utmost integrity, my lord, but you must agree that you cannot tell your sisters apart much of the time."

Daniel hated to admit it, but it was true.

Mr. Pettigrew bit his lip to keep from tittering, but a giggle escaped anyway.

"I do not find it amusing, Mr. Pettigrew! What has happened to these fellows?"

"Perhaps it is the pressures of war which have diminished their judgment, my lord."

"That may excuse some of their odd behavior, but it does

not explain their total disregard for the schedule which I have set up. I can see only one alternative."

Mr. Pettigrew had a feeling he was not going to like the solution. "What is that, my lord?"

"I shall have to leave my residence here and move my field headquarters into Terrace Palace where I can keep closer surveillance myself."

The secretary's eyes widened.

"You are not pleased, Mr. Pettigrew?"

Mr. Pettigrew tried to swallow the lump in his throat. His lordship might disapprove of his spending so much time with Lady Georgette. "I am just surprised that you would consider it, my lord."

"Well, Tilbury will be overjoyed. He has done nothing but complain about never knowing where I will end up spending the night. So I will inform him that we shall move into the East Wing of Terrace Palace this afternoon and stay there until the Season is over."

"Very well, my lord. Should I tell Mrs. Vervaine and Beetleworth to expect you for dinner?"

"No, we have that appointment with the detective, Mr. Slipperson, and we don't know how long his report will take. He said in his letter that he has turned up some very interesting facts he could not put in writing. In the meantime disciplinary action must be taken. Tell Mrs. Vervaine that the girls are to be grounded for the night. Alert their escorts that they need not report for duty until I send for them."

"As you say, my lord. Is there anything else?"

"That should just about do it, Mr. Pettigrew. I am anxious to see what it is that Mr. Slipperson deems so surprising."

Eighteen

Mrs. Vervaine sniffed and jingled her keys before making her announcement. "Lord Chantry said that he and Mr. Pettigrew have a meeting to attend and will be away for the evening. He has left orders for me to send you ladies to your rooms as soon as supper is over."

Freddie could not believe that the earl had made it so easy for them to sneak away on the very night that the jubilee was to be celebrated at Vauxhall Gardens. Their abigails were dismissed early—except for Flora, who slept in Freddie's and Georgette's dressing room.

As previously planned, Flora and Sukey helped them to slip out of the house by way of the servants' stairs.

It was still light out when the girls left, so it did not take them long to make their way to the river where several wherries and sculls were bobbing in the water waiting for passengers. Rebecca, Ruth, and Georgette had practiced their manly strides and made fine-looking young bucks in their smart black coats and breeches. Babette and Antoinette had brightened up the earl's somber wardrobe with bright-colored neckcloths made from their own pretty scarves, and Georgette pasted a fine curly brown mustache under her pretty nose. They had also borrowed three of their brother's walking sticks and persisted in swinging these with a jaunty air as they marched into the Gardens.

"Isn't it beautiful!" squealed Mary who had been warned a dozen times over not to draw undo attention to themselves.

Already at seven o'clock the entrance was aglitter with thousands of lights. The three "gentlemen" gallantly paid their fees and the girls entered a fairyland of long colonnades festooned with colorful Chinese lanterns.

It had been decided beforehand that Rebecca and Ruth would each play escort to one dark-haired and one redheaded twin so as not to draw the attention which look-alikes generally attract. Georgette and Freddie went as a couple.

A performance by a ballet troupe and a display of horsemanship were scheduled before the concert. In the meantime the sisters planned to walk in the gardens, observe the artwork, and enjoy the rockeries and fountains.

The orchestra was to play at eight o'clock in the raised shell, and it was agreed that the two threesomes, and Georgette and Freddie, would go their own way instead of trying to stay together. A certain crooked tree with colorful ribbons entwining it was chosen as their final meeting place, from which they would watch the fireworks and then make their way to the river where the boatmen had promised to be.

"I'm hungry," declared Margaret, sniffing the air.

"You are always hungry," said Mary.

Freddie was glad she had divided the two youngest sisters. "There are supper boxes in the colonnades," she said. "We had best buy something to eat now if we plan to get anything at all."

"I am told there are usually five thousand visitors a night," Ruth said. "But I'm sure more will be here for the special display."

"Just make sure you *ladies* keep your masks handy in case you should see anybody who might recognize us and tell his lordship," whispered Freddie.

"If that should happen we would really be in a stew," Georgette said, lowering her voice to a deep masculine tone while twirling the ends of her mustache.

"Until the fireworks then," Freddie said, taking Georgette's arm. "My handsome gentleman friend and I are off to see the sights."

* * *

Daniel had just been given some startling information. "What do you mean, she's not my sister? Of course, Lady Winifred is my sister."

He and Mr. Pettigrew were seated on one side of an ugly but serviceable oak desk, in a tight little office down a narrow street not far from Covent Garden; the detective Mr. Slipperson sat opposite them.

"No, Lord Chantry, she is Miss Hendry. It is true that her mother was your father's third wife, but as you know she was a widow at the time of her marriage. She and her first husband, the Honorable Frederick Hendry, had a daughter Winifred. Mr. Hendry's father is the Earl of Bellingham. The Landry family seat is in Northumberland, somewhere near the border, but from what I found out, Mr. Hendry was disowned when he married your stepmother. His family has had no contact with his wife or child for over twenty years."

"You are telling me then that Lady Winifred—that is Miss Hendry—is not Georgette's twin sister."

"No, she is not. Miss Hendry would have been about one year old when your father married her mother, his third wife."

"I shall strangle the little brown-haired minx. Surely her mother told her," said Daniel, "but I have seen no indication that my sisters knew. They would have been too young to realize that she was not my true sister. It must have been mother and daughter who continued the hoax. To think that all these years she has reaped the benefit of my father's wealth and title and now she is having her Season at my expense as well. Oh, she is a sly one."

Mr. Pettigrew was having a hard time accepting this interpretation. "I cannot believe that Lady Winifred could be as wicked as you are painting her, my lord. The young ladies did not seem to be living in a great deal of splendor when we visited Knocktigh."

Daniel refused to consider any other explanation, not when

he'd already set his mind on this avenue of thought. "Miss Hendry could have been hiding the blunt somewhere, waiting until she was rid of my sisters."

Mr. Pettigrew persisted in digging a little deeper. "Perhaps Mr. Slipperson can enlighten us as to what he found out about the estate."

Daniel conceded. "Yes, you are right, Mr. Pettigrew. I don't know why this has hit me with such force. What did you find out about the disposition of my father's Northumblerland property?"

"Nothing."

"Nothing?"

"There was not one person or one scrap of evidence I could uncover that could point me to the ownership papers. The friends of the late countess were mostly from Edinburgh, where her first husband was employed in government work. The people of the villages around Knocktigh knew very little about the personal life of the family."

"What was the countess's family name?"

"That I couldn't find out either. Her Christian name was Gilliane. That's all I could get from the staff at Knocktigh. I went there first, you see, to find out what I could. Sometimes servants have information they don't realize they have. All I learned was that she and Hendry ran away and were married somewhere in Scotland. They came to Knocktigh soon after. It wasn't Gretna Green or you could go look up the records. They may have been married by Scottish law. That is where a couple only has to claim they are married in front of two witnesses. Completely legal."

"Well, Miss Winifred Hendry must know what her mother's maiden name was, and when I confront her I shall find out why she is playing this game. I must have had a premonition that something of the sort would turn up when I made all the girls stay home tonight. Come Mr. Pettigrew, I've had enough of this playacting. We are heading back to Terrace Palace. I am going to confront that hoyden and demand she explain this chicanery."

"My lord," Mr. Slipperson said. "There are a few more details I'd like to speak to you about. Knowing of your family's position in Society I was at first quite surprised to observe how badly the estate had been permitted to run down. I began to make a search into the reasons." The detective stopped for a moment and began to shuffle through his satchel.

The expression on Daniel's face altered completely. What a fool she took me to be, he thought. All that the mother acquired from my father by charm and stealth, the daughter hoped to reap as benefits. "The reason why is evident to me. As soon as my father died the little thief sold off all that was of value. In all probability if I had not arrived when I had she would have disposed of the manor itself—and left my sisters to fend for themselves."

With a look of satisfaction Mr. Slipperson pulled out a sheet and held it under the candle. Frowning, he shoved that paper to the edge of the desk, then reached back into the case for another wad of papers. "I do think you had better see the accounting I have done of the situation, my lord."

Daniel held up his hand. He'd had enough disappointing news for one evening. Besides, there was something more urgent on his mind. "I shall check your inventory and financial report at another time, sir. It is late and I have some unfinished business to take care of at home. Mr. Pettigrew will make another appointment."

By the time the coach rolled up to the front of Terrace Palace, Daniel knew exactly what he was going to say. He'd been rehearsing his speech ever since he'd left Mr. Slipperson's office. He didn't even wait for the footman to open the door of the carriage but leaped out, ran up the steps, and pounded on the front door with the hard silver handle of his walking stick. Mr. Pettigrew followed as quickly as he could.

When the sleepy-eyed Williams responded, Daniel rushed past the startled servant, continued on toward the library without taking time to remove his hat, shouting, "I want to see *Lady* Winifred in my study immediately!"

Once inside the room, he paced up and down, his hands behind his back. "Why should she have executed such a dastardly act, Mr. Pettigrew?"

"I'm sure she had her reasons, my lord."

"Selfish ones, yes. She was stealing my sisters' inheritance."

Before Mr. Pettigrew could respond, a very distraught Mrs. Vervaine arrived, *sans* chatelaine, *sans* keys, *sans* jingles. "Lord Chantry . . . My lord . . . Oh, dear . . ."

"Finish your sentences, Mrs. Vervaine. I am afraid my patience is running short."

"She is gone! They are gone! All the girls are gone!"

"Gone? Gone where? I said they were to stay in their rooms this evening. Does no one obey orders anymore? Where is her abigail?"

"She is in my lady's chambers flooding the carpets with crocodile tears. I cannot get a word out of her."

"Well, I shall. Bring her down here."

A few minutes later, Daniel had the story out of Flora.

"Good lord! Vauxhall! Tonight is the display of Chinese fireworks. They expect at least ten thousand people there—perhaps more. A haven for pickpockets and thugs. Anything could happen to young ladies alone, and no one would be the wiser."

By now the entire household was awake and stirring. Beetleworth was ordered to send out houseboys with the message for the earl's former officers to head posthaste to Vauxhall Gardens and take the young ladies in hand. "No matter where they find them," Daniel roared.

"Williams, send word to the stables that Parks is to saddle my Scots Grey, and I want two coaches to follow fully manned. We will meet at the Gardens and bring those termagants home."

Within half an hour Daniel was on the back of Perseus, Parks on the dark bay, heading for Westminster Bridge. "I am angry . . . I am angry . . . I am angry!" Daniel kept repeating. However, it was something other than anger which drove him to urge his great stallion to go faster. Since he'd never experienced the feelings roiling from the pit of his stomach into his throat and back down to the area around his heart, he didn't even attempt to define them. All he knew was that his sisters were out there, unprotected and possibly in danger.

Minutes later two of his coaches rumbled from the stables. Mr. Pettigrew sat in the first, clinging with one hand to his hat, the other to the strap to keep from bouncing off the seat. He was not going to be left behind when his sweet delicate Georgette may be in danger.

Freddie had never thought to see so many people crowded together in one place. She and Georgette had been jostled and spun about until they were holding their sides from laughing. They had eaten their fill of sugar buns; they had seen the dancing waters, and climbed about in the rock gardens—although she supposed his lordship would not think it very ladylike. Now their game of hide-and-seek among the statues had led them deeper and deeper into the garden until she could not find her partner at all. Up until now Georgette's tall beaver—or rather, the one she'd borrowed—had given her away. Babette had stuffed the shoulders of his lordship's black riding coat so that her sister looked quite elegant. The black breeches tucked into the tops of a pair of black riding boots had made her receive quite a few shy glances from pretty maids along the darkened pathways.

Many of the couples were now heading back toward the center of the park for the fireworks, and Freddie knew it was time to meet their sisters. She circled about the dense foliage, and was coming out on the opposite side, when she saw her, half-hidden by a large hedge, facing the path as if fully expecting Freddie to be among the throngs of merrymakers hurrying toward the raised shell.

"I've got you," Freddie cried, throwing her arms around Georgette's waist, nearly taking her down as they catapulted into the bush.

However, it was not a squeal of surprise but a growl—a deep masculine growl she received in return as a strong arm flew out to grasp a tree to keep them from falling.

"You!" he rasped, spinning about and seizing her by the shoulders.

Screeeeeeee . . . Pop! Pop! Pop! POW! The fireworks had begun.

"Oh, my goodness!" Freddie cried, looking up into the searing eyes of Lord Chantry.

BOOM! BOOM! BOOM!

Daniel wanted to shake the living daylights out of her, because of all the terrible things he'd pictured happening to her. Instead, he clasped her tightly to his chest and held her there for a second, breathing in the fragrance of her hair. However, he remembered that he was supposed to be angry and thrust her out at arm's length. "You are not my sister," he yelled above the explosions of fireworks and cries of delight filling the air around them.

Freddie shook her head in silent agreement. *He knows. Somehow he's found out.* Although she felt this fateful knowledge sealed her doom, she wished with all her heart that she was back in his arms. She tried to think of something to say, but his lordship was obviously not going to give her time to gather her wits, for he was already striding down the walkway pulling her behind him.

"We found my sisters gathered together as sensible young ladies should be. Not running about like Gypsies. But you are not sensible are you, Miss Hendry? No—you take chances. Now you will have to reap the consequences of your gamble. You have a lot of explaining to do, and as soon as I get you back to Terrace Palace I want some answers."

Shhhhhhhhhh . . . Sheeeeeeeeee! POP! POP! POP! BOOM!

Not long after, Freddie stood facing Lord Chantry in his study. His sisters had been scolded for their part in the escapade, then sent to their rooms. The servants had been dismissed, Chantry's friends sent home. He had told Williams to leave the candlestick on his desk and turn in for the night. He now confronted Freddie.

"Mr. Pettigrew is the only other person at this moment, besides the two of us, who knows that you are not my sister, Miss Hendry. I do not even wish to go into the matter of Knocktigh being stripped of its treasures in so short a time after my father's passing, or the manner in which my sisters were forced to live. Whatever your motives may have been, they would not affect my sisters as much as what you have done in London. Do you have any idea of the harm you will cause them if the scandal should get out that their brother has kept a young woman who is not his relative under his roof. Or that I have represented such a woman to be someone she is not? The girls will be shunned by Polite Society."

Freddie's eyes grew larger. She had never thought of it that way. She had only desired to see that her sisters were happily settled with good husbands who had comfortable incomes. How could she have guaranteed that this would happen had she been left behind? If she did not find a husband for herself—and her wishes along those lines were becoming less and less of any interest to her—she would go back to Knocktigh, if his lordship had no objections.

Daniel could almost feel sorry for her. Even his horse was taken in by her big brown eyes. *Hell!* Daniel himself was more than attracted to her, and he knew he should be wary. Napoleon was small and had been very charming when he wanted to be. "Go now, Miss Hendry. We will sort things out in the morning."

Freddie bobbed a curtsy and left the room. The world had begun to fall apart right before her eyes. Just as she'd feared, she was being cast out. She could already see herself thrown into the street, destitute and lonely.

Daniel settled back down at his desk and watched his candle burn down to a little flickering flame. When it finally sizzled and went out, he just sat and stared into the darkness. The clock in the library had long-ago struck midnight. Then one. And as he was waiting for it to strike two he heard a slightly familiar scraping sound . . . like wood scratching wood. Like a window whose latch was loose, opening.

There was only one other person in the house who knew of the window with the broken latch. *Hell's bells! What was the termagant up to now?* Was she going to run away? The thought of what would happen to her on the street frightened him. Daniel moved to the door and listened through the crack. Yes, there was the scraping sound again. He narrowed his eyes and looked into the blackness. The candle in the sconce on the wall had burned out, as had the one on his desk. He eased into the library, making certain to stay against the wall of books, while straining to catch any sound. Nothing.

Then a *Crack! Crash!* and *Bang!* followed by a deep-throated oath told Daniel this could not be Miss Hendry. The only other possibility was that a thief had entered the room and knocked into a heavy piece of furniture.

Daniel reacted instantly, throwing himself in the direction of the noise. His body smashed against a solid boulder that reeked of grass, earth, and strong spirits. He and the rock let out a few more oaths as they rolled together over the floor breaking more furniture, and cracking a bone or two, before a light appeared in the doorway.

Williams, holding a candelabrum, was the first to come running in, Beetleworth close behind, followed by a string of manservants, and Daniel suspected every one of the females in the house was now outside the library as well.

It took four men to subdue the wild man, three more to hold him once they had him upright. He looked like the original man, made of earth and clay, with a mass of shaggy red hair. Indeed he was the scroungiest, raggediest, wickedest, hairiest malcontent Daniel had ever seen. A living bramble bush in a tartan.

Daniel whipped out his handkerchief and held it to his bloody nose. "Let no one else in," he shouted to one of the footmen standing in the doorway. "We've caught a burglar. Call the police."

"I ain't no thief," said the ruffian. "An' dinna ye be callin' the police neither."

"Then who are you?" Daniel said grasping the man's shirt front.

"They call me Clach, and I dinna want yir gewgaws."

"Then why were you breaking into my house?"

"I only cum fir the lasso."

"What lass?"

"The teeny-tiny, bitty one. The one ye call Winifred."

"You were going to kidnap Lady Winifred?" shouted Daniel quite forgetting that he had just divested her of the right to be addressed as such.

"Her grandfather wants tae see her. He sent me to collect her."

Daniel lowered his arm. "Good lord, man! What kind of fool do you take me for? If that were the truth you would have only had to walk up to the door and ask to see her."

" 'Tis not our way."

Daniel could not believe that Lord Bellingham would have sent such a disreputable character to claim his granddaughter. There had to be more behind it. "I understand that her grandfather is the Earl of Bellingham. A Hendry, I believe."

"Poof!" spouted the man. "I spit on the name. 'Tis the Earl of Gloaminlaw I represent, the MacNaught hisself."

"And where does this lord of yours live?"

"Haw! As if ye dinna know. All the world knows he lives at Castle Naught."

"Where is that?"

"Dinna all you *Sassenach* wish ye knew so ye can capture him, put him to the horn, and declare him an outlaw, as ye did the first Gillie MacNaught. All I'll say is hit's him wot wants tae see his granddaughter."

"Good lord!" Daniel rasped as the thought struck him. Winifred was the granddaughter of the irascible scoundrel Gillie MacNaught, still fighting his own battle against the English

from somewhere deep in the Cheviots. That made her a direct
descendant of the original border outlaw of the 1600's.

Freddie had heard it all from the corridor, and ducking under
the arm of the footman standing guard at the door, she ran into
the room—without stopping—until she stood right in front of
the strange man himself "My grandfather?" she cried. "I have
a grandfather in Scotland?"

"Winifred, I ordered you to stay out." Daniel countermanded
her wild charge.

Of course she ignored him and cocked her head in recognition
of the stranger. "Why, you are the man who followed me out
of the Farley estate." She thought she detected a smile under
the walrus mustache.

"Aye, lass, and ye led me a merry chase, ye did. In and oot
o' aw those alleys like a rabbit in his warren."

Daniel's face turned purple. "You mean you have followed
my sisters before?"

"Not yir sisters—only this 'un," he said, inclining his head
toward Freddie. "She's a lass wot wud make a MacNaught
proud."

Freddie smiled, her face full of happiness. "Oh, sir, I would
like to meet my grandfather. Truly I would."

She'd said it so eagerly, with her big brown eyes pleading,
Daniel could not explain the feelings which shot through him
when he thought of Winifred going out of his life forever. All
he wanted to do was shout, *She's not my sister! Thank God
she's not my sister!* He didn't know if that meant he was relieved
that he did not have to claim any relationship with the termagant
or that he wanted a deeper one.

Daniel thought of the other seven beautiful imps, who at this
very moment, were peering in through the doorway. While he
had been trying to make proper, biddable, obedient wives of his
sisters they had somehow wrangled their way into his affections.
Especially this one. He knew what he felt for Winifred was far
different from what he had felt for his mother and his sisters.
Very much so.

When did it happen? How could he have fallen in love with a thief and a liar? The granddaughter of the border rogue who thought nothing of snatching her from under his nose?

Daniel looked at all the expectant faces around him, including the Scotsman's, and barked an order. "I want everybody back in their rooms. Beetleworth, take Mr. Clach to the kitchen and see that he has something to eat. Williams, give him a room in the servants' quarters and find him a replacement of clothes. Mr. Pettigrew, stay in the doorway, if you would, while I speak a word to Lady Winifred."

Mr. Pettigrew stepped into the corridor and discreetly turned his back.

Freddie was sure she was in for a scold, but that didn't stop her from saying what was on her mind. "May I go, your lordship," she said, placing her hand on a sleeve. "If my grandfather wants me, then I won't have to bother you anymore. Perhaps you can say that I have taken a trip around the world. Then I can live with him and no one in Londontown need know that I was not your sister."

That thought made Daniel feel worse. He did not want to lose her. He didn't even want her out of his sight—out of his house. He wanted to marry her. Good lord! He had fallen head over heels for a regular female thatchgallows.

But Daniel had no intention of letting her go so easily. He would have to let her know that he forgave her, of course; and with his guidance, in time she would overcome this propensity of hers for thievery. Yes, that was what he would do.

"Miss Hendry," he said, "you must stop thinking that telling such clankers will cover up your deceptions." He meant only to give Freddie's fingers a reassuring squeeze, but his hand became glued to hers and he found he could not remove it. He didn't know what possessed him to do what he did next, but he drew her to him and buried his face in her hair. Quite reprehensible behavior to be sure, but he found that he was enjoying it. "I love you, Winifred," he whispered hoarsely. She was very, very quiet. He wondered if she had heard him. "I am sure that

I have gone utterly insane. All I know is that I want you her with me. We will work something out. Perhaps after a whil you will find that you care for me a little too."

"Oh, but I do. I have forever and a day," Winifred said, hug ging him back while hoping that he would hold her against hin a bit longer. "And I'm sorry if I caused anybody any harm."

Daniel's heart soared. She was sweet and witty, and brave an well meaning, even if a little misguided. He wanted to believ her when she said she was sorry. Early tomorrow Mr. Pettigrev had agreed to meet with Slipperson to collect the statements he' prepared and to compare notes on what the secretary remem bered of the furnishings that had existed at Knocktigh at the tim of his last visit to the manor house. That should give Daniel ai idea of how much the estate had been worth when the countes died, and how many things the little prigger had pilfered. Th thefts had obviously been going on over a long period of time But he'd sworn to forgive her.

Daniel gave her soft little body another hug—to give he assurance of his support, he told himself. Then feeling quite ir charity with the world, he sent Winifred back to her chambers

Freddie stared back at his chin for a moment—for she di not trust herself to look up into his eyes—then left, nodding t Mr. Pettigrew as she did so. Lord Chantry had said that he love her. She decided she was not about to figure out the earl. Jus when she thought she had all his habits summed up and stacke in a little box in her brain, he did the most astounding things— like scolding her sternly one minute, and then giving her a ten der hug the next. The latter, she had to admit, had sent the mos pleasant sensations she had ever experienced through her.

What did he mean by it? Was it only his way of stopping he from going to see her grandfather? She would just have to wai and see.

The next afternoon Daniel looked up from the househol accounts Williams had left on his desk earlier.

"Come in, Mr. Pettigrew."

"I think you should see this before you read the itemized list that Mr. Slipperson and I made up, your lordship," the secretary said, handing the earl a single sheet of paper.

"The other pages you hold are the listings?" Daniel asked.

"Yes, my lord."

"How many pages are there?"

"Twenty-five."

Daniel's eyes turned black as pitch. "Then let me have the sheet of paper," he said, taking it from the secretary. It was short—only a paragraph and as he read it, Daniel's face alternated between white, scarlet, gray, and red. "According to Mr. Slipperson's findings no money was sent to my sisters for four years?"

"Not according to what he could ascertain."

His father had not sent his daughters anything to live on for four years. He was not perfect after all.

"How did they survive, Mr. Pettigrew?" Daniel held up a hand as if to ward off the truth being written in the air in front of him. "Of course! They had to sell off the furnishings of the house." Daniel thought of the much-mended frocks, the age and plainness of the servants. Draperies gone from half the windows in the house. Threadbare rugs. No paintings or ornaments of any kind on the walls. Crockery dishes instead of fine china.

It had not signified at the time when Daniel first noticed how the servants at Knocktigh and his sisters had all seemed to turn to Winifred for directions. It was the little mouse who had held them together. If she stole or sold anything it was to keep them alive. Oh lord, how he had wronged her. Would she ever accept his apology now? Would she accept what he wanted to ask her? To stay with him and be his wife?

That evening as Daniel was preparing to have dinner with his sisters he looked with distaste at the black, black, and more black attire his valet had set out for him.

"My wardrobe is beginning to look quite boring, Tilbury."

A little spring of hope rose in the valet's chest. "You are the one who has insisted on the importance of protocol, my lord."

"Aye, I suppose I am," Daniel said. Now he wished he hadn't. "I've tried all my life to be perfect, Tilbury. Do you think perhaps I have overplayed it a bit?"

"I believe one has to accept imperfections, my lord—in oneself as well as in others."

"I thought my father was perfect, and I tried to be what I thought he expected me to be. Have I seemed nearly perfect to you, Tilbury?"

"I believe you are nearly, my lord. I don't believe I have met anyone as nearly perfect as you."

Daniel mused over that a moment. "But I don't want to be perfect, Tilbury. 'Tis a demme nuisance. One is always expected to do the right thing, and I am finding that it is impossible to get it right every time."

"That I cannot say, my lord. I have too many imperfections to make judgment on someone who has so few."

"My year of mourning is almost over. You don't think I'll be cheating if I put on a white neckcloth for dinner, do you? And perhaps one of my little diamond stickpins? It is part of being the Earl of Chantry, is it not?"

Tilbury hastily returned to the chest of drawers and began rummaging through the earl's cravats, tossing the black ones out this way and that, until he found a white neckcloth in the back.

Daniel nodded his acceptance as the pudgy man waved it in the air. "We shall take that for a starter, Tilbury, and if you wish you may choose whichever waistcoat you think would look rather eye-catching. I have a very important question to ask of someone tonight so I would prefer not to look somber when I ask it."

Nineteen

Daniel thought dinner had gone very well. He tried to be attentive to his sisters and did not criticize them or deny any request concerning their entertainment for the following day.

Instead of having port and cigars with Mr. Pettigrew, he asked that gentleman to again play chaperone. Then he invited Freddie to follow him into the drawing room, where he wished to have a few words with her. He smiled as charmingly as he could, but was disappointed to see that it didn't completely wipe away the wary look in her eyes.

"Miss Hendry," he said, as soon as he had settled her on the rose-colored settee, "I wish first to apologize for any discomfort I may have caused you yesterday."

She sat with her hands folded in her, lap looking at him as if she expected him to fly up into the rafters at any minute. He could tell that his speech and manner had not produced the proper mood which he had hoped for, even though he was trying his very best not to be so stiff and proper. "It was my misconception of circumstances, not yours, which caused the problems. I'm sorry." He took a deep breath and sat down beside her.

"I should have known when you told me how you had always been guided by *The Book* that you could not have been a selfish person."

Freddie's interest was now sparked. "Oh, yes," she said. "I am certain that you must have read it—or your mother read it to you—when you were little."

"Perhaps I should start reading it again," he said, trying to find a mutual avenue of consensus to make her more amiable toward his suit.

Freddie's eyes were now alight, and Daniel wanted to keep them that way which is why he was ready to promise her anything at that moment.

"I will fetch it now if you like," she offered, jumping off the sofa.

Daniel had not meant right away, because he had other things he wanted to say to her. "Well perhaps another—"

" 'Twill only take a second," she called back as she flew out the door.

Daniel wondered if she actually did have wings because she was back almost before he knew it, a book nearly as big as she cradled in her arms. "It belonged to Mama," she said, placing it on his knees before she settled upon the settee again. "Mama always told us that all the wisdom of the world is in its stories and songs. Remember the night in the library when you handed me the volume on ancient Greek mythology? You suggested that I read *The Book* more often, and I have been. Mama said that you could always learn something new no matter how many times you have read it."

The book jacket was leather and very old. The gold letters on the front barely visible anymore for many little fingers had traced over them, but he could still make them out. Daniel's eyes glazed over as memories flooded back. His lips began to twitch, he felt his hands shake.

"Well, don't just stare at it. Open it," Freddie said. If he was so touched by just the cover, she was eager to witness his re-action to the inside. "It is illustrated."

Daniel laid back the cover to reveal the title page. The lettering was much clearer: *NURSERY RHYMES of the Ages.* He shut his eyes; closed the book, and set it to the back of the settee, willing himself not to laugh. All these years they had been reading nursery rhymes. The "Looby-Looby." "Twinkle,

twinkle little star." "Hickory, dickory dock." It had been there all the time and be hadn't seen it.

He meant to have another go at it, but she turned those chocolate eyes on his face and he watched, mesmerized, as her gaze traveled from the top of his head, down one cheek, across his chin, up the other cheek, and down his nose until it settled on his lips.

Daniel gave a whoop, threw protocol to the winds, started laughing, grabbed Freddie by the shoulders, laughed some more, pulled her toward him, and blurted out, "Oh, hell's bells, darling, I'm so sorry. Will you forgive me for accusing you of being mean-spirited?"

Freddie started to speak, but the minute he held her, Daniel's emotions began rolling downhill so fast they could not be stopped. "If you do find it in your heart to forgive me will you marry me and be my countess?" He placed a finger on her lips, which again prevented her from speaking. "Don't try to say anything right now, because I'm going to kiss you."

And he did.

Freddie let out a sigh.

"I hope that is a *yes*," he said after several minutes of kissing most every spot on her face that he could think of.

"How can you want to marry me? I have no dowry to offer you."

Daniel tried not to show his amusement, which amazingly was coming to the forefront more and more since he'd made the acquaintance of the little brown mouse. "I believe we can struggle along on my income. Now, is the answer to my question *yes?*"

"Oh indeed it is, my lord," she said.

"I would like to hear you call me Daniel."

"Yes, Daniel. I shall marry you. But I suspect that you are deliberately trying to distract me, and you cannot. I still want to meet my grandfather."

That sobered Daniel a bit, and he sat back. "All right, but I shall accompany you. I won't have you going unprotected into unknown territory."

It took a few heated discussions before Clach, the Earl of Gloaminlaw's stubborn henchman, could be persuaded to give Daniel directions to Castle Naught, which proved to be only a matter of thirty miles or so west of Knocktigh. As to why Winifred's mother had never told her that her grandfather was alive was a puzzle Daniel wished to pursue. After all these years of thinking she had no family except two half sisters, he did not want Winifred to find more disappointment and another rejection.

Within three days Daniel and Freddie, with Tilbury and Flora, were on their way toward Cornhill-on-Tweed.

It was decided that they would stop at Knocktigh, then cross over John Smeaton's bridge into Scotland at Coldstream and follow the Tweed westward through the Cheviots to Castle Naught. Freddie said she wanted to see everybody at the manor first, and Flora could visit her mother.

Daniel rode Perseus alongside the coach much of the way, but with the added attraction of his beloved, he found it quite a pleasant interval now and then to ride inside.

Clach had been given a horse and sent back to Scotland to tell the MacNaught to expect the arrival of his granddaughter within two weeks' time.

Although summer was upon them it was still cool at Knocktigh. The hills were clothed with heather and bracken. The trees, in full leaf, formed havens of shelter around small pools of water nestled among rocks. Butterflies fluttered over wildflowers and birds hovered and dipped in the air. Just as the old manor house came into view, they caught a glimpse of the chestnut mare. She stood on a craggy hillside and watched the coach and his lordship upon the great Scots Grey. Perseus—or Precious—saw her too and perked up his ears and let out a loud, Neeeeeeeiiiighhh.

"I agree with you, she is very pretty," Daniel said, slapping the big stallion on the side of his neck. He mentioned to Freddie soon after they had alighted in the kitchen courtyard that it was a pity to let such a valuable animal run wild. Anything could happen to her. "Would you like to have her brought to London for you to ride?"

"She is a mountain horse," Freddie said. "She would not be happy in the city."

"Then I shall have her caught and sell her to someone in the area who would appreciate her."

Freddie looked shocked. "Oh, no, you cannot! That is Mama's horse."

She seemed so upset that Daniel decided not to pursue the subject at that time, but a valuable horse like the chestnut would bring a good price and he hated to see prime horseflesh wasted in the wild hills where it was not appreciated.

The whole staff at Knocktigh were delighted to see his lordship and their little mistress; and they all remarked on how well turned out Flora looked in her crisp new uniform. Mrs. Doone cooked to her heart's delight, for now that the earl had left substantial funds in Mrs. Ash's hands their fare was much better.

It was really Granny Eizel whom Freddie had come to see, and as soon as she was settled in her old room, she made her way to the upper floor. She raised a hand to knock, knowing that she wouldn't have to touch the wooden door before she would be invited in.

"Oh, Granny Eizel," Freddie said, kissing the soft velvety cheek, "you will never guess what has happened."

"Granny never has to guess, lass. You know that. Were ye a good lass who did as Granny Eizel said? Did ye study his lordship?"

"If you know everything you do not need to ask," Freddie said.

"Yir a naughty one, aren't you?" Granny quipped, cackling softly.

Freddie was too full of her happiness to act the coquette.

"His lordship is wonderful, Granny, and he has asked me to be his countess. Now he is taking me to see my grandfather. Why did you not tell me that he lived so close by?"

"I promised yir mither not to mention that name after he cast her out. Ye dinna make the vow, so 'tis now yir choice to make what ye will of yir grandfather's gesture."

"It is all right for me to talk to him, isn't it?"

"Aye, as ye choose, lass. But be forewarned. Yir problems are not over yet. Remember that yir grandfather turned his back on yir mither when she went against his wishes. He is a man who likes to have his own way."

Freddie agreed that he must be. "I can think of no reason for him to dislike Daniel, though. There is no blood feud between them as there was between the MacNaughts and the Hendrys."

"The decisions ye will have to make are more far reaching than blood feuds. Ye will have to deal with the depth of yir sense of family loyalty."

"I am sure that my grandfather loves me if he has sent for me, Granny. But there is one thing that does bother me. Daniel wants to catch Mama's chestnut mare and sell her to a good stable."

"What are yir thoughts on that, lass?"

"I know that Mama rides her mare over the hills at night, for I have seen her."

The old woman smiled. "Then dinna ye fret. Yir mither won't let anyone take her horse away from her now. Wait and see. My Gilliane always had her ways of turning the trick on the other fellow."

"Then I shan't fret," Freddie said.

"There is something I want ye to do before ye go," Granny said. "In the cupboard under the eaves is yir mither's chest. I want ye to take it with ye."

The old woman's urgency concerned Freddie. "Oh, Granny, you are not going to leave us, are you?"

"Nay, lass. The box has yir mither's keepsakes. Ye're goin' tae be married now, and she left some jewelry for each of her daughters. It will be yir responsibility tae see that Margaret and

Mary get their pieces when they are married. There are also some tidbits from yir mither's past that I'm sure she wud want ye to have. I know there's a rag doll, a button collection, and some papers that she saved: some watercolor sketches and letters . . . that sort of thing. I have kept them for ye and now yir auld enuff to be in charge of them."

Freddie got down on her hands and knees and pulled out the box. It was not very large, handpainted, with a little gold latch.

After they had chatted awhile, Freddie tucked the chest under her arm, kissed the old woman on the cheek, and quietly closed the door.

As Granny Eizel usually did, she began to sing a little ditty:

> *"Ride a cockhorse to Banbury Cross.*
> *To see a fine lady upon a white horse."*

The following morning they prepared to leave early. Freddie hummed as she entered the back courtyard and sang as Daniel handed her into the coach. " 'Ride a cockhorse to Banbury Cross, to see a fine lady upon a white horse.' "

"Are you singing that for me, my darling?" Daniel asked when he thought no one would hear him.

Freddie looked at him and laughed. "I was singing it without thinking."

"Surely you are hoaxing me," he said. He could tell by the expression on her face that she wasn't. "You didn't know that I am also Viscount Banbury? That is one of my titles. The Durham seat is in Oxfordshire just south of Banbury. I thought you knew."

"Well, I know now," said Freddie, giving him a sassy smile. *And I should have known Granny Eizel was up to something when she was always singing that nursery song.*

"Speaking of cockhorses," Daniel said, pulling on his riding gloves, "I wonder why Parks is taking so long to saddle Perseus?"

As if he heard his name, the groom—not the horse—came hurrying from the barn, a harried look on his face. "He's gone."

"Who's gone, Parks? I hope you mean that white menace with horns."

"You know who I mean, your lordship. The rascal opened the latch on his stall and left."

Daniel's good humor took an about face. "Perseus?"

"Can't find him anywhere."

Daniel had managed to avoid the barn the few days they were there, but he now entered the dark building. Tweedle-dee was nearly full grown and her appetite for leather had grown in proportion to her belly. She had welcomed his lordship with enthusiasm the first day they'd arrived.

"Why wasn't the barn locked?"

"You know they never lock anything around here," said Parks. "He's nowhere about. Loof hasn't seen him since last night. He could have run off anytime after he was fed."

Daniel strode back into the courtyard and scanned the horizon. "Run where? He likes the comfort of his stall. Demme! We can't wait forever."

"I see him," said Freddie, pointing toward the hills. "I don't think you will be able to get Precious back to the stables until he is ready." All eyes followed her finger. The big Scots Grey towered over the chestnut mare, with that silly grin on his face and a tuft of heather hanging from his lips.

"I'm afraid we will have to leave him if we are to get to the Earl of Gloaminlaw's castle before dark," said Daniel, walking to the edge of the cobblestone courtyard where he leaned over and broke off a piece of heather growing up between the cracks. As soon as he climbed into the carriage he handed the flowers to Freddie. "For you, my lady. It seems that Perseus knows the way to a female's heart better than I. We will have to leave him here with Loof until our return trip to London."

Their journey into Roxburghshire along the basin of the Tweed—though not far in miles—was an arduous one and consumed much of the day. When Freddie first saw Castle Naught she thought it a splendid thing. The castle sat neither at the bottom nor at the top but in the middle of the side of a mountain and overlooked deep valleys, lush foliage, and rushing streams. The amber light of the evening sun bounced off the stone walls of the rounded watch tower entwined with ivy and honeysuckle vines.

Even Daniel fell under the spell of the remoteness and sensed that he had stepped back into a time of medieval routs and brawls.

The castle itself was four stories high and built in an L-shape. They were evidently expected because the minute the Durham coach circled up to the tower, the two wooden, iron-studded doors were opened and the majordomo of the household met them on the steps. Servants came running to unload the coach, and Flora and Tilbury were led away to be shown to their employers' chambers.

The circular stairs were in the corner tower and led up to the chieftain's Room. It was a large Hall festooned with banners, the walls covered with weapons and portraits of past chiefs. Their path was lined with kilted men and a few women in woolen dresses of a more practical nature than what was being worn in London.

Freddie had eyes only for the man sitting in a high chair on the raised dais at the far end of the room. He was in full Scottish dress his plaid secured with his clan brooch, and a large sporran of fur and gold at the front of his kilt. There was no question in Freddie's mind who he was. His shock of wiry hair was more gray than red, but from under heavy, almost black brows his keen blue eyes—so much like her mother's—fixed her with a fierce scowl.

She broke away from Daniel and ran across the vast room to stand in front of him. "Grandpapa," she said. "I have come to see you."

He rose from his chair, indeed an imposing figure, but Freddie realized he was not as tall as she'd first thought him to be.

His voice thundered from somewhere deep down inside him and filled the room. "What happened to your hair?"

"There is nothing wrong with my hair," Freddie said, raising a hand to her head.

" 'Tis nae red as it ought."

"It is brown. That is good enough for me, sir."

"Bah! A MacNaught canna have brown hair. 'Tis the fault of those Hendrys. Traitors—the whole lot—mixing with the *Sassenach.*"

"That was two hundred years ago, Grandpapa, when the Scots' own King James the Sixth sat upon the English throne. Mama told me that."

"What else did your mama say?"

"Mama told me how nice and handsome my papa was."

"I mean what did she say about me?"

"Mama never mentioned you. I did not even know I had a living grandfather until two weeks ago when Mr. Clach came to London to fetch me," Freddie said. "Granny Eizel said that you forbade Mama to ever speak your name again. That was very mean of you, Grandpapa."

" 'Twas her own fault. Yir mither ran off and married a mon that I forbid her to see. I disowned her." The MacNaught, the Earl of Gloaminlaw, glowered at his granddaughter to silence her. It did no good, he saw, so he turned his back on her. That did no good either, because she kept right on scolding him.

"I think it made her very sad, Grandpapa. Now you said that I should come see you. So here I am. What is it you wanted to say?"

Since he would rather look at his granddaughter than the wall, Gilbert MacNaught, laird of the borderland MacNaughts, turned back around.

"My only son and his wife died in an epidemic, but they left me a grandson, Robert MacNaught."

"I didn't know that I had a cousin," Freddie said. "Is he here?"

"He died, too," he said sharply, then nodded toward the two lines of people whom they'd just passed. "The Council of Clan

Leaders has met here today to tell you that they have chosen you as the next MacNaught and heir to Gloaminlaw. You will cuim here to live with me and learn our ways."

Freddie's gaze swept the Great Hall. She stared out the window at the sweeping view of tree-covered valleys and then back to her grandfather. "All this will be mine? What happens if I say I will not do it?"

" 'Tis yir duty—yir loyalty—yir pride!" roared the Mac-Naught. "If you do not take it the earldom of Gloaminlaw, the Castle, and all the holdings your family has taken over the last four hundred years will pass to another clan. A MacNaught will no longer be high chieftain. 'Tis yir duty to cuim to Scotland and marry a Scot." That was the most ridiculous hum Daniel had every heard. He stepped forward to give Winifred his silent support. It was then that he saw it—the brooch holding the old man's plaid. True, it had three feathers signifying high chief, but the engraving on the badge was a silver lion's head. The same as the one Edgar Buttons had brought wrapped in the scrap of cloth.

"My lord, if you will allow me to interrupt," Daniel said. "That badge you wear—that is the MacNaught crest?"

"Aye."

"How did your grandson die?"

The old man looked at Daniel as if he weren't seeing him at all, but straight through him to something on the other side. "He were killed in the Englishmen's war with the French."

"Is there an inscription—Latin—*nia Fort?*" Daniel asked.

The old man looked at him ominously. *"Omnia Fortunae Committo:* I commit all things to fortune. The MacNaught motto. Why do you ask?"

"I believe it may have been your grandson who saved my life," Daniel said and quickly related the story about the red-headed soldier's wild ride into the Battle of Quatre Bras, his loud battle cry, his strength.

Only his eyes showed the deep emotion going on inside of MacNaught. "That do sound like my Robbie," he said.

"But he wore the Gordon plaid. I have a piece of it."

"His mother were a Gordon, and he insisted that he was going to join the 92nd Highlanders whether I liked it or not. The pigheaded fool."

"Well, he was a brave warrior, your lordship. You can be proud to know that he died fighting. When I get back to London I shall have the badge and piece of his uniform sent to you. I'm sure you would like to have them."

"Obliged," he said. The MacNaught chewed the tip of his mustache a while longer and studied Daniel, then Freddie. "So this is the *Sassenach* Earl of Chantry that ye brought with ye? Clach told me it was at his house ye were staying in London."

"Yes," Freddie said, putting her arm through Daniel's, "and I have accepted his proposal of marriage."

"I will give my permission for you to marry my granddaughter under one condition."

"What is that, my lord?"

" 'Twas my Robbie, my heir, who died for you."

"That is something which I shall always be grateful for, my lord."

"Well that you do remember," said the laird. "You may marry my granddaughter as long as you cuim to Scotland to live and take the name of MacNaught. For then the MacNaughts will continue to inherit Gloaminlaw with Castle Naught."

"What!" said Daniel. "That is impossible. I am the Earl of Chantry. I have large estates, business interests in England."

"You forget that I am also an earl," answered the old man. "Being clan chieftain is far more important. Winifred's responsibilities will be great. If you want her, you will have to cuim here."

The two men glared at each other until the laird turned to his granddaughter. "It is you the Council have chosen to be my heir. You will be the next chief of the clan MacNaught."

"You wud cuim to live here regardless," said her grandfather.

"You have two other granddaughters, Grandpapa. Mary and Margaret."

"You are the next in line. They say you are the one who must accept."

Freddie was more practical. "Can't I do both?"

Daniel was beginning to wonder by the looks on the other chieftains' faces if they were going to let them leave. "No, you can't do both, my dear. I have asked you to be the next Countess of Chantry. Your name would become Durham."

The old laird's scowl became deeper.

"But here I will be the MacNaught. I will be the chief of the clan," she said.

Daniel did not want to give her up any more than he wanted to give up his own name, title, or holdings. He pulled her off to one side. "Let us go back to London, Winifred. The Season is coming to an end, and I need to be with my sisters."

"That is just it. You have seven sisters. Grandpapa has no one. Oh, Daniel, don't you see, he has lost everybody who ever meant anything to him. He is an old man. I have nothing to bring to you now. At least I could come live with him and take care of him. After that I will be the High Chief. I can marry whomever I please."

"I have an idea the old curmudgeon is going to be around for another twenty years or more. Do you want to wait that long to be married?"

Freddie had not quite calculated it in years. To her, anyone over forty was ready to stick their spoon in the wall. "Not really," she said, taking his hand in hers and giving it a squeeze.

"Don't do that, Winifred," he said, removing her hand from his. " 'Tis not proper." He did not want to tell her what it did to him.

Freddie raised her eyebrows. "Are you going to be so stuffy when we are married?"

He couldn't repress his smile. Hardly, he thought to himself.

She caught the glint in his eye. "Well, I hope not."

His voice became serious. "We will go back to London. You need time to think the matter over. Then you can make your decision as to what you will do."

Epilogue

When Daniel and Freddie returned from Scotland a letter was
waiting, addressed to Major Daniel Durham. It was from Lieutenant Edgar Buttons telling him of a strange encounter he'd
had with a young farmer in Belgium.

The man had no memory for almost a year since the
last battles of the war. He married the Belgian farmer's
daughter who had cared for him and has born him a black-
haired son. He said that his memory began to return when
he heard bagpipes being played over the unmarked graves
in a field adjoining his father-in-law's pasture. I happened
to overhear him telling of his experience in a tavern in
the nearby village and asked him to repeat his story.

He claims to be one Robert MacNaught of the 92nd
Highland Regiment and placed himself at the Battle of
Quatre Bras. I questioned him and came to believe his
account of remembering hanging onto the stirrup of a big
smoky white horse. From your accounting of his having
fiery hair and the disposition of a bull, he fits your de-
scription. I told him that I had been in your service during
the latter part of the war and that I was the one who had
pulled you off the battlefield.

He plans to return to Scotland and bring his wife and
son with him. I hope it is all right with you that I gave
him your direction in London and said that you were the

officer he had protected with his body. I know that you
will want to thank him personally for saving your life.

Daniel read the letter to Winifred and watched for her reaction.

"Grandfather will be so happy," she said.

"What about you, my love? It means that you will not be the
next MacNaught."

Freddie threw her arms around Daniel's neck quite forgetting
that it was not the thing to do at all in the presence of Mr.
Pettigrew. "If what this man says is true and he is my cousin,
Grandpapa will have his heir and three granddaughters as well."

"And you can marry me, my sweet, without my having to
change my name."

"If you want me without a dowry."

"I believe we can struggle along on my income," he said.

Their happiness was so catching that Mr. Pettigrew became
overcome by the emotion of the moment quite forgetting his
timidity and boldly asked for Lady Georgette's hand. Daniel,
so caught up in the relief of not having to find a way to cir-
cumvent a very sticky situation of name-changing, not only
agreed but generously offered the couple a wedding present of
the Sussex manor house and four hundred acres which his father
had won with a turn of a card. With Georgette's dowry, which
Daniel had no thought of shortening now, the couple could easily set up housekeeping in the country and Mr. Pettigrew could
continue his artistic endeavors.

Perseus or Precious, depending on who was speaking, had
already made one decision as to his future, and Loof told them
that he would keep an eye on the chestnut in the spring and let
them know when she foaled.

Another unexpected significant occurrence as far as Freddie
was concerned, and a bit of an embarrassment to Daniel, was
the discovery in her mother's chest of the missing deed of ownership for Knocktigh. The entire estate belonged to Freddie. So
she had done nothing illegal when she had sold off the furnish-

ings and family heirlooms. On the contrary, Daniel said she had acted most generously in providing for his sisters, and therefore, in consequence of his father's neglect, he had many of the treasures hunted down and bought back—sometimes at thrice what Freddie had sold them for.

The end of the Season saw a double wedding for Lord Chantry and Miss Winifred Landry and the Honorable James Pettigrew and Lady Georgette Durham. The Honorable James Pettigrew who had been nothing more than a humble secretary for most of his life was married in all the pomp and circumstance allotted to a peer of the realm.

The Earl of Gloaminlaw, the high Chief and Laird of the once-pronounced outlaw clan of MacNaught, was persuaded by his grandson and heir, Viscount Pitdearg, the red Pict, to step foot on English soft to give the bride away. He brought his own pipers and insisted his granddaughter be piped to the altar properly.

Major Daniel Durham, Viscount Banbury, seventh Earl of Chantry not only gave his sister Lady Georgette to his former secretary, the Honorable James Pettigrew, but was himself a part of the wedding party.

Lord Chantry said that he was considering several offers for his other sisters, but that he was not ready as yet to make any formal announcements. His interest at that point in time was his own honeymoon trip with his bride to places he would not specify. The truth of the matter was Daniel hadn't the foggiest idea of where he and Lady Chantry were going. She said she was planning several surprises over the next few weeks, and she wasn't going to tell the bridegroom about any of them until their wedding night.

For those who do like to follow the goings-on of the Fashionable World there was an interesting tidbit which had recently reached London. Durham Hall in Oxfordshire had been opened again, and on one particularly lovely afternoon in August the lord of the manor was seen riding into Banbury with a lovely little lady upon a large smoky horse carrying a bouquet of wild flowers in his mouth. They stopped at the old Banbury Bakery where her ladyship picked up a basket of Banbury cakes to take back to the manor. It is said that Banbury cakes had been a very favorite treat of his lordship's when he was a little boy. Her ladyship left an order for a fresh basket to be delivered to the manor house each morning for the length of their stay. As they rode away it was said that they heard Lady Chantry singing:

> *"Ride a cockhorse to Banbury Cross.*
> *To see a fine lady upon a white horse."*

Another rumor began circulating, though it may have been pure nonsense, that his lordship was seen to ride up beside her and kiss her in full view of anybody who happened to be watching, which was of course most of the village. But then some folks do enjoy embellishing a story until it gets all out of hand, so it probably didn't happen at all.

Dear Readers,

In *The Sister Season* I present a whole new set of characters. Like the old woman in the shoe who had so many children she didn't know what to do, I could not possibly spend time with all of them. Three successful pairings in a Regency Romance, I feel is a very good record for one story. So maybe there will be more of the Durham sisters in later books.

Those of you who have read my previous Regencies know that I love a fast-paced, light-hearted comedy. *The Sister Season* is no exception, and I hope you like this one.

I enjoy hearing from readers. Your letters make it all worthwhile. If you wish to write to me, I may be reached at P.O. Box 941982, Maitland, FL 32794-1982.

Elegantly,
Paula Tanner Girard